A Jack Bur

CASH-TRAP

TIM SHORT

A Jack Burgoyne Novel

CASH-TRAP

TIM SHORT

CASH-TRAP

© Tim Short 2023

Inspired by actual events

PROLOGUE

Everything she was doing, she had done a thousand times before. There was just one change, but it made all the difference. The routine was not calming this time, because she knew that one mistake, one typo, even one delay, and her husband and daughter were dead.

She had taken a gas-powered auto-rickshaw to the office, as usual, because they told her that everything had to be the same as on any other day. It was hot and humid and oppressive even though it was still February in the South Asian capital. Part of the humidity came from the fact that the city was in a delta and surrounded by four rivers. It was still three months to the monsoon though.

The three men had come to her house and told her what to do. They would stay there until she did it. She only had to do her job they said. It would be easy. They each had a gun and only one of them said anything. He spoke English with an accent she couldn't place but also with great precision and even greater economy. The other two just looked alert and responsive but also more quiet than any men she had seen before in her kitchen. All of them were wearing balaclavas, which must have been very uncomfortable in the heat. None of them appeared to care. They also looked relaxed about the guns they were holding.

She had arrived at the Central Bank where she worked. The guard was so used to seeing her that he barely looked up. It was relatively unusual for anyone to come in at the weekend, but it had been quite busy lately so that probably explained it.

She went in to the windowless office with the terminal. They called it the bunker. You could get in with a pass card. Twenty people had cards. Everyone who worked in there plus their supervisors plus the big bosses, who never used them but thought they needed the kudos of theoretically being able to go in the bunker. But actually, it was so dull that they never did.

There was nothing in there apart from a hefty and outdated computer with a screen that was very much not flat. The keyboard was also about 20 years old. There was a printer that would be too ancient to be in use anywhere else. But nothing complicated or pretty or interesting was being done with these devices. Type text and print it out. Send simple messages down a secure wire to a small number of pre-registered addresses. You didn't even have a wide choice of messages. It really was dull to look at if you didn't know what was happening. If you did know, it was terrifying.

She looked at the piece of paper the men had given her and started to type. She had two things to do. The first one was to send some payment instructions. So far, everything was still the same as any other day. One difference was that her fingers slipped on the keyboard. She didn't normally sweat at the office. But there was no-one there to see, so it didn't seem to matter much. Her hands were shaking as well so she used the delete key more than usual. The computer was not sophisticated enough to have a key logger installed, so that wouldn't matter either.

Then came something new. She had to open a particular window and type in something she didn't understand apart from the name of someone she had seen in the canteen. In the roped off section for the top guys.

The man in her kitchen had been very clear that this typing had to be perfect. One letter wrong and the consequences would be severe. The way he put it was 'one mistake, one finger.' It also had to be right first time. She typed it in very slowly and checked it against the paper three times. And then three times again. It looked right.

$ yes astrid223 | sudo -Su sakhawat.moula rm -f r

That just left the one other difference between today and other days. She wasn't authorised for any of this.

CHAPTER 1

CHIANG MAI, THAILAND

The problem is, you can't see the money any more. In the old days, we could see a million dollars walking down the street," I said. I was trying to explain how I saw the situation to Gas Station Susie. It wasn't quite clear why she was called Gas Station Susie, but one theory was that it had something to do with the fact that she was from Houston. We were sitting in the cavernous lobby area of the Pang Hotel. This was old-school four star but quite cheap because it was attached to an equally enormous but derelict shopping centre, which put some people off.

I was not one of those people, however. I quite liked the view from the gym which showed trees and plants taking over the building as it decayed slowly. There were still ornamental dragons just visible in its ponds through the undergrowth. I wondered who if anyone was paying for the maintenance, and what would happen when the dragons realised they were free.

The great thing about this hotel, apart from its almost total lack of clientele, which made spotting people easy, was the food. There was a guy around the corner in the Nimman food court with orange hair who only made two things. I don't know what the other one was because I never got past the first one, which was Khao Soi Gai. Gai meant chicken. It was a speciality of Northern Thailand and it seemed to have two sorts of noodles: crispy and soft. I didn't really understand how it was done but I knew how much I liked it.

The dish was fresh but spicy even before you loaded it up with chilli and he was charging THB60 for it. One of the habits I had retained from finance was always using the three letter acronyms, or TLAs, for currency, so THB or USD it was. This price was criminally low for a dish of that quality. It was fairly low for anything that would just keep you alive. This was much better than that.

Gas and I both tried to avoid having it every day, not always successfully. In my book, he could have charged that amount just for the availability of fresh lime to squeeze over the dish. Gas said that I had seafaring blood when I did that, which might have been a subtle US/Anglo dig, but was also probably true, since I had been born in Bristol.

"We don't always know what people are trying to say when they say things. If they are in fact in a position to say anything," I said.

I explained: "Sometimes communication failures can be quite subtle, so you don't know what happened really even afterwards. There was that time when I was supposed to meet a girl from a dating app here in Chiang Mai, and she specified "Central Airport." So I said, 'Cool, and that I would go to Entrance 3,' because that's what Grab Taxi said was a popular destination at the airport. I went there but she went to some shopping mall which may or may not have been near the airport. Or that's what she said later. I didn't have data and the airport Wifi wasn't working so that was that. Catfish, troll or error, I don't know." Gas interjected: "All three. Beaucoup problemas."

"There might be a digital native thing going on," I continued. "I would never have told anyone to meet me somewhere which had 'airport' in the name which wasn't the airport . . . but also I would not expect to be able to recover from imprecise location details with realtime comms. Everyone else does nowadays. It's an advantage in general but it means people don't have any real world moves."

Gas replied: "What were you doing trying to get a date on an app? Karen doesn't have a smartphone."

Gas worked on the principle that if a remark was relevant and accurate, you should probably say it. I couldn't quite work out why this wasn't always helpful. Or more precisely, I couldn't say what the third criterion should be in any concise way. After all, part of conversation was information exchange. "You know that's not helpful, right, Gas?" I used to say in the first years we had worked together. It didn't make any difference so I stopped saying it.

Maybe it was something to do with the difference between what the words said if they were written down and what they actually meant when someone said them to you. In a real place, with some context.

I had started out in sort of the same place as Gas but had evolved to more-or-less the opposite position. Information had value in our game and therefore it would be wise to hold on to that value. So you could either say things that were not exactly false, because you would get found out doing that, and also either vague enough to obscure the key points. Or you could say something completely precise but about something slightly different that happened somewhere else. That seemed to work out fine mostly.

Then of course though you had to remember what happened where and that was hard enough with normal straightforward events like lunch and much harder with money or crypto where you couldn't always say clearly what was happening while you were watching it happen. But that was what we got paid for. That and our ability to find the money.

A kid wandered through the lobby wearing a t-shirt that had "No Cats, No Nietzsche" written on it. I inevitably spent a few seconds trying to work out what this meant before deciding it couldn't be done and returning to the issue at hand.

We had been following a sequence of unauthorised SWIFT payments which ended in the Philippines, as far as was known by the general public or law enforcement. We had added a stage to Chiang Mai.

SWIFT was the payment network for banks, including Central Banks. It moved vast amounts of money around. It didn't actually have any money itself. All it did was facilitate secure messaging between those it did, and even what you could say was restricted. It was basically what banks did when they were wiring money to each other, like what individuals did to make an online payment. Just much, much bigger and global and all the banks pretended to trust one another, most of the time. At least, it turned out that it was a big problem in 2008 when they openly didn't any more.

The big innovation in the SWIFT system was that it took out ambiguity, in much the same way that conversations between air traffic control and pilots are now standardised. You can only say specified word which have agreed-upon meanings. This could be known as message type constriction. Every message type had a name, which helpfully enough would be a Message Type Number, MTXXX.

As I had explained to Gas, "People think that the imposition of message type constriction in SWIFT was a disadvantage, but the free-for-all with TELEX before 1977 was the real problem." She loved this sort of thing. Numbers, dates, data. I was kind of fond of it too, because of what we could do with it. She had got heavily into the message formatting on a previous thing we had done in Brazil a few years before.

"Before people would send anything or something close enough they thought to what they wanted to happen and then someone on the other end would have to jam it into a category. They wouldn't always get it right. Now it's basically you specify a message type and it requires you to fill in some boxes and that's it. A payment is like "How much to who?" and then that's all you can do in that category really. Much better. People are forced to be more clear."

I knew what the system did approximately but I had never worried about message formats much. Gas was all over the plumbing that did that. "Can you just send some free text asking for money to be moved?" I asked.

"You can send an MT 299 free format message, but..."

"Doesn't that mean you still have the disadvantages of the old system, though?" I interrupted.

"No, it doesn't. If you want money to move, you send an MT 202 Request for Transfer. If you send anything that's not a 202, no-one is going to execute it. OK, you could do an MT 203, but that's just a set of 202s."

"This would be quite useful with people you are trying to go on a date with," I said. "Like there could be an MT for date location and date time and the only allowable contents of the first one would a location code in some standard format."

"Depends on whether you want to date a person or a robot."

I had to allow that point, though I mentioned that robots were getting sexier. Later I realised that I should have responded by including a requirement to specify individual type in the code that would set up a date. Human or Robot. But that was later.

Hacking the system was supposed to be impossible. Access to it was only possible via air-gapped computers located in concrete bunkers with a ton of access control. Air gapping meant that there were no connections to the internet from anything inside the bunker or indeed any connections at all to anything apart from an actual physical cable to the printer.

Access control to the bunker however was not like in the movies with iris scans. An old-fashioned ID swipe card was good enough for most purposes. That kept bad actors out. But it didn't help if you got to someone who was supposed to be there. No system could catch that.

The only realistic way to get to a SWIFT terminal was via what was euphemistically called "social engineering," which might mean being nice to people but often involved threats, extortion and violence. Certainly in the case of SWIFT, access to a terminal would be lucrative enough to justify any course of action. It handled 42 million payments a day. It was claimed that the US Treasury had once estimated the volume of transfers at $5 trillion a day. Proving that that was the right amount was hard, but the number was certainly unimaginably vast. This was a playground for all sorts of activities of all sorts of size.

We had been asked to look at an incident in the Central Bank in Dhaka, Bangladesh. The problems there had begun to appear when a printer stopped working. Ideally, in a Central Bank, especially anywhere near the SWIFT bunker, any changes at all would bring immediate investigation in their train. In the real world though, printers run out of paper all the time.

It hadn't run out of paper though. Printers have a way to tell you they are out of paper. What the printer actually said was "file NROFF is missing or changed." The problem of course is that that sort of language was only spoken by people like Gas Station Susie, and there weren't too many like her.

Because the printer wasn't working, there was no immediate printout of the previous day's SWIFT transactions to check. This introduced a crucial source of delay. Delay can be a big deal when money is flowing with silent and deadly rapidity through the world's virtual financial conduits, with some of it sometimes slopping over the sides or winding up in some of the wrong places. Sometimes all of it would end up in the worst place imaginable. Wherever it was, it was bad enough that it didn't go where it was supposed to, let alone to somewhere where it would be actively employed in generating outcomes that most people would call negative.

It was the weekend: a standard Friday in February. Staff thought that probably nothing much was happening and didn't check again until the next day. Someone tried again with the printer. This time they found their print command was locked up with the "file changed or absent" message. Now they were paying attention. The thieves had known that Friday was the start of the weekend in Bangladesh.

One of the things they were now paying attention to was a bunch of messages from the Americans. Inevitably, the US was by far the biggest and most important player in the international financial plumbing, simply because of the size of the US economy and the dominance of the dollar.

These Americans kept asking why all this money was being moved in an unusual sequence of transactions with a strange recipient, but not even the absence of a response meant they had grounds to interrupt a sequence of $10m transfers. They were holding the cash on behalf of the counterpart Central Bank, but it was definitely that Central Bank's money that they could do anything with that they wanted and the Americans were getting valid instructions from a genuine terminal in that bank.

Any messages inbound to the SWIFT terminal would normally just show up right on the screen. Whoever had sent it would have some lengthy code identifying themselves which the terminal would convert into a short name for the institution. So you would know who you were talking to.

Often the failover from a failure to write messages to the terminal screen was nothing. It was "piped to dev/null" in Gas's jargon, which meant something like "put straight in the bin without looking at it" as far as a computer was concerned. Here, someone had been smarter. They had piped any messages that didn't make it onto the screen to the printer that was in the bunker. Which they had disabled.

"So you would have to have actually been sitting in the room when the question was asked," said Gas. "Very clever."

Eventually the Americans wanted to know why there was all this money going to a charity. They didn't say anything about the first one. The second time they sent "PURPOSE YR LAST?" in an MT 295 Query format. They kept saying that about another six times, then they sent a bunch of MT 292s, which requested that the receiver *considered* cancelling previous pay orders and then they concluded with a rare MT 299 Free Format "SUSP PEND RESP" which meant they were going to stop doing stuff unless an actual person talked to them and said something reasonable.

We knew all this because we had scans of the printouts. Gas got them on actual paper immediately. "This is some bizarro super faint font from a dot-matrix machine; it's a nice nostalgic dive bar touch," she observed.

I didn't know any of those still existed in working order. I had done a bit of coding but I was mostly a spreadsheet guy and not a technical specialist any more, like Gas was, or had been.

We had fun imagining what it was like for the guy who got the printer to work on Saturday to see a) a whole bunch of massive transfers out being confirmed and b) a similarly large number of messages indicating the Americans were kind of freaking out. These were Americans in serious institutions who were known for a general aura of Zen and calmness.

INTERPOL had given us the printouts. Why did they do that? Because they couldn't look at it themselves. Not exactly because they lacked capacity. They had lots of competent, dogged investigators. They had some very smart people. But they didn't have any former investment bankers like me, because they weren't allowed to pay for them. They might have been able to find some detail-oriented hacker/fixers like Gas, but again they got very expensive if they were any good. Plus they tended to have intense anti-system views.

Another important reason we had the printouts was that if INTERPOL looked, everything would get political. Another was money itself. We were effectively bounty hunters, paid by results, with no result meaning no money. INTERPOL, as a public sector organisation, had to follow rules about excess salaries. There weren't any rules about percentages being deducted from what were known as "recoveries" before they were returned and indeed recovery percentages weren't even reportable and in a lot of scenarios not even knowable by anyone apart from the bounty hunter. So that was nice.

Everyone would be complaining about foreign investigators poking their noses into stuff. Whereas no-one would particularly care or notice if a former English bond structurer in a Motörhead t-shirt and a current American hacker with aggressive hair were wandering around apparently on holiday even if they appeared to have a fairly unusual level of South East Asia experience.

A correspondent bank in the Philippines had received $81m from these transfers which were concerning the Americans. It was normal for a ton of banks to be involved in moving large amounts of cash around, but it didn't make our job any easier. None of the banks who handled the money had done anything wrong because the instructions were apparently valid. $31m of the $81m had been delivered to a guy claiming to be called Weikang Xu at a casino.

This was very smart because large amounts of cash are delivered to Chinese high rollers in casinos all the time, and they get it in chips which they can effectively launder immediately. Laundering is the process of turning dirty money into clean money. If you gamble with chips and win new chips, those chips are clean. They have no history. The system doesn't remember anything about them. You're home free.

We thought we'd found the next move: this Xu guy was in Chiang Mai. Except of course he presumably didn't really exist. All we really knew was that the money had moved here after it had walked into the casino in the Philippines. We had no idea how far along we were in the chain.

It was pretty unusual for Central Banks to be wiring a charitable foundation; much less a "Fandation." Normally they would be making balancing payments to each other or dealing with their own local banks. At this point we were in a position to draw a number of conclusions.

This was a sophisticated operation employing multiple cells in different jurisdictions with seamless control of the operation from a central point allowing for good synchronisation.

There were zero native English speakers involved: any 14-year-old kid from Brooklyn or Hackney would not type "Fandation." This was actually a very strange error which only needed spell-check. Given that these guys had done stuff that was ten times harder, it was odd they dropped the ball on that. Clearly the guy in the woman's kitchen hadn't been on that part of the job.

Another terrific effort was with the printer in the SWIFT bunker. I asked Gas what this NROFF stuff was about.

"That stands for New ROFF. ROFF means Run Off. It formats text on UNIX based terminals for printing to old-school printers like dot-matrix. Completely deleting the fucker is like super aggressive but effective. And totes difficult."

"How do we know they deleted it rather than changed it? Both are compatible with the error message." We were standing outside the steps to a temple. There were many of these in Chiang Mai, and we had paused in our walk while we discussed the position. It's not clear we had noticed we were doing this because we were focussed on the problem.

"Since it's the same error message, their risk of detection is the same. They are relying on no UNIX guys being in the room at the weekend or ever. Deleting it means definitely no printing going on until someone finds out what that file is supposed to have in it, compiles it and loads it. Not that hard for the right guy, but you got to find that guy and he has to find probably a floppy disk or something insane in a storeroom. It might be 20 years since someone last compiled a file on that system and kids these days don't use compilers and link libraries so they can't do it. They've gotten slack."

The operation was relaxed about employing violence that amounted to terror. They had got to a female employee who had legitimate access to the SWIFT chamber. One of the perennial problems with any highly secure system like this was that actually operating it was a mundane task. You couldn't have some team of Navy SEALS typing away in a bunker. They'd get bored, and shoot someone, or themselves. Our thieves had got to the woman's home. So we knew that they had the ability to do that, and that they didn't care much about hurting people.

They also had been able to be confident about what would happen to funds arriving at a Foundation, which was in a different geography. So that was the second team.

Finally they had been on the ground in the Philippines, so they had at least three teams. The last one might have been one guy, but he was probably at least backed by some serious ID fraud operation. You couldn't just walk in to a casino and announce "I'm Weikang Xu, you have some chips for me" without showing some identification. Unless of course you showed up in a white stretch limo with four models and a lot of coke and it was $31m of chips you were looking for. Because then clearly no-one was going to look into anything in case you found it upsetting or dull.

Eventually a German bank got in the way of the heist with a masterful piece of pedantry. The thieves spelling caught up with them, in a great piece of recruitment for spelling bees the world over. They had been wiring some of the money to a "Fandation" and the Germans asked them if they wanted to fix the spelling just to avoid any difficulties at the other end with the Foundation that was apparently getting the money. Now the authorities all over were on the case; these transfers of about $100m had been interrupted which was progress, but it also became clear that the target amount for the heist was approaching $1bn.

The actual total amount was one of the things we couldn't work out. But we knew what had happened in the additional stage. There are arrangements for high rollers in casinos.

"If you win say $100m, the casino doesn't really have that in loose change and anyway, even if you are in Mayfair, do you want to walk onto the street carrying that? Bear in mind that you don't actually ever carry anything. You have people for that," I said.

But it might be that you are going to be in a different casino in Macau in a couple of days. Or longer if you are using your yacht. So it would be quite handy to have some chips there. So, chip swap agreements sprung up between the casinos.

"What do chip swap agreements do?" said Gas.

"They give you time to arrange for wire transfers behind the scenes, so no-one has to deal with vulnerable armoured trucks full of cash in known locations, and the high rollers are good to go again in the new location," I explained.

This was another clever part of the scheme, and where the fourth team must have been. The casino attached to the Hotel Pang was also derelict, or at least overgrown and closed. There had been few Chinese tourists to Thailand since the pandemic, and they hadn't yet returned in the huge numbers previously seen. Someone had reactivated the chip swap agreement for the Pang casino. This person had also used the Weikang Xu identity to get the chips.

So much Gas and I understood. But as she said, "I don't see what they do next. They've just got a bunch of chips for a casino that isn't operating." We had thought that if we turned up and looked around, we might be able to see what happened next. But we had and we couldn't. In fact, it had got worse. We couldn't even work out how the chips would have been obtained, because as we could see, the Pang casino was completely dead.

"A lot of what you need to do with a chip swap agreement takes place in the legal ether," I said.

"Doesn't that mean that they never even needed to be here?" asked Gas.

"I think they must have been here once. You can't just magic up a chip swap agreement from hyperspace. You need something, a guy on the ground, the original document..." I explained.

By this time we had finished our walk and were back at the Pang Casino. There was a large peeling poster of Jason Statham on the front. The name of the movie was in Thai, so we couldn't read it. It must have been the last film that was on before everything shut down.

There was a guy sitting in what would have been the security checkpoint when it was open. It was now also semi-derelict, but the lack of distinction between inside and outside in Thailand meant that it could continue in operation. You didn't need walls, because it was always warm. You had to go up a mountain for the temperature to fall to 15C. The Thais thought that was freezing; I had spent most of the previous decade in London and I thought 15C was a holiday. What you did need in Thailand was a roof, for the rainy season.

The guy was wearing long trousers and a shirt with a collar, which indicated some level of seniority. Everyone else was in shorts and a t-shirt, especially the Farangs. "Farang" was the potentially slightly pejorative Thai word for people from abroad; presumably it had developed from 'Foreigner' or maybe 'Français.'

I asked the guy about CCTV. He looked blank. I got the transition app up on my iPhone and had it pronounce "CCTV" in Thai. This turned out to be nothing like one might expect, not even with any identifiable acronyms or repetition. The guy still looked blank. I gave the guy a THB 1000 note. The guy looked extremely interested. "TV no have" he said.

"Even if we it existed and we got it, it would show us nothing. You just torched a thousand Baht for a less than meager return," pointed out Gas.

"I had to cover the base."

"It can go on the expenses I guess. But you could have got "TV no have" from him for a couple of hundred probably."

"You need a bank. A real commercial one, not a Central Bank which doesn't deal with casinos," I said. "And it needs to be easy."

I thought about the Prussian military dividing its people into four categories. The quote in question was often ascribed to one of the von Moltkes, but actually it was from a General called Hammerstein-Equord. He had a two-by-two matrix with the axes being lazy/diligent and non clever/clever.

He said that the lowest ranks do not require the highest levels of diligence and intellect, which made sense. Diligence was required for NCOs, but regulations could stand in for brains. What Hammerstein-Equord said next was the unexpected part that made his matrix memorable. It looks up to this point like he has two figures of merit and the top guys in his opinion are going to be the ones who score well on both.

But what Hammerstein-Equord says surprisingly is that his third category up, junior officers, are the conscientious and intelligent. He thinks that the lazy and intelligent are the ones who are suited to the highest levels of command. This had always appealed to me since I felt I belonged in that category.

The idea was that regulations are not needed for creative thinkers, providing you are certain their aims are aligned with yours. Someone who is diligent and intelligent will get a lot done, certainly, but they will do it by the book. Your lazy person on the other will do creative, rule-bending and unusual stuff if it does the bare minimum required to achieve the objectives *especially* if it involves them doing nothing much themselves.

This was one of the differences between Gas and I. She liked procedures and she loved detail. There couldn't be a missing item on the list. Because then the algorithm would fail. I just wanted to get out with whatever I could call a result with the smallest possible amount of effort and risk. I would cut any corners that I thought could be cut whereas Gas couldn't see any differences between the corners. They were all real corners and you would have to go around them in the right order. At least, that was how I saw it. She just thought I was a cowboy. But we were coming together slowly on this point.

I looked across the road from the Casino, basically in the same direction as Jason Statham was staring in his somewhat dilapidated state. He was wearing a tuxedo and looking as stern as he always did. I saw the Sukhothai massage parlour, one of the newly legalised cannabis dispensaries "Garage 420" and a bank.

"We need to go over there" I said.

"You want hand relief and a blunt right now?"

"I always want those things, but also we could go look in the bank," I clarified. "Because if you're the floor boss of the Pang Casino, how far do you want to walk with cash? What if the guy was clever and lazy, like Hammerstein-Equord was looking for?"

"Nice," said Gas.

We walked over to the bank. There was a smart-looking Thai lady wearing dramatic German geometrical glasses.

I asked "Did that casino used to bring you cash?" Gas was looking like she was sceptical about me getting an answer to a direct question like this which moreover involved a point of customer confidentiality.

"No, they not bank with us. We too small."

So this was progress of a sort. I had not given out another THB 1000 note without getting anything back. The woman spoke pretty good English, but it was difficult for Thai people because they did not use the Roman alphabet and it was phonetically a long way distant. Similarly very few Farang spoke Thai with any level of facility.

That meant I did not pick anything up about the statement. It had the standard abbreviation/simplification methods of many foreigners speaking English: no tenses and no verbs. After a while, native speakers sometimes adopted this. After all, it looked like you could say the same thing quicker and with fewer verbal keystrokes as it were. Another victory for Hammerstein-Equord.

Gas picked up the tense thing. "They not bank with you now? They bank with you before? Before they close."

"No, they with other people."

This was still looking like present tense.

"Where other bank?" continued Gas.

"Not other bank. Lawyer. Same same for us."

'Same same but different' was a ubiquitous and useful phrase in Thailand for reasons that were unclear. It was on t-shirts. You could use it at any point in a conversation to gesture at the basic ineffable profundity of reality or get a gin and tonic if your companion had just ordered one.

"We'd really like to talk to him," I said.

"She in town. Maybe have address."

This was my cue. I handed over another THB 1000. We got a post-it note with an address on it and left, gratefully.

The centre of Chiang Mai was based on square fortifications from the 14th. Century, which were impressively well-preserved. The quadrilateral in the middle formed the old town, and we were going just past the edge.

"We'll have to go to the Maya Center to get a tuk-tuk," I said. "That means the traffic lights."

The Maya Center was a very new, very impressive shopping centre on a corner just up the road from the Pang Hotel. The traffic lights were odd. There was quite heavy traffic, which probably explained the oddness.

Only one direction of four at a time would get a green light. And also that situation would persist for 90 seconds. That meant if you were queuing to cross as a pedestrian or waiting in a cab, you might have to wait over eight minutes. I had even managed to do worse than that one time before I knew that the cycle went anti-clockwise.

"What is that thing with the counter-clockwise?" asked Gas.

"It does that so we have to," I replied. "If you go the other way you get more wait cycles." We did it the right way and found a tuk-tuk, one of the ones which was basically a shack with seats strapped on to a moped. They were quick and not as dangerous as they looked.

All of the metalwork holding on the structure would protect you in a crash. All the injuries were drunk Farang kids on bikes they hired. Or possibly stoned, now.

We got to the address. It was on the Loi Kroh Road, which by night was the centre of Chiang Mai's relatively restrained bar girl scene. By day, as we now saw, it was dead. In fact, the whole of Chiang Mai was very sleepy when compared to the insanity of, for example, Soi Bangla in Patong on the island of Phuket.

The first thing we saw at the location was a 'Super Rich Money Exchange.' It was also the second thing we saw because there was nothing else there. A woman sat behind the counter playing a game on her phone.

"Lawyer here?" I asked, somewhat confused.

The woman replied "You can leave letter."

I wrote my email address on a piece of paper together with "Request meeting re: legal questions." I used the email provider Protonmail which had end-to-end encryption, so you could use it for field work. It had been designed in Switzerland by people who had been in particle physics like me, and it was expensive, which was always reassuring. Gas had ten separate addresses but I thought that was probably excessive. Basically the standard moves these days were Protonmail for email and Signal for messaging. But it was always worth remembering that nothing could stop a guy reading over your shoulder apart from standing with your back against a wall. In the dark.

We retired to a coffee shop to decide our next move.

"This isn't great," said Gas. "We can maybe be relaxed about the letter getting there, but there's no guarantee she will come back to us or see us or tell us anything."

"I suppose we have to try," I said, without much enthusiasm. We went back to the Hotel Pang.

In the morning, we went downstairs for breakfast. The same kid with the weird t-shirt from yesterday was getting an omelette with chilli and nothing else, which I thought was aggressive. This time, his t-shirt said "Where's that Henge?" I tried to think of a scenario in which someone might say that. They could be lost on tank manoeuvres on Salisbury Plain, perhaps. Maybe the kid just had a gift for incomprehensible t-shirts. Maybe he didn't speak English. Maybe he liked t-shirts made by people who didn't speak English. There were enough examples of kids getting tattoos which were supposed to mean "peace and persistence" or something but which actually meant "minimum octane rating 94" or "danger high voltage." Which was probably just as good.

My phone pinged.

"Hey, I have something," I said. Surprisingly enough, our piece of paper had produced a rapid effect. Super Rich Money Exchange must have scanned it and emailed it. Very efficient.

The response was also from a Protonmail address. It read: "Meeting Hà Nội, Vietnam. $100 per hour in advance. Huỳnh."

I showed Gas my screen. "Looks like we're going to the 'Nam," I said. "$100 is actually cheap. I used to pay £1000 an hour for a partner and there would be six of them. Huỳnh is the name I imagine."

"You mean your clients would pay," said Gas.

"Exactly. OK, let's go to the airport and sort out flights."

"Do you mean the airport or the airport shopping mall?" asked Gas.

"That's not funny," I said, though it probably was.

CHAPTER 2

HÀ NỘI, VIETNAM

We booked into a hotel called the Miranda Boutique and Spa on Ma May St. The streets were often called 'Pho Something' which was odd because the excellent main national dish also seemed to be called the same thing. In fact though, the spicy soup had an accent so it was properly 'Phở' and pronounced more like the French 'feu'

but with the accent mandating a touch of wah-wah pedal upwards on the last letter.

The Miranda was a very well-appointed hotel in a great location. The taps and other bathroom plumbing were made by the 'Fukyoo' company. I wondered if this was an American having fun but decided it was too on the nose. That must really be some guy's name. Anyway, the products were good.

They had to be here, where there was a street called 'Sink Street.' Or that's what I assumed it had to be called. It was a long strip of stores selling only bathroom and kitchen fixtures. It wasn't far away from Santa Claus Corner. Shops here seemed to congregate by type, which always stuck me as hard to explain, economically speaking. Gas though that 'Fukyoo' was at least better than 'Kumho Tires,' and I couldn't disagree.

The meeting was set for outside the Water Puppet theatre the next day. This was a local landmark on the lake where you could see puppets animated from under the water showing the local history. It was actually quite spooky. There were dragons that could breathe fire both above and below water and also strangely disturbing grey man-babies that did a lot of backflips. The music was good. It had that Eastern set of pitches that seemed to be different to Western music and somehow 'in between' it.

The puppets sat squarely in what is known in robotics circles as the 'uncanny valley.' If you made something indistinguishable from a person, people would interact with it like it was a human, no problem. If it clearly wasn't human, that was also fine. People would deal with it like they would a spoon.

The problem came with where the robotics people were at, technically. They could make androids that weren't human but looked like they were trying to be. This is what people didn't like, so the designers had to deliberately fail in the task of making the androids look a lot like people, until they got better at it.

While we waited for the meeting, we hung around. "We have to do the thing with the train," Gas had said, so we were doing that. This involved sitting at a distance from a train track which appeared inadequate when there was no train there and also seemed to have even less than that inadequate level of adequacy when there was a train coming.

You also put the lid from your bottle of Hanoi Beer on the track and the wheels crushed it as the train went past, inches from your feet. That was the plan.

The bar owner came round first and moved you so you were sitting sideways. Westerners thought this was unnecessary caution the first time until they actually tried it. What we were doing would be completely banned anywhere normal and boring. They didn't know that here, this game was serious and you should pay attention to safety advice.

"How do we know the beer bottle lid won't fly off and blind us?" I had asked, but Gas responded "You're wearing glasses, so you don't need to worry about it." I wasn't completely reassured, but it was a good point about trajectories and probabilities, so I had to go with it.

The train came incredibly close to where we were sitting, to the extent that it would have hit us had we not been aligned with the wall. The noise was extraordinary, and was added to by repeated long blasts of the horn. We picked up our flattened and oily beer caps, which were also hot.

Having done the train thing, we needed a new bar. We wandered around and the first place we found looked super-posh and oligarchic. I liked the look of it, but Gas wasn't sure.

"That might be a bit upscale. I haven't exactly got my eyebrows on fleek," said Gas.

"I have no idea what that means, but I know what you mean," I replied.

We continued and found somewhere more low-key. I ordered Bia Saigons for both of us. We also got some mango, which was served differently here than anywhere else. Instead of the idea being 'ripe and sweet,' it was under-ripe and therefore sharp and citric. But the mango pieces came with a powder to dip them in which was simultaneously salty and sweet and slightly fishy. It was delicious, and it made you drink more beer, which was presumably the point of bar snacks. We sat in the road on very low plastic stools.

A pair of women who appeared to be Indian tourists showed up. They ordered drinks, but then immediately whipped out phones. One of them took a very leisurely video scan of the whole scene, completing three full revolutions at a speed slow enough to get good resolution on all of us.

I was often surprised by what tourists did. I could understand them going on a trip where they saw four sights in five hours; after all, they had limited time. But what was this woman going to do with her video? I didn't see what value there was in having filmed a load of strangers, or at what point someone would say, "Now is the time to look at a clip of people I don't know in a bar," or, "hey, this is what a bar looks like." Maybe I had been in too many bars to find them unusual.

The filming disturbed me slightly. I took note of who else was disturbed. Three guys, not sitting together, looked unhappy. Only one did the classic "yawn into hand/smooth hair/turn slightly away" to avoid being filmed move. Another person did the "sudden bend down to tie shoelaces" trick that features in hostile environment training but that kid was so transparently a drunk Farang backpacker who actually had undone laces that I discounted him. He would have to be very, very good indeed to be anything other than what he appeared. And really, who knew we were here and who would care? No one cared enough to pay for a fake Farang of that quality when there was so much real Farang around.

Yawn guy was either Russian or skilled at looking like it. You can't fake a jawline easily. You could still see huge Soviet era GAZ jeeps rolling around downtown. They were now carrying tourists rather than Viet Cong artillery advisers, but that and the whole Communism thing made the Russians feel right at home. That was true for some of them, anyway. It was not the hard core iron rice bowl Communism any more. It was Capitalism with a lot of crimson haberdashery.

A siren started up in the background. The bar staff started to move quickly and chivvied us all off the stools. We didn't particularly have any space to move to and some tourists were older, slower and confused so the operation was not a great success.

The police came past in force. They seized a lot of plastic chairs and threw them in the back of a beaten-up pickup. Someone had put a sticker on the side of the police vehicle. It read 'Ganz Ulm haßt die Polizei,' which meant 'All Ulm hates the police.' This was either remarkably post-modern or subtle self-mockery by the local force, or someone had looked up the word 'Polizei' and decided the sticker was apt, especially given the fierce German eagle on it. A pair of presumably Deutsche tourist girls grinned, as did I.

The whole thing with the seats was odd. The police would come through three times an evening to clear the streets, and the bar owners just regarded it as a cost of doing business.

"I don't see why cars should have priority or why they should have to be in narrow streets in the first place," said Gas. "The bar owners have to make a living. There's like 200 tourists and locals buying beer and one guy wants to drive a car through here and everyone has to move so he can do that."

I agreed. "Apart from that, that's 20 officers doing nothing actually useful and hassling people. Still, the money is probably good."

The next day, we were outside the Water Puppet theatre at precisely 1800. This was about the busiest time to be there. One show was ending and one was beginning. The area was busy with people strolling past the lake and buying small doughnuts, which I did and paid the equivalent of $4 for. This unbelievable markup struck a passerby as so outrageous that she remonstrated with the woman who had sold them to me. At least, I assumed that that was what it about because it ended with the second woman pulling my sleeve in a way that suggested sympathy. This probably meant I had been overcharged by a factor of 10. A factor of four would be normal for a Farang penalty, but 10 was on the unreasonable side.

The Vietnamese currency had a number of unusual features. Firstly, it was called the đông. There had been a Danish wind power company called that but they got bored with the jokes. The exchange rate was something like VND 25,000 per USD. No-one used the thousands, so most prices would read "100" and they would mean 100,000. There was no obvious reason why the currency was not simply multiplied up by 1000 to get rid of all the numbers, since the exchange rate appeared not to have moved much in decades. There was a very good non-obvious reason though, because it would mean trashing all the old bank notes and issuing new ones and not having that whole process incur a 50% corruption/inefficiency penalty.

A woman on a moped came up to us. She said something I could tell was "Burgoyne?" I said yes. The woman asked for $100 which I handed over in the form of a Franklin which was so virgin, clean and fresh that I was sorry to see it go off into the world to get smudged edges. She gave me an envelope. Inside it was a card with an address on. It was slightly back into town. We started walking after looking it up on our phones.

Traffic in Hà Nội was different to that in Thailand. It was more old school in that it was still dominated by mopeds. There were positive and negative factors in negotiating it. The biggest negative was that people would come at you from all directions. The saving grace was that they weren't going very fast and they were expecting obstacles, such as pedestrians, the odd tuk-tuk, and random overflows of detritus, life and business on to the road.

We got to the address which was over a bánh mì place. This was fortunate because I was starving. Bánh mì was chicken in a baguette with pâté and some sort of specially zingy salad. The quality of the baguette was always excellent and critical to the dish. I assumed that the French had something to do with this.

We finished our lunch and headed to the stairwell which would take us up to the office. We hadn't been given a time so I was hoping we therefore couldn't be late. The stairwell was on the nondescript side, but it was clean. It had a fan rotating below a light, which meant I was glad not to suffer from epilepsy, and that was it. It did not appear to see a lot of traffic. At the top was a door with a small sign that had 'Huỳnh' written on it and nothing else.

"Guess she doesn't need anything beyond that," said Gas.

We pressed the doorbell. A well-dressed Vietnamese woman opened it and ushered us in. The office inside was a great deal more impressive than we had expected from the outside. It had marble flooring and a lot of heavy wooden furniture that looked vaguely French. It may well have looked precisely French to someone who knew anything about antiques. But that wasn't me.

Equally impressive was the woman herself, who introduced herself by name, which was pronounced Hoàng or Hwang. She moved and spoke quietly and precisely.

Once we were seated behind a highly stable desk, she asked: "How can I help you?"

"We're interested in chip swap agreements between casinos," Gas opened up. "Is that something where you have experience?"

"I do indeed."

"There's one in particular we would like to know about. Anything that relates to the Pang Casino in Chiang Mai," continued Gas.

"I cannot discuss details of individual clients with other potential clients. Confidentiality requirements," said Huỳnh.

"Of course," said Gas, "but we would be interested in a case study based on actual experience. We wouldn't want to pay a lot for work that was more ... theoretical."

"I have a great deal of relevant experience on chip swap agreements and I could have a report prepared."

"That sounds excellent. When could we have it?" I asked.

"It could be ready in about three days. But it would be a great deal of work and would represent a significant amount of high value IPR. So I would need to charge $10,000 for it."

I was sort of shocked by this number, but also not. People who hadn't instructed a lot of solicitors had the wrong idea about how the charging structure worked. It did not always depend on hours worked, though the lawyers themselves made it look that way by charging out per person per hour by seniority. But if you wanted a work product like this which was going to be based on work already done, you were paying not so much for the work or for the information solidity but, critically, for the fact that the law firm would stand behind the opinion. So effectively you were paying an insurance premium.

If the law firm told you something which turned out not to be true, and you relied on in and lost money, you could sue them. That was the theory anyway. No one in the history of the world had ever sued a law firm and come out better off. Though I had once sued a dead guy using a legal opinion and had won without going to trial. So there was that.

"We might be able to find that sort of money, but it would be very helpful if we could have some sort of indication in the report as to the nature and foundation in reality of its provenance," Gas said, but this appeared to be too opaque. At least, I wasn't completely sure what she meant. But Huỳnh was on the case. She could see that we wanted to know something about specific counter-parties.

"A special report of that nature would involve additional technical security measures and would therefore cost $15,000."

I wasn't clear on this either, but what was clear was that these numbers were going the wrong way; however it looked like Gas and Huỳnh were inking a deal.

Huỳnh wanted payment upfront, but we agreed on the standard basis of half now and half later. I would have to go to the bank to begin the laborious process of acquiring a pair of bankers drafts for $7,500. It was really hard if you had the money. Presumably it was even harder if you didn't.

It wasn't great giving large amounts of cash to people you didn't know. But Gas checked on the registry of lawyers, and Huỳnh featured as a solo partner. She wasn't listed at the location above the bánh mì store, but she was in a place we looked at which turned out to be a corporate mailbox provider. "That will have to be good enough," concluded Gas. "She exists and she is a lawyer. Unless she just borrowed the name and paid for a nameplate."

"And some furniture."   It was the furniture which convinced me. And the fact we didn't have a choice.

"We've got three days to kill now.   What shall we do?" asked Gas, after I had dropped off the first $7,500 draft. These were a better way of paying people large amounts of money than wiring them because wires could go astray.   In fact that was the whole basis of the operation we were in. So it kept us in employment at least.

Banker's drafts had a payee name on them so they couldn't be cashed by anyone else.   Though there was that famous case where enterprising British postmen had opened up bank accounts in the name of an Italian guy called "Inlando Revendi."   They had then paid a lot of slightly doctored cheques made out to the Inland Revenue, the UK equivalent of the IRS, into this account and bought a lot of stereos and TVs. Then they went to prison.

"We can check out the war museum; after that let's go on a cruise in Hạ Long Bay.   It's beautiful and if that Russian guy wasn't just a Russian guy, it will throw them off. Tourist stuff. Maybe I'll get some board shorts."

So that's what we did. The bay was filled with enormous stone pillar islands that rose vertically out of the water but were also somehow covered with trees and vegetation. We drifted around and drank a lot of pretty good Mojitos. At night, the water turned from a vibrant milky green colour to a deep aquamarine blue, with the golden lights from other ships forming bright paths towards us. Occasionally new boats would turn up. Some of them were quiet, like ours, and others would have American spring breakers doing 'Rage Against The Machine' covers on the karaoke with some enthusiasm and actually quite a lot of rage.

There was no Wifi on the boat so I checked my phone when we returned to Hà Nội three days later. I had an email from Huỳnh. She was typically terse. "Report ready. Water Puppets 1800 tonight."

I got the document from the same woman on the Moped as before. Having checked that the folder she gave me contained some paper with writing on it and not old newspapers, I handed over the second banker's draft and brought the report back to the Miranda, where we were staying again. Gas was waiting on my first floor balcony over-looking the street restaurants. The street was always busy but the room was quiet.

"It's big," I said, "this is going to take a while."

"OK," said Gas, "see you in a couple of days."

"You don't want to stay and help?"

" 'How?' and 'no' are my two initial responses," she said as she exited.

That's how long it took. The report was a very good piece of work and it focused on the legal concept of novation. This was when an existing contract was modified in that some of the counter-parties changed. Basically, if everyone in a contract agreed, then a person or entity that had signed a contract could be replaced by a completely different entity. Getting people to agree to this generally meant paying them, even if they would be better off with the change. The world was in fact so cynical that plenty of people would charge you for giving them money if they knew that you needed the alteration more than they did.

I learned that English law was often used for these chip swap agreements, because that was a good venue with clear law understood by everyone and impartial enforcement. You didn't want to have an agreement between, for example, a casino in Thailand and a casino in Vietnam under Thai law because one guy would have a natural advantage, and not just because he would be working in his native language. I thought that the example of a casino in Thailand and another one in Vietnam was enlightening given our situation.

The last 30 pages were an appendix which purported to be a draft chip swap agreement. It was mostly unredacted apart from the parts upfront which named the parties to the contract. I tried holding those pages up to the light but there wasn't anything to see.

The report had a bunch of footnotes throughout. Mostly they were pointers to English law precedents. But the third footnote among five, on page 157 of 256 was something that looked like a link but also looked like an incomprehensible piece of garbage, as far as I could tell. When Gas came back from wherever she'd been, I asked her what it was.

She said "That's a burner link."

"Which does what?"

"Don't know until I hit it. But it only works the first time and will probably go somewhere that has all the feels of a dungeon full of trapdoors," she said. "Maybe it will be a proof of life video or an extortion demand. It's probably not a cake recipe."

"I like cake."

"You wouldn't like this cake."

"OK. Sounds lovely. Let's hit it."

"I need to do a couple of things first," said Gas. "The first is setup a sandbox. I don't want to get spiked by some piece of malware."

I used a MacBook, because it was clean and quick and easy-to-use and synced up well with my iPhone. Gas's laptop was basically the opposite of that on all parameters. It was squat and ugly and, as if embarrassed, the manufacturer had not bothered to put its logo or name on the device. It could only have looked more Soviet if it had had a hammer and sickle on it and been made of concrete.

The only thing it could do was execute code extremely quickly, because it didn't waste any time on fripperies like a graphical interface or anything that might make it user-friendly. It wasn't even obvious whether the thing was turned on or not. It probably indicated that it was in operation by flashing a black light on a black background. But only once, and only during non-daylight hours. It maybe also had beeps, but they would be well north of 20 kHz so only dogs could hear them.

I'd seen Gas do this sandbox thing before. She had explained it to me once by telling back to me a story about a time I had overdone the weed in Phuket. There was a strip off the main bar street in Patong, called Soi Bangla, which had a bunch of strip clubs and additional bars. A long time ago, someone had added an additional set of bars above the main ones. It appeared that the planning philosophy was that you could never have enough bars on Bangla.

However, it turned out that you could. The ones on the upper level had been dormant for a long time. Even the extra effort required to go up the stairs detracted from footfall. And there was no USP. All of the bars had a whole bunch of people outside trying to persuade you to go in, based on the cheapness of their beer, which they displayed on signs. This meant that the beer market was hyper-efficient: there was probably not going to be a 5 baht difference between any two bars unless they were offering something else on top, like a ping pong show, or dancers, or ladyboys who would beat you at Connect 4 a hundred times in a row if it paid.

The prime spot on the upper level closest to the main street had been dormant like the rest, but recently it had been taken over by a weed entrepeneur, who was, inevitably, from Amsterdam. This guy would roll you a joint and advise you depending on your requirements. I got some called lava cake. I later found out that the THC content was 24%, which was way higher than the 'red leb' and 'black rocky' that we had at college.

I had made the classic error of smoking half of the joint and on nothing much happening, continuing to smoke the other half. This resulted after about 20 minutes in a phenomenon I could only really describe as 'hearing the angels' sing. It was unusual, synaesthetic, intensely enjoyable but with a significant undertow of paranoia all at the same time.

This was all fairly standard, but the interesting point about how I got home and the way I'd explained it to Gas was that it was some kind of internal sandbox thing happening. It was like there was one part of my mind, the major part, which was thinking 'we need to go home now' and somewhat freaking out. Another part of my mind was saying 'that's no problem, I can make that happen for us.'

I had asked myself the question how I was going to get back to the hotel safely, given that I was hearing colours and seeing sounds. Or we had, since we appeared to have become plural. The answer came in from somewhere 'walk down the stairs, go right, right along the beach and right and that's it. Don't do anything else. Don't fall in any holes. One step after another. If you see any Hotel staff, smile and move on.' It was like mentally running some software using my mind as the hardware environment around it.

Gas had explained that a sandbox on a computer was basically a safe area where anything was allowed. "It's like you have decided to do something stupid and dangerous, like you maybe did, but you have done it in a location where there are limits to how far the stupidity and danger can spread. Outside the sandbox, there's always something or someone or an aspect of personality left in control that can step in and prevent any damage or data-loss or security breaches."

"It's kind of lucky I have this sandbox feature in my head. What happens if you don't have it?" I wondered.

"I guess you wake up dead or broke or you don't do these things. But no sandbox means no Navy and a bunch of other stuff."

How she actually created the sandbox apparently involved something called a 'virtual machine' but I was happy enough with the analogy.

"What's the other thing you need to do?" I asked.

"We need a record of what happens," said Gas and switched on screen recording. This was one of the few concessions to modernity available on the Gas laptop, which grudgingly allowed something like a prehistoric window to be formed if you tried really hard, when on all other occasions it was pure Command Line Interface:

there was just a % prompt and you could type things in like ps -aef and something would happen.

That was one of the few commands I understood. Gas told me it showed the processes running on the system. It was actually very straightforward. ps was the command to show processes and the flags after the hyphen modified that command. -a meant show all processes, not just your own, -e meant show them even if they did not have a controlling terminal, meaning no-one human was home and -f meant show full data on the processes.

If she didn't like the look of anything, she could type kill -9 which was better than just kill. Kill -9 meant terminate immediately with extreme prejudice and don't think about it or raise any caveats. This was the Apocalypse Now of UNIX commands. It was so evocative that it sometimes emerged from Gas's technical sandbox into her conversation: "We need to kill -9 that" meant that an something I had started was very bad. Usually she was right. She didn't use it for bad ideas I proposed, because she said "you can only kill a process, not an idea for a process." Somehow it was in the right font even when she just said it.

"OK, vamos," said Gas.

She typed in the link from the footnote:

```
https://one-time.link/?t5ZZ-AHg#KtZgLrFs-
qQb4ptC
```

This took a long time because it was so cumbersome. Gas stared at it for about 20 seconds and stared at the report for a similar amount of time to make sure she had it right. Then she hit enter.

That was an anticlimax because what came back was something very similar to what she had typed in. It was another burner link, together with some advice:

This message won't be displayed again.
Copy it before closing this page, as necessary.

"Yeah, too right," said Gas. I wondered about the 'as necessary.' It was like they were remarking on the point that it might be necessary for us. They could have said 'if you like' or they could have said nothing. Gas hit the link again to see what would happen, and got the following:

The message has been removed, or wrong URL.

"The great thing about that," said Gas, "is that it's the same error message for situations where that link never existed and where it's already been accessed. So no-one will be able to tell the difference from now on. And they certainly won't be able to follow us. But the sender of the message can see it has been accessed."

"How many times are we going through this loop?" I asked.

"Three times. If in doubt, three is always the number."

She was right. We went through three burner links and the third one opened a picture. It was a fairly low quality photo of the back of an envelope with "DragonWorld" and an address in Phnom Penh written on it.

"That's our counterparty, presumably." I said.

"I know what you're going to say next," said Gas.

"Yes. Airport. No, wait." I searched for DragonWorld and got the address, and then I looked at the redacted counterparty names at the start of the sample chip swap agreement. One of them had approximately the same number of characters and line breaks in the same places as what was written on the envelope, including a six-digit Cambodian ZIP code. ZIP codes in Thailand were five digits. They were also six digits in Vietnam, but that didn't appear to be a problem. "That works. Or it's consistent, anyway. Indeed, airport."

I had a penchant for booking flights actually in cabs on the way to the airport. It took me back to my time as an investment banker, where we had an entire department that did nothing else apart from move us front-office types around the board, often with the plan changing in real time as it was elapsing. It was fun and it didn't really move the dial on expenses.

The other thing we did in the airport, apart from load up on free booze in the lounge, was contact our INTERPOL handler. This was Brynjar Pettersen, who was a big, bluff, slightly cynical Norwegian who had a habit of saying "Uff da" quite a lot. This apparently meant something like "that's unfortunate" and it was true, quite a lot of things were. He said the first word like you had punched him gently in the gut and the air was sighing out of him.

He was unusual in that he didn't regard being posted out of Kripos into INTERPOL as a punishment. He hadn't had to move far; he was still sitting in the National Central Bureau in Oslo as the local lead for INTERPOL's Financial Crime and Anti-Corruption Centre. He was also unusual in that he was probably the only cop in the world with a philosophy degree. This sometimes meant he seemed to be operating on a different level to everyone else, either above or below or beyond or sometimes orthogonal. But he got results.

I had never really understood why people avoided an INTERPOL posting if they could, because it looked at least like the work was more interesting. But apparently it didn't do much for your career prospects because you were simply effectively absent from your home force, so net generating seniority in the usual fashion of sitting on your ass, and the silo mentality meant it was even more difficult than usual to get any cooperation. At the same time, when the system could be forced into action, it could do impressive stuff. And no one else could really do anything cross-border, so the field was wide open and becoming more significant all the time.

Brynjar would do anything for you as long as it did not involve any paperwork, approvals or allocation of resources. This wasn't because he didn't want to help. It was just that if you asked for anything requiring a positive decision, nothing would happen. Like many public sector organisations, it was a lot easier to do nothing that could get you fired. You couldn't get fired for not doing anything because no-one could see you doing that. They could see you signing a document which led to a blown operation or some wasted resources though. They could also see you turning down an operation which it later transpired should have gone ahead. So all in all, the most skilful operators stayed away from any actual decisions that would be recorded and have consequences. You could sometimes force things through, but Brynjar needed to choose his battles and the absolute best case for a decision was a month, which was often the same as 'never' on internet timescales.

Brynjar gave us the details for a local freelancer who could give us local colour and fix stuff. He was called Jimmy MacAllister so he was probably Scots. I didn't know Cambodia very well though both Gas and I had at one time been to Siem Reap. Temple skills were unlikely to be helpful where we were going however, though the ability to appeal to some wakeful gods or protective Nāga might have been.

CHAPTER 3

PHNOM PENH, CAMBODIA

We had got hold of MacAllister straight away, who turned out not to be Scottish. He was instead a lawyer from Dagenham, which is a strange if not incoherent juxtaposition. British lawyers were normally posh and from posh places. Dagenham was much more about ducking and weaving and this was reflected in MacAllister's life story. He had made his money importing 'reasonably kosher' wheel trims for BMWs and then had branched out into Chinese fireworks. These were also 'reasonably kosher' but they certainly provided a proper big bang, and one with may have exceeded local regulations on bang size. And that was what people wanted. Nothing he had done was causing Brynjar a problem in having him named as the local unofficial contact, but then Brynjar hadn't really heard of any of us in an emergency.

We went for beers to get a view of the place. The expat community was noticeably slightly morose. It was as though they felt they'd drawn the short straw in the South East Asian lottery. Sure, it was cheap, but you couldn't really make big money unless you were one of the guys from Aberdeen in the oil business. There were lots of them but they gave off the same aura people used to have in dustier parts of the Middle East in the old days 'I'm just doing my time and racking up the chips; I will live later on.'

The climate was a bit too sticky. There weren't any pavements. Or none you could use, because a lot of business activity spilled out on to them, or they were damaged by years of traffic and climate erosion, or there were a million mopeds stacked up on them.

But the big problem was the food. As MacAllister put it, "there's a reason the world is full of Thai restaurants and there are no Khmer ones." I had not really thought about this but I would have assumed it had something to do with the availability of capital or the amount of tourism. But the locals as well as MacAllister were all adamant that you had to eat the French food, which was expensive but excellent.

Gas and I decided to test this theory, which looked suspect. Surely an entire national cuisine must have some bright spots. We looked up online the name of the most highly rated restaurant and persuaded MacAllister to come with us. He was not greatly enthusiastic but agreed so long as we could go to a French place the next evening.

We got a tuk-tuk to the restaurant, which turned out to be in a very impressive colonial mansion with a garden surrounding a pool. We got a pretty impressive Californian Chardonnay which was certainly the best glass of wine I had ever had in South East Asia. I was beginning to think that MacAllister could not possibly be right about the food.

"So is all this part of TORAID?" asked MacAllister. This was a project that aimed to use Japanese money to expand on work done under a previous project, TORII, which aimed to Trace, Obstruct, Recover Illicit Inflows in South East Asia. MacAllister had had some people come through from Brynjar in connection with it.

"We let Brynjar classify it. I think he probably just puts our whole operation down as 'Sundries and Consumables' if we actually need him to front up some cash, but mostly he just doesn't ask questions about any differences between the initial recovered amount and the final remitted amount."

"That's helpful."

"It is, but sometimes it creates documentation problems. Gas sorts that sort of thing out. I think one time we were 600,000 toilet rolls. Brynjar is world-class at virement."

"I might have some work for you," said MacAllister, looking at Gas.

"Fine," said Gas. "I'm not that busy while Burgoyne is thinking or chasing trails. Then other times it briefly gets super busy. It's like the Navy."

"Is there going to be a crypto stage?" asked MacAllister.

"Bound to be, since there is $24bn a year of crypto money laundering," I replied. "I'm dreading it," Crypto always seem to be part of the trail these days. It was invariably complex, stressful and difficult all at the same time.

"The only thing worse than crypto is if it disappears somewhere on K Street, because then we can see it but it's the other side of kryptonite plexiglass and we're finished." K Street was the locus for Washington lobbyists, representing another financial sink hole where money went and was never seen again.

Following a money trail was a bit like looking at the Loch Ness monster. This was a probably mythical creature which was usually drawn as having a long serpentine body which would alternately dip below the waves or be visible above them. You could see a part of the path the money followed, and then it would disappear into the system, and you would have to do work to find out where it went. If there was a crypto stage, things could get a lot more opaque, depending on the level of sophistication of the operators. And it didn't look like our guys were going to drop the ball any time soon. And even idiots could be hard to follow just as a result of the sheer volume of madness going on daily.

MacAllister though any crypto stages would be elsewhere. "It probably won't be here. We've got some floating around, but those guys are highly mobile and they would only really have one reason to be here, which is invisibility. And that's not a USP."

"Worth having though. And the Portugal tax angle disappeared so some people might move." The Portuguese government had forgotten to pass legislation making crypto returns liable for capital gains tax. A number of crypto bros had moved there having interpreted events as meaning that the government wanted to encourage a dynamic innovative industry, but no. They just forgot. And then they remembered.

"Sure. So what exactly do you think is happening?" enquired MacAllister.

"We think a chip swap agreement between a casino in the Philippines and a defunct one in Chiang Mai has been reactivated and novated, which means that the parties to the agreement are now the original casino in the Philippines and a new one here," I explained.

"So what does that mean is happening?" MacAllister wondered.

"Basically if you had a way of getting cash into the Philippines shop, you could buy into local chips there and then you could almost automatically trade those in on a real-time basis for the ability to receive chips somewhere else. The fact that the original casino on the agreement is no longer active doesn't really matter."

"I've seen contracts like that but I've never seen one with a novation.   But I suppose if the original parties agree, it's going to work."

"Indeed," I said.   "We think the new party is DragonWorld, here."

"That's a pretty big outfit.   HoldCo is listed in Hong Kong.   Nice location, overlooking the confluence of the Tonlé Sap river, which is actually a freshwater lake, and the Mekong.   There's a strike going on there at the moment."

Our food arrived. I was forced to agree with MacAllister that it was pretty disappointing. The local speciality was called Fish Amok. This name wasn't great marketing to start with. Beyond that, as a general principle fish sauce needed to be citric and acidic and zingy, and this was sort of turgid and creamy.   The fish was also over-cooked. It came overcooked and then they brought it on a contraption which included a candle to ensure that it became progressively more over-cooked as you ate it.

You could get a much better seafood experience at any beach shack in Thailand, and also you would pay less by a factor of 10. I worked out that I was going to pay the equivalent of $57 for this experience; which didn't make any sense even allowing for the wine. It made even less sense when you considered that this place was much poorer on average than Thailand. Or maybe it did. Anyway, I got bored with figuring out why the fish was bad and just accepted I wasn't going to enjoy it.

"I will never contradict your opinions on local cuisine every again." Then I asked, "Who is striking?"

"Good move. The local staff in the casino. Apparently they are paid according to standards obtaining around here. But they see all these dollars flowing past them and they think they should have a taste of that. I can see their point, but of course the company just says that it doesn't want to pay more than it has to and these people can easily be replaced."

"Right."

MacAllister continued: "They are all out the front banging drums and blowing trumpets. You could go and see if any of them want to talk, taking some cash of course. There's a lot of security overseeing the situation so you would need to watch that."

"Disgruntled employees who like dollars. Perfect."

The money situation in Cambodia was in flux. The Riel traded at around 4,000 to the dollar, so it was more big number maths like in Vietnam. Historically it had been a fully dollarised economy, but efforts were underway to change that. Low value transactions were in KHR and big ones continued to be in USD. It was noticeable that while this generally worked out, people were much happier giving you KHR than taking them from you.

"So is it the usual game with these guys?"

"Yes," I responded, "they always want the same two things. Not getting caught and winding up with clean laundered cash they can spend and where we can't follow them and neither can anyone else."

What we were tracking was known in the Anti-Money Laundering trade as 'layering.' This meant mixing up legitimate and illegitimate cash as much as possible and in a long sequence of transactions so that you ended up with clean money. AML and Diversity were the only two items of mandatory annual training for investment bankers. It was taken seriously nowadays and the times when senior guys on the desk would get interns to take it for them were gone the same way as the five-hour boozy lunches and strip clubs. Underground.

Gas had once asked me if I had ever made a report to the AML officer. I had done it once in my career.

"What raised your suspicions?"

"Nothing. I was just trying to piss someone off internally by getting them into some paperwork." The semi-Swiss bank I had ended my career at was notoriously buccaneering even in the generally piratical world of investment banks. I had often been involved in legal situations, but the Swiss outfit was the only one where I had been threatened with litigation by my own swaps desk. It would later go bust and get bought by the other Swiss bank.

"Nothing like actual bent money coming in the door ever really happened. We were too big to deal with individuals. We used to get emails round from Compliance telling us not to open a bank account for Muammar Gaddafi but he never asked so it wasn't a problem. But nevertheless, we were trained to death on it, which is useful now I suppose."

Also my speciality in banking had been as a securitisation structurer. That had been all about transformation of cashflows into other cashflows or asset types, and we saw a lot of that. Cash in investment banking was like energy in physics; neither could be created or destroyed, if you understood all the sources of friction, but both could take on an infinite array of appearances. Sometimes I would meet people from more conventional areas of banking who thought that principal could only be principal and interest could only be interest no matter how many transformations you went through but I didn't care: any cashflow could become any other cashflow. The accountants could worry about definitions later on. I just wanted a cool structure.

Gas had asked whether this made me any different to the money launderers.

"I never did anything illegal," was my response to that. "But a lot of cashflow transformations might involve transferable skills between the two arenas I suppose."

"So what's our next move?" asked Gas. "Go talk to these strikers?"

"Yep. But let's get a translator first."

MacAllister said "I could get you a real translator, but you could just get a tour guide if you want to ask people for info rather than end up with an admissible document. That's also more low-key."

"Sounds good."

MacAllister thought again from the perspective of keeping a low profile it would be good to source a tour guide by actually going on a tour. Rather than drive south to what was known in English as the Killing Fields, we stayed in Phnom Penh itself and went to the Tuol Sleng prison museum.

Our guide was called Chamroeun and was a young, friendly graduate in tourism with good English. We went around the museum which was if anything even more depressing than otherwise since the building had originally been built as a school. It was easy to imagine kids running around the grounds. There was a wooden structure supporting baseball hoops which had been converted to a gallows. There were fountains and shrubs. There was an imaginary smell of death that had lingered for decades.

The rooms were all basically bare with fading orange and cream floor tiles, concrete walls, iron beds and the odd box of 5.56mm 10 clip bandolier B40 cartridges. Rudimentary brick cells were added to many rooms. They were of a size where a person could maybe stand up in them but that was about it. The mortaring was really bad, but presumably that had not been a major concern of the desperate denizens.

Some rooms were full of skulls. It was particularly striking that some of the translated reports from prison guards used an inanimate pronoun to dehumanise their victims. An example that chilled me was "it did not eat rice because it decided to die." 20,000 people went through Tuol Sleng and 12 survivors are known.

None of the prisoners seemed to have really done anything. One guy had been studying in Japan when the regime appealed for people to go back and help with reconstruction. They tortured him to death because he had been in Japan and therefore couldn't be trusted. Guns give stupid men power, I thought, not for the first time. They could have just left the guy in Japan.

Chamroeun took us through all this with good humour and at the end I asked him whether he was free tomorrow and wanted to make $100. "Nothing illegal, no sex, no problem."

"Police?"

"No police. Just talking to people. We work for the BBC in London. We want to talk to the strikers at the casino."

"Just talk?"

"That's it. Nothing more," I reassured him, and he agreed to meet us the next day at our hotel in the Boeng Reang district. The hotel was fine but had some slightly odd features. The gym was enormous but carpeted. They had quite a good whisky selection but the barman had clearly never actually sold any of the premium stuff because when I had tried to buy some, he couldn't find how to do it in the till. It took long enough for me to realise that I would get a hangover and think better of it. There was a fair amount of 'stuff that looks good but you may struggle to actually get it to happen' around.

"Do you think I should do this or you?" I asked Gas.

"Why don't I do it?" she said. "Might make a change and I can be fairly unobtrusive. Security are still less likely to see or care about a woman."

"That's a mistake, but sure, let's run with it," I said. "You might not need to actually do anything other than observe Chamroeun."

I spent the day reading the FT, doing the crossword and putting on some desultory trades on the Nikkei. Nothing particularly worked but I did finish the crossword. Gas came back at dinner time.

"SITREP is positive," she said. This was good. Many SITREPs were 'NTR' for Nothing To Report which was the worst thing because you didn't get any new cards and you might have to think of something.

Chamroeun was good," she reported. "We got some street food to make it look like he was someone's brother delivering supplies. It was balut which is fertilised duck eggs. You mash up the embryo with rice."

"Wow. I don't really have a good argument for this, but I am putting that up there with shiny fried cockroaches on a stick." These were sometimes hawked around in Phuket but I'd never seen anyone try one. Maybe the sports teams and stag parties did it as a bet.

"So he wanders around the strikers. He looks legitimate and like he was supposed to be there. I hung around some way across the road in a doorway. Security don't care about me or him."

"Great. What did he get?"

"He spoke to a bunch of strikers. I told him probably we wanted croupiers and it took him a while to find any because a lot of people there were kitchen and support staff. We were interested in two things: anything weird and anything involving amounts of money like $30m."

"What did you get?"

"Firstly, the definition of 'weird' in a casino is slightly off-kilter with normal life. Some of the high-rollers want unusual stuff. Like paying hookers to snort coke while they watch."

"That is indeed more unusual than snorting the coke yourself and then thinking of something to do with the hookers," I responded. "Or you could snort coke off the hookers. I suppose that's just too last year now."

"Right. But the real lead we got didn't come from the croupiers, only two of whom were out there. One of the women who worked in the chow shop said that she has a cousin who works in the chip dispensary."

"This is gaming chips we're talking about now, not the edible sort?"

"Why would I be telling you about French fries now? And I wouldn't be calling them 'chips' would I?" retorted Gas.

"Fair points. I got confused with the kitchen stuff. So what did the cousin say?"

"She is reluctant to meet us. Doesn't want to get fired. She's not on strike. I've spread some cash around Chamroeun, the kitchen woman and her cousin and I am saying we would like a meet but we'll take a call. Chamroeun is going to see what he can come up with."

A couple of hours later Chamroeun showed up and said we could do the call. But the cousin would only take a call from his mobile, would only speak to him and didn't want to say anything confidential.

"OK," I said, "let's see what she's got."

Chamroeun put his phone on the table and set it to speaker mode.

"Just start by asking her for more, anything really, on this unusual thing that happened," I said to Chamroeun. He placed the call and spoke Khmer briefly. There was a long response during which Chamroeun took notes. Then he summarised for us.

"She say many reasons she think this is weird thing. Number one, big money, and $31m like you say. She see million dollar many times but this big, she sees only see a few times a year. And also number like your number. Number two, not the normal way. Normal way is that a man comes in with money, he gives her money, she gives him chips. Then he goes and gambles with the chips. After that, sometimes he comes back with chips and she gives him money again. Not many times he comes back with more chips, but sometimes. Mostly they lose all the chips and buy some more."

Chamroeun got to the weird part. "But this time the chips come from the sky, she says."

"What?" Gas asked. "Oh wait. Does she mean she just got told to give some dude chips?"

"She say no dude. 'Dude' means 'man' right? She say no man. They have system to record balances. Man come in, he win chips, sometimes he takes them, other times he leaves them in system and he can play with them next time. This is different. Account in system with lot of chips but no man. Man somewhere else. System says that this account is in Vietnam but it does not belong to a person. Third weird thing."

"OK," I asked, "so she's got these chips, or this system credit that represents chips, but she's got no customer in front of her, so what is she going to do with them?"

Chamroeun continued: "this is the weird thing. She say the chips come from the sky and go to the sky."

I was getting the picture. It fitted with what we had found about the chip swap agreement. These chips had come in on an automatic mechanism and they were going to go out the same way, with no person showing up at the desk. Gas was on the same page but was looking perturbed. She was probably thinking what I was thinking, which was this could go on forever. Or at least until they ran out of casinos.

"So what happens to these chips?" I asked.

"She says there was a flag on the system. It says any balance on this account is to go to another account. She presses a button and the system does it. No real chips in her hand. They go to the other account. She says this would even happen automatically often, but just with this big number, she has to say yes."

"Where do the chips go to?"

Chamroeun spoke some more. He got an answer he didn't seem to like very much. He asked more questions. He looked confused for a while. That didn't clear itself up. Finally he spoke to us.

"This is nonsense now. She says the chips go to America and Korea or America in Korea."

"Some of them go to the US and some go to Korea?" asked Gas.

"No she says *all of them* go to America and Korea. I don't understand," clarified Chamroeun.

"It has to be one or the other."

"That I say to her. She is very insistent."

"OK, can she get some kind of printout from the system? On the transfer?"

Chamroeun again spoke at length, and managed to reassure the contact. It was going to cost us $20 and we would get it the next morning after she came back from work; she worked until early in the morning. I was happy with this arrangement.

"Tell her we have a deal. Here's $50, please go get it and pay her and the rest is for you," I said.

It looked like our guys were transferring an amount close to $31m every time. They were not 'cutting it into shapes.'

"So what is this shapes thing?" Gas had asked.

"I once almost got into a serious amount of trouble in relation to large transfer amounts and breaking them down. That's the 'cutting into shapes.' I had done a deal in Dublin for €525m. My client had sold Irish mortgages to that value and I had securitised them, meaning that I had sold €525m of bonds backed by the mortgages."

"OK."

"This was all fine, except my client wanted their money first thing in the morning, which technically meant I had to sort of borrow it, because I wouldn't get paid by the bond buyers until various points during the day. But they were all highly-rated, so I didn't really have to worry about them going bust. The money would be coming to me in London from Ireland, because that's where the Special Purpose Vehicle company we had setup to buy the mortgages and issue the bonds was based."

"OK," said Gas again. She somehow managed to retain all of this stuff I mentioned so sometimes she would correct my memory because of a time I had said something years before.

I moved on to borrowing conventions. "In The City, you can borrow money for nothing, for a short time. The infamous and now on the way-out LIBOR is the interest rate you pay for borrowing from another bank in The City. That's what it stands for: London Interbank Offered Rate."

"Oh this sounds like a flash loan, where you borrow money online and it can be any amount with no cost provided you pay it back in the same single UNIX command," said Gas.

"Sounds like it. How does it work?"

"A flash loan is a smart contract," explained Gas. "The critical point is that all the parts of the contract get executed, in a pre-determined order, in a batch job on Ethereum or something. And it's on an all or nothing basis: either everything happens or nothing does."

"What can you do?"

"You can borrow money or tokens or assets without putting up any collateral. It all happens, initiate, execute, wrap up effectively in zero time. So it can be very powerful if you stack a bunch of them up."

"What's great about this," I observed, is that you don't have any credit risk, or liquidity risk. In banks we spend half our time worrying about who we are lending to and whether they can pay it back. And you just don't care here. Plus it sounds like you don't have to concern yourself with any tedious Know Your Customer bollocks."

"That's right. It's pure instantaneous capitalism," said Gas, who was after all Texan. Apparently her middle name was Dixie. I wasn't sure what that meant.

"So this is like that but in real time. There is a sort of Gentleman's agreement in finance that says if you borrow money and you give it back by lunchtime, you won't be charged interest. So I was expecting to get this €525m I had given to my client by lunch so I could basically give it back to the London system before the 'end of lunch,' which was vaguely defined and generally understood to refer to the old days of lunch, which could mean anything but definitely before 'Close of Business' for the day."

"I think I am beginning to see the possible problem here," said Gas.

"Right. The cash didn't show up. Apparently there was some offsetting arrangement people wanted to do, which involved cutting my money 'into shapes' and netting it off with other major transactions going on that day between the UK and the Republic of Ireland. The problem was that I was by far the biggest thing happening that day between those two states. And the guy doing the cutting into shapes was a guy called Seamus at AIB Baggot Street and he had gone for a sandwich."

"What could it have cost you?" wondered Gas.

"I wasn't sure. But overnight LIBOR was about 5% or 500 basis points as we would say, with a basis point being 1/100 of a percent. I would presumably have only paid for one day, but there were are 400 days in a year approximately so I would pay maybe a basis point and a quarter."

"That's terrible maths, but I guess we don't need the exact number," said Gas.

"Just the rough number was scary enough, because I was out €525m. Multiplying that by a 5% annual rate even for one day gets you to €70,000. I had no idea where that was coming from and potentially the answer was my pocket."

"Plus you didn't know how long this was for. If it didn't show up one day, maybe it wouldn't show up the next day either. Or ever," added Gas. "What happened?"

"Seamus came back. I assume he enjoyed his sandwich. He actually didn't cut the transfer into shapes once I mentioned lawyers and the €70,000 number. I don't know if I could actually have pinned it on him but anyway, it came through in once piece by around 1400 London time, which was comfortably within the parameters of 'lunch.' And that was that. I was in

Munich Airport at the time, but I generated a proper phone bill."

"Less than €70,000 on the phone though, I guess."

"Sure. The other thing was that this was in the days before mobile phones worked internationally, so I had to exit back to landside through security having been airside."

"How did you do that?" asked Gas. "This is Germany, international home of regulation.

"I had to show them where because of my PhD is says 'Dr' on my credit card and say "Es ist eine Frage von Leben und Tot' meaning 'It is a question of life and death.' I suppose that they way I looked pale like I might die was probably good for adding to how convincing it was."

While we were discussing this and enjoying the American breakfast with a ton of coffee, a guy showed up on a moped. Basically a person on a moped was a cheap and efficient way of moving anything around the city. It was sometimes quicker than email, it was definitely more secure and the sender knew the message had arrived. Photos could be exchanged for assurance purposes and Chamroeun had taken one of me yesterday. Now we could see a guy in the lobby next to the breakfast room looking at his phone and at the few guests having a late breakfast. He worked out he was looking for me and came over with an envelope. He didn't say anything but just handed it over and left.

We opened the envelope, which had the printout in it. It was confusing. There was the usual bunch of numerical codes. I recognised the formats though not the individual codes. There was an amount, which was close to $31m. So far so good. It looked like our people were paying any charges or cuts they needed to effect the transfers separately in order to preserve the main figure. This had costs and benefits for them, but basically it made it much easier for us to track them. So they clearly didn't think anyone could possible be this close.

"Our guys may not be cutting into shapes either because like I said, it can be a major pain in the ass even if you are doing a legitimate sequence of transactions. And it makes the accounting really difficult if you have to show someone a whole bunch of transfers which add up to the specified amount." That of course we both knew depended on whether they were doing any accounting.

The tricky part on the printout was the part where I would normally expect a named destination to be. This was there alright, but it said

AMERICA TOWN, GUNSAN

"So where the hell is that?" said Gas. "I can see why she was confused. It might be a Casino in a place called Gunsan, which is maybe US owned, or it might be in the US and Gunsan is a person..."

"You would rarely see an individual named on one of these. Even if you were effectively paying an UHNWI, it would go to one of their companies or a family office," I said, using the acronym for Ultra High Net Worth Individual, which was polite private banking language for 'someone who gets whatever they want.'

Gas started searching online, and got hits immediately.

"It's in Stars and Stripes," she said, referring to the US military newsletter, "and it's not called that anymore. But maybe they didn't change the name of their receiving identity."

"Changing these codes is next to impossible and probably not worth it. The airport code for Ho Chi Minh City is still SGN for Saigon, and that horse bolted after the Americans left," I said. "Is it a casino?"

"It's not a casino, it's a place. Sort of. It's been renamed International Culture Ville," said Gas, staring at her screen. "It looks like it's some kind of R&R place for airmen from a base nearby which is called Kunsan. Kunsan base near Gunsan town, it looks like."

"Name is same, same. Do they have a casino?"

"Not obviously," said Gas, looking at some US military database listing posting details for service-members. "The billet is described as 'remote/unaccompanied.' This place is going to be like Soi Cowboy in BKK. Total mess." She searched some more. "I mean it looks like there could absolutely be some late-night shebeens with flyboys playing poker, but I don't see anyone's late night illicit card game getting $31m of chips."

"Though the sky part is appropriate for the air force. Actually it doesn't have to be chips this time. It could be cash. This is just a standard transfer message," I said, looking again at the printout.

"Would she have that kind of cash -- in the casino here?" asked Gas.

"She wouldn't physically have it on her routinely, unless they were expecting someone special, but she wouldn't need it. She is in a cash dispensing office. She could wire it out without needing physical dollars on hand, if she had an offsetting source. Maybe the casino's bank here just says something like 'if you get chips from a specified source, we will treat that as a legitimate offset for cash transfers out." '

"So we've effectively got cash being wired out to a bar zone? Maybe it just got spent. Maybe someone bought 31 million beers and put them on a plane."

"More than one plane. And where would you fly that plane to?"

"Thirsty people. Are we going there?," said Gas.

"I don't know. It sounds like a fun gig, but I don't know about the food situation. Kimchi is fantastic, and it's like saké, in that it's a range of things not one thing. But otherwise I think the idea is they bring you raw food and you cook it on a barbie thing at your table."

"What's the problem with that?" asked Gas.

"I'm paying them to cook my food. I don't want to do it. I'm competent at eating but that doesn't make me competent at cooking. I might poison myself. If I went to the garage with a carburettor problem, I don't expect them to hand me a wrench and say I've signed up for 'a mechanic experience.' I expect them to fix it. Otherwise I could just stay home, slap myself in the face with an oily rag, throw $300 on the fire and do nothing with the problem."

"That's pretty intense as an objection. What are we going to do instead?"

My idea was to get more information before we decided our next move. "Let's maybe get Brynjar up to speed and see if he knows anything about the place."

Gas accepted this and returned to the topic of International Culture Ville. She said, "Apparently even when it was still officially called America Town, everyone actually called it A-Town."

"What do they call it now?"

"They still call it A-Town."

Gas used the standard mechanism for sharing material with INTERPOL, which was a sort of dropbox affair with triple-password protection. For added security, she encrypted the photo of the printout itself before putting it in the box. The encryption password was 'Astrid,' which meant 'divine beauty' in Norwegian and was the name of Brynjar's cat. I had asked Gas whether this was adequately secure, but she said it was fine as an extra layer.

What you could easily get from Brynjar was file data, whether historical or recent. There were no procedures to go through, assuming the information did not relate to live operations. In fact, the problem was the opposite; you would get Gigabytes of data and would have to work out what, if any, of it was relevant. Often there would be diamonds or at least emeralds in the rough, but I had an abiding suspicion that we missed most of them.

This was a reflection of my standard approach when asked by regulatory authorities for information. I would disclose absolutely everything that could possibly be relevant. This meant I definitely wasn't going to go to jail for failure to cooperate and also meant that they would never find anything. There was never anything to find, anyway, of course.

It was also useful to remember that we had been told that paper serviettes did not fall into the category of writing materials and therefore not subject to subpoena. But people freaked out if your desk had a 70cm layer of serviettes on it.

"Do we need to be here any more?" asked Gas. "Couldn't we wait for Brynjar to deliver in Krabi?" Gas named her favourite part of Southern Thailand, which had incredible scenery and the thing she liked doing more than many things, scuba diving.

"Fine by me," I said, but it was more than fine.

CASH-TRAP

CHAPTER 4

EAST CHINA SEA, 34.77°N, 125.02°E

There was a clear indicator for captains of merchant vessels if what they were about to do had any question marks around it. That was if the client instructions included the command 'turn off transponder' in them. That really meant 'transceiver.' Both words were portmanteau terms, one being composed from 'transmitter/responder' and the other from 'transmitter/receiver.'

The first type of device would ping back if you pinged it, responding with basic information like who you were and where you are. The second type was more chatty and didn't wait to be asked. All cargo ships over 300 Tonnes Gross had transceivers, which were periodically broadcasting that data to anyone who cared to listen. There were no legitimate reasons to switch off either system. The illegitimate reasons were that you didn't want people to know who you were and where you were and the only reason for that was because someone wanted to obscure what you were doing.

Moving ships around at night was fairly easy, if you had instruments. Lights were also good. Clients sometimes wanted lights out as well. This just meant you had to be slower and more careful than usual, but it was basically fine.

Moving ships close to other ships was starting to get trickier. And then connecting the two of them at sea by large flexible pipes was really getting into the 'quite tricky' domain. Doing that in the dark without transponders added up to 'probably not worth it' under normal circumstances. However, in this as in all other fields, you got paid proper money for doing stuff that no-one else could, or would, do.

There were no unacceptable risks, just inadequately compensated ones. A game of Russian roulette probably was a good trade at maybe $10m, if you could persuade yourself. I'd said something like that to Brynjar once and he had asked me "when you are persuading yourself, who is the persuader and who is the persuadee?" which seemed like a good question but I got hung up on whether 'persuadee' could be a word.

This particular nocturnal maritime intertwining risk was adequately compensated, which was why two vessels were dancing around each other in the East China Sea for four days with their transceivers switched off, connected all the while by huge pipes as they drifted with the current. Occasionally they would run the screws to avoid entering crossing a territorial waters boundary, but mostly drifting together with the currents was acceptable and cost nothing.

Four days of transfer time meant you could hook up at night no problem, as the client wanted, but you would still be hooked up the next day. The client had wanted disconnection every morning and reconnection every night. But this meant doubling the transfer time and doing it eight times. That was just too much grief. And anyway, where were you going to put the ships in the meantime?

That was why the way the two ships danced around each other was seen by a satellite. Just in the optical spectrum, nothing fancy. And then that data was in the system, if you knew where to look for it.

AO NANG BEACH, THAILAND

Ao Nang was almost the place that you would be thinking about if someone said 'beach in Thailand' to you. Unless you jumped straight away to Leonardo di Caprio and that great track by All Saints from the eponymous movie. That particular beach, or The Beach, was in fact not far away in Maya Bay. That had benefited greatly from being closed during pandemic and now the Thais had very sensibly placed some limits on visitor numbers. It was still basically like Piccadilly Circus in board shorts however.

Gas had mostly been diving. I had been developing a ranking of restaurants. All of the Thai ones were great, as one would expect. I had been going through the

various combinations of protein with red/green/
massaman/Penang curry. I had decided that my
favourite option here was massaman, the local name for
Muslim, which involved a turmeric led sauce and potato,
although it was nothing like a vindaloo. There was also
surprisingly enough a good Swiss place. I was having
some rösti when Brynjar popped up on my phone, so I
had to stagger out to the nearby beach to hear what he
had to say. To a first approximation, all of human life
took place on the beach here. I had no objections. An
advantage for us was the large and transient western
population, which made us totally invisible.

Brynjar wanted to talk about the US armed forces. "This
Gunsan place is basically just the American Air Force.
Nothing much else happens there and all of the local
economy is dominated by the Americans. There is a
port. It's probably best described as mid-sized. But that
could still be enough for what we are talking about.
There's plenty of legitimate through-put."

"OK. Are there any casinos?"

"Not exactly there. In fact, the legal position on
gambling is odd in South Korea. You aren't allowed in a
casino if you are Korean. Or there is one you can go in,
in Gangwon. That's basically the other side of the
country from Gunsan. Otherwise you have to be foreign.
Or you can be an expat Korean and count as foreign. We

don't think casinos are interesting here, although they are clearly bizarre from a regulatory perspective, so some guys on my team think it should be looked at."

"If not casinos ... I wonder what sort of institution could handle cash like this," I asked.

Brynjar was looking like a highly smug cat at this point. That meant he knew something.

"You look like you know something," I prompted.

It wasn't going to be that easy.

"Are you going to tell me what it is?" I asked.

"I can't tell you. In fact, we don't *know* anything, but possibly we [know] something."

"OK great, so is this call about something? Or shall I go back to my rösti?"

"Your what?"

"Swiss dinner. It's great, basically onions and potato sautéed. Don't worry about it."

"So I'm going to tell you a story," continued Brynjar, "which is not related to anything in particular and is probably outside our jurisdiction."

This was interesting, because technically nowhere was outside Brynjar's jurisdiction. There was a flagpole in somewhere like Angola which had been demised to East Germany in perpetuity, and then not mentioned in the reunification of West and East Germany. It was highly unclear who owned this flagpole now; potentially the answer was still the GDR, which didn't exist. That flagpole might be outside Brynjar's jurisdiction. At one time we thought Antarctica was as well, until someone committed a murder there, and it had to be given a jurisdiction and that right quick.

I always thought there must be some great tax angles to the GDR situation. But they might involve living up a flagpole in Angola. You should never let the taxation tail wag the investment dog. Unless the tax angle was magnificent, which sometimes happened.

"In fact,' said Brynjar, "on reflection, I am going to tell you nothing at all. I will ask you some questions."

"All very mysterious."

"What do air forces consume in great quantities?"

"Planes, people, food, aviation spirit, spare parts ..." I guessed in a fairly random order. "That's more a question for Gas."

"What quantity of aviation spirit do you suppose the USAF consumes?"

"No idea, but it must be immense."

"Are you aware that different grades of fuel and crude oil can be swapped for each other?"

"Yes." This I knew. There would be a conversion factor between grades possibly also with a side agreement specifying cash settlement of any difference.

"Do you remember me telling you that Gunsan is a big seaport?"

"Sure."

"Right, see you later," said Brynjar and hung up before I could complain that he *really* hadn't told me anything even beyond the fact that he hadn't told me anything.

Gas rocked up at the restaurant by the picturesque method of walking up the beach straight out of the sea. She dumped her snorkel and mask on my table. I gave her a glass of house red and a brief overview of what Brynjar hadn't told me.

"So let me get this straight," said Gas. "There was some guff about jurisdictions, then there were four questions and no statements. Assuming that a question cannot be a statement."

"Brynjar could correctly tell a superior, and I could accurately testify if subpoenaed, that he questioned me. That's a routine operation. He questions people all the time. He questions offshore assets like us all the time. The function of a question is to obtain information, not to convey it," I said.

"Is anyone going to believe that Brynjar was asking you questions?"

"They *should* believe that. It's true. The meta-question is whether they also believe other things. And then the other side have to prove things about implicature. Brynjar knows about implicature. And this is all after the transcript of the call has got into the official record. So this is all fine. Good lawyers could obfuscate this into oblivion before breakfast."

"OK, let's assume you're right," said Gas. "So there were four questions, the first two of which were about air force supply, and then there was one about swap possibilities between different flavours of hydrocarbon molecule, and one which could have been an underlining of the fact that Gunsan is a port."

"That's about it."

"So let's try this as a hypothesis," said Gas. "Cash arrives into Kunsan which is some type of air force satellite town. The air force procures a ton of aviation spirit and will always be doing that. Aviation spirit can be swapped for crude oil. Gunsan is a port. Can it ship out crude oil?"

"I'm sure it can," I said. "You might have a process here. But we wouldn't have a chain of evidence because of this jurisdictional opacity."

"Does all that fit with what Brynjar told you?"

"He didn't tell me anything, remember," I pointed out.

"If he had told you things, would that hypothesis fit with those things?"

I decided to agree with this. "Yes, but would these links in the chain be good enough or would they be like ungraspably tenuous phantoms that break the whole chain? We don't have a solid evidence process."

"We wouldn't really need that though, would we?" responded Gas. "As long as Brynjar can see it and maybe disclose it in some closed court format. Or maybe he doesn't care and just wants us to keep chasing the trail because he's confident it passes through here somehow. Or maybe he has the locals on it. It looks like it needs that, international cooperation and all that. He might be happy for us to just carry on while he fills in some of the other blanks. I mean this is the sort of vague crap I hate but you're fine with it."

"That could stack up. He's certainly acting like he thinks that."

"Let's assume that's the story." Gas was still looking quizzical. "How much is a shipload of oil worth? Could it be on the sort of scale we are looking for?"

"I think so. Depends on a bunch of factors including the size of the ship, and the quality of the product," I replied. "There are a few standard sizes depending on where they can go. They biggest ones you see a lot are VLCCs. You probably came across a few of them: Very Large Crude Carriers. There's a size up from that called a ULCC but hardly anyone can handle it. Only Louisiana in the US and even then, it's way offshore initially. So practically you want a VLCC. That's a ship that can actually go normal places with still a pretty decent amount of oil."

"I knew a guy like that once. Too big to be be useful," said Gas.

"Really?" I asked.

"I didn't know him biblically. I just heard about it."

I couldn't decide whether she was being ultra crude or just very crude, and I didn't really mind, so I went back to the question of valuation of oil cargoes. "The US oil benchmark is called WTI. Just like you -- you are also kind of West Texas Intermediate. It refers specifically to light, sweet crude. I'm not sure how many of those epithets one could legitimately ascribe to you."

"Not that many unless you want a kick in the cojones. What's the limey benchmark?"

"It's called Brent. Some nondescript location in the middle of the North Sea. You can't particularly make an insult out of it."

"I could. Brent sounds kind of like a boring Canadian dude who likes sports," said Gas.

"You're right. That's quite insulting. But doesn't seem to apply to me. Anyway, a VLCC will typically hold a couple of million barrels of WTI."

"How much is that worth?"

"The key variable, which is properly variable, is the price of a barrel. That's all over the place. It even went negative one time in a central pipeline hub in Cushing, Oklahoma."

"That can't be right," objected Gas. "It's a valuable asset."

"The value of an asset consists also in where it is, when and in what format. Futures markets are all about the idea of an asset, not the asset itself. Sure, they derive their value from the value of the asset but that's different. Storage tanks in Cushing were full. So a guy who was showing up tomorrow with a thousand barrels needed someone to take it off his hands because there was nowhere to put it. Not too many people can just say, 'sure, I will be ready tomorrow to take delivery of that oil' who didn't know about it months ago and weren't already busy. It didn't last long," I explained.

"So how much are we talking about normally? Under the circumstances where you have to pay cash money for this asset?"

"You could sort of use $100 per barrel as a reasonable approximation."

"So one ship could be $200m. That's an interesting sort of number for this process."

It was. The next question was how you would get into the system and out of it. It was obvious how you would move it around. You would fill up a ship and then sail the ship somewhere. But cargoes and ships were quite trackable.

"Can we see ships moving?" I asked.

Gas replied "A lot of that is Open Source these days, so we could take a look, no problem. Satellite imagery and transponder data. But that's a problem for our guys, right? They can't be seen just loading oil and off-loading it later somewhere else, it would be too trackable. But..."

Gas thought. Then she said "What if one ship transferred an oil cargo to another? Maybe they can do that at sea. Then you wouldn't necessarily easily see a cargo moving from one port to another."

"What would that look like," I asked.

"We couldn't exactly see the oil move, I guess, but if the locations and timestamps are consistent with that plus one ship loads a cargo at a location and the other offloads a similar or identical cargo then that would be suggestive at a minimum. In fact, it would be at least balance of probabilities and maybe even beyond reasonable doubt if you could get some additional background. Sometimes you get draught changes from the automatic transponder. If a ship is riding a lot higher in the water, then its cargo has been unloaded."

"Can you take a look for all this or anything like it?"

"OK. That's going to take a while."

I left her to it and went out for roast duck. I met a couple of Americans who said they sold software. I was always sceptical of this because of the high number of large men who said this in Phuket. It was apparently given out as a bland suggested cover story for military types that would discourage further questions on the grounds of being too boring. It turned out that none of these very large Americans could answer the next two questions, which were 'what does the software do?' and 'in what language is the software coded?' The other thing you could do was ask them about Camp Lemonnier in Djibouti. Anyone not associated with the US military had probably not heard of Djibouti and had definitely not heard of Camp Lemonnier. These guys however could answer the software questions and were a normal size, so I gave them a pass and we enjoyed chatting over dinner. We didn't talk about Djibouti.

I spent the day reading and got a massage. In the evening as the sun set, Gas knocked on my door and then rolled over on a lounger on my balcony with the air of a self-satisfied Gekko. We had lots of those. They all looked pretty happy with themselves as well. We also had something I had never identified but that I called 'the disappointed bird.' Its call had a downward cadence that you could transliterate as 'uh-uh, uh-uh, uh-uhhhhh...' That bird never got what it wanted. Or if it did, it wasn't admitting it.

I'd spent most of the day on the balcony listening to this bird and looking at the scenery. It was pretty dramatic around southern Thailand. Vast limestone karsts projected vertically upwards from the land or the sea. Life went on around them. They were mostly covered in trees at the top, which was a testament to the persistence of plant life. You normally couldn't get up them, but I had once walked 1280 steps to get to a big buddha. A week after I did it some German dude had a heart attack at the top, which must have been inconvenient. Not so much for him, because he died.

"I have something," Gas announced. "It's got a fair number of jurisdictions involved in it. And I got a couple of texts from Brynjar on what I've been working on."

"That's a good sign with the jurisdictions," I said. The two things almost always involved in a money laundering layering chain were multiple geographies and SPVs scattered around like confetti. SPV, or Special Purpose Vehicle, was a company you created for a specific purpose and listed somewhere cool like the Caymans. This and other popular locations required local offices with local directors so the places were notorious for hosting single shacks with 2,000 company nameplates on the door and a fax machine. Given you could setup an SPV company quickly and cheaply in many jurisdictions, you might as well. It all created extra steps for the pursuers.

Gas outlined what she had. "A South Korean company chartered a Russian tanker. The ship left the port of Gunsan in South Korea and headed out to the edge of the Chinese EEZ, but staying just out of it." States had Exclusive Economic Zones stretching out of their coasts into the sea. They were often a source of unresolvable disputes and otherwise incomprehensible behaviour like creating artificial islands or bulking up intertidal reefs into something more substantial. Nothing like getting an EEZ around an otherwise pointless rock, strategically and hydrocarbon-wise.

"It looks then like it hooked up with a Chinese-owned ship. Which is flagged in Togo."

"Togo? That's exotic. I don't think I've seen that come up before," I said. "But it doesn't matter that much where a ship is registered. Or it does matter, but it probably isn't going to help us very much."

"Togo," said Gas, "is a bit like Mauritania. Neither place seems to have ever generated any news activity."

"Does the ship go to North Korea?" This would be an endpoint event for us, but this rarely happened with actual non-state criminal actors. North Korea was certainly not going to get you on anyone's radar but it was also totally impossible to get anything done there that connected to the outside world. So if you had a stage there, it was totally secure, but only in the same way that burning $100m in an oil barrel in your backyard was totally secure.

"No, it doesn't. The manifest says it was going to, but you can file that and not do it."

"So where does it go?" I asked.

"I don't know yet, but I should be able to work it out. I've got to track the transponders, once they get switched on again."

"Is this process repeatable? It can't be, right? We can see it happening so you couldn't do it again."

Gas said "It is and it isn't. This exact same thing maybe can't be repeated, but you don't need to do the exact same thing. You could do an analogous thing with different ships, different ports and a different handover location. You could even change the nationalities involved but you probably don't need to."

"But we can see it happening," I objected.

"Sure but how does that help? First up, we can sometimes see it happening in real-time but that is not advance notice. And even if you had that, what would you do? To interdict the transfer, which may not even be illegal, you would need a couple of warships. They have to get there. Whose would they be? The Chinese and the Russians are getting paid for the ship charters, and they are pissing off the Americans, more to the point. The diplomatic consequences would be huge for everyone involved and people have much bigger fish to fry."

I tried to think of further objections.

"The South Koreans are getting a cut and the North Koreans don't know they are being used. Maybe they aren't every time. Maybe they get a shipment every other trip. There's a port in the North near a place called Nampo which is basically in business solely to receive illicit oil shipments according to Brynjar. And he has a satellite photo of the two ships next to each other."

"Not exactly a smoking gun, but not far off," I said.

"Right. With all these players, that just leaves the US Navy as people who might get involved on the side of screwing things up. Maybe, but they have to go through a bunch of inhospitable places first."

"Yeah," I agreed.

"And the reason this transfer was done on the edge of the Chinese EEZ was to make it easy to get in there in an emergency. But they weren't actually in it so no-one can say there's a diplomatic situation. And no one ever wants to be in the North Korean EEZ. Not since the USS Pueblo."

Gas was referring to an incident when the North Koreans had seized what was admittedly a US spy ship. The timing was pretty excruciating, coming a week before the Tet Offensive of the Vietnam War in early 1968. The ship was still in North Korea today which showed how long it could take to sort out anything diplomatic and controversial. I continued to try to think of objections.

"Where was the Pueblo thing?"

Gas looked it up. "39°N 125°E," she said. "No, wait, that's where it is now. Probably. The file photo is from 2012. Anyway -- close on a global scale, close to where we're talking about."

"Spooky."

"On top of all that," said Gas continuing with her objections to the idea that someone could stop these transfers, "you are asking for military involvement to resolve what is effectively a commercial dispute. A big one, and maybe a sanctions busting one, but...it isn't going to happen."

I realised what this could indicate. "So all of this means we might only be seeing one cycle. This whole process could be run multiple times. The total amount of money involved could be ..."

"Yep. Huge. In fact it has to be multiples of what we can see. Because they have gone to a massive amount of effort to set this up. You only do that if you are going to use the chain more than once. In fact, dozens of times."

"So what's next?" I asked.

"I can't see any transponder location data. They must have left it switched off. But I can see it getting pinged."

I said "So what is this ping system, anyway?"

"Formally, this is the Automatic Information System or AIS Transponder mandated by the International Maritime Organisation for all cargo ships over 300 tons on international voyages. There are some exemptions available to flag states in specified circumstances," explained Gas. "Basically turning it off is very unhelpful to you and everyone and not at all legitimate."

Gas was looking at a list of data and its format specification. "We get a standard data package which contains the ship's identity, type, position, course, speed and navigational status, which could be O for 'underway using engine,1 ' for 'at anchor,2 ' for 'not under command,' for example.   6 for 'aground' is perhaps the most exotic.   Where 'exotic' means 'bad.' Aground can also mean 'underwater,' which is stretching it a bit."

"Both are pretty unhelpful, but underwater looks terminally unhelpful," I said.

"Yep.   There's also rate of turn indicator output if you have one and a calculated value from the compass otherwise.   The data goes to other ships and aircraft nearby plus shore stations with the right kit.   Basically your data is like the price of access to the system which then gives you access to everyone else's data."

"Where do these data go?" I asked.

"It gets off the ship via a specialised AIS VHF antenna, which really doesn't like being near anything else playing the same ball game like radar or radio telephone. After that...," Gas paused for a second. "Well, the IMO is super unhappy about people broadcasting it on the web," explained Gas, "which used to happen and sometimes still does.   Because piracy.   But the data is collected in a bunch of places.   The US Coast Guard has whet they call a marine cadastre but it will be easier to hack an environmental protection agency.   In fact, I already have credentials for that. One of them is notoriously lax and have been since they installed their system. I could get a Coast Guard login from the dark web, but I'd have to pay and it wouldn't be all that admissible if we care about that."

After about another fifteen minutes, Gas looked happy. "Got it. Or rather I have the space where it should be."

"What do you mean?"

"I mean they turned off their transponder, and they are not supplying any data. But the system still wants to play with them, so it sends pings."

"Is that helpful?" I asked.

"It could be. I at least know how many of them there are. I can see the system asking for a handshake every hour. Or a type 15 Interrogation -- Request for special response to be precise."

"This sounds a bit like that MH17 situation," I remarked, talking about the missing Malaysian plane.

"No, MH17 is the one that was shot down by a Russian BUK over eastern Ukraine. You mean MH370. This is slightly better than that in that the ship will eventually show up somewhere."

"Right. So what are we going to do with these pings?"

"Basically add them up and see where you might get to. I already have too many pings for where they claim to be going."

Gas downloaded a tool that calculated sailing distances between ports. Then she fired it up and squinted at it. "The largest port in North Korea is Chongjin. Getting there from 35 North 125 East means going around the southern tip of Korea and heading up the West coast. A direct route would be about 707 nautical miles. At 15 knots, that's going to take one day and twenty-three hours. In other words, 47 pings."

"And how many do you have?"

"103, which would be four days and seven hours. Way too many. At 15 knots again, you're going to do 1557 nautical miles."

"Which gets you where?"

"Could be a bunch of places. I might be able to write some code to do it, but basically it's probably easier to just put some lines on the map."

She worked on that for about twenty minutes, making odd sort of snuffly 'I'm working, leave me alone' noises. I was used to this. I waited and drank coffee.

"It's too far for anywhere sensible in Japan, which would be your obvious northern objective. You would have to keep going. You could get to a place in Russia called Bogorodskoe." She did some more typing. "Looks like that has a factory museum of wooden toys but no obvious port. Maybe the south side of Japan..."

She drew more lines. "No, that doesn't work either. You end up going right past Tokyo and hitting the Kuriles. That's disputed territory. Could be a possibility."

"I like disputed locations," I said. "Let's keep that one on the list."

"Heading west, you get nowhere. Just no-man's land, or no-man's sea I guess, between the Philippine Sea and the North Pacific.

I asked: "Philippines -- do they work?"

"Maybe. Subic Bay is the obvious to look at. US Navy were there forever, then got kicked out. They're back again now. Looks like ... nope, too close, 1347 nautical miles."

"Further south in the Philippines," I said, now leaning over her shoulder.

"Furthest south port in the Philippines is Davao. That would be...1954. Too many. Further north, we have...Surigao. That makes 1627. Zamboanga. Too far. Cagayan de Oro." She zoomed in and moved the lines around so they passed through sea lanes. "Yes. That's possible."

"We've already been in the Philippines. Or the chain has. It's not impossible for the chain to go back, but it's less likely," I said. "It would introduce potential recursive problems for the managers. Like 'are you talking about Philippines I or Philippines II stage?" '

"You could head more-or-less south west from the start point. That means crossing from the Yellow Sea to the East China Sea, skirting the coast of China, passing between Taiwan and the mainland, going past Hong Kong. You definitely can't get to Malaysia or Indonesia."

"Right."

"But...looking at big ports...Đà Nẵng, Vietnam. 1557.7 nautical miles from the start point. Spot on."

"So it's somewhere obscure in the Philippines again, Đà Nẵng, which is in Vietnam once more but a new location, far east of Russia or disputed islands north of Japan?" I summarised.

"That's about it. But actually I have more. They switch the transponder on again later. They are in Singapore VLCC Terminal after another 85 pings. Three days 11 hours."

"That should tell us the answer, right?" I interjected.

"If you stay fairly close to the coast of Vietnam initially, which is the obvious thing to do, and then go south around Bintan Island, which you will probably do, you get to 1254.8 nautical miles as the sea distance from Đà Nẵng to Singapore. Three days 11 hours. That's it. There's no way you can get there in that time from further away in the other candidate locations in a tanker that isn't going to do routinely or at all much better than 15 knots. It's definitely Đà Nẵng. We just need to find out if the oil got dropped there or went on to Singapore."

"Let's start in Đà Nẵng," I said. "Singapore is a lot of fun, but we may as well be methodical. There's still an open question though."

"What's that?"

"How much of this cargo is now our guys," I answered. "They could in theory just have a $31m slice of the whole $201m. They could equally in theory have that be disposed of separately to the rest of the cargo."

"But that's awkward, right," said Gas. "And it's a piece of awkwardness that doesn't help them much in terms of covering their tracks."

"Maybe it does help with that, but this is looking more and more like we're seeing parts of a bigger picture. I'm going to check in with Brynjar."

The Norwegian answered promptly, as he usually did. I explained that we were now looking at potentially a bigger number. I was careful to not actually specify the precise $201m number we had calculated based on pricing on the relevant day and exact capacity used according to the draught reports and the ship types. Brynjar needed deniability on that so that he could disclaim any knowledge of the reasonable commission that Gas and I would charge. I told him that we were now looking at something like 7x the original number.

"That doesn't surprise me. The updated number for SWIFT transfers out of Central Bank in Dhaka is now $101m. We don't know for sure what the real number is; that's a lower limit. For those at least we have printouts which I can drop-off for you. But on top of that I have some reports for you of similar events elsewhere. I will stick all this in the usual place."

This meant the dropbox. I emailed Gas even though she was in the same room because she was on a call. She got hold of the files, after a brief interlude where I could tell she had been talking to her mother. This usually involved her being told that 'it is time to settle down Susan' before it was too late. I couldn't understand why you wouldn't call Gas by her real name. I also did not know why parents thought their life choices were the only ones possible.

There was a file called 'Liberia.' Brynjar had taken the slightly unusual step of giving us read access only, so we could look at the file but we couldn't copy it. Gas had coded a workaround, which involved opening the document, taking a screenshot, saving the screenshot, adding the screenshot to an an accretion file, opening the next page etc. We had never actually used it because we didn't want to screw Brynjar.

And also, while we technically would not be in possession of a hot document, merely pictures of each page of a hot document in a new document, we would be in possession of hot content and that was clearly something we didn't want even on the Soviet concrete laptop without good reason. The argument that we had pictures of text and that did not become text until you put it through an OCR did not look seriously appealing legally. Even assuming you could get a lawyer to understand it. Lawyers were great at what they did but they absolutely had no idea about technical points or numbers.

I only had time to start looking at the Liberia file before we left for the airport. Gas took a look at the same time. It was a fairly short file written in INTERPOL language, which meant a maximum level of terseness and as many acronyms as possible. We could have read some more in the cab but reading while moving didn't agree with me.

The story was supposed to be that there had been exactly $100m in freshly-printed Liberian banknotes due to go to the Central Bank in 'containers and bags of money' that had moved through the port at Monrovia and Roberts International Airport. The authors of the report, who were unidentified INTERPOL dudes, had put 'containers and bags of money' in quotes and underlined it and applied bold font to emphasise how much they couldn't believe this. But I wondered to myself, 'what else is the money going to be in? I mean, maybe have some other security features but bags are good at some level.'

It reminded me of something called an 'in-tray exercise' that I had done when I had failed to get a job at the Bank of England for reasons I regarded as spurious but ultimately fortunate.

That particular day had started on a questionable note because I had flown in from Hamburg without an appointment. There was a guy on the door of the Bank of England wearing a top hat and a pink tail coat that looked like it was standard for the 18th century. He was pretty sure I wasn't coming in, and I thought he was probably right, but somehow I talked my way into him calling someone and whoever that was turned out to be less hidebound. So I was admitted, and had a chat to the guy about moral hazard, and then he put me into the recruitment channel.

The start of that was what was called an in-tray exercise. This was actually a quite reasonably valid test of prioritisation and resistance to panic. A job interview was one of the few situations where the simulation could approach the reality in terms of affective import because everyone except me is always really stressed in job interviews. I never was, for reasons I didn't fully understand. Maybe I didn't care that much. I didn't do a lot of it anyway, because being an investment banker is like being a football player. People call you. They want to be your agent.

The exercise took the form of a bunch of emails that you might have in your inbox at the Bank of England on a particular morning. You had to classify them in terms of whether you would do anything about them, if so what it was, and then you had to say what order you would do things in. There was a lot of distractor guff about visits in three weeks that you were asked to write a presentation for. In real life, that would be significant, but in the context of the exercise you could just dismiss it under the rubric of 'write the presentation at an appropriate later date.' Then there was a lot of other stuff that was completely unimportant, to do with redecoration schedules in your corridor.

The only way through all this crap was to flick through everything quickly. The classic error made by impressionable undergraduate perfectionists was to do irrelevant stuff like write the outline of the presentation. In the half hour you had. If you did that, you didn't get to the email two-thirds down a stack of 100 where it said there was a consignment of gold coming in to Heathrow that morning and the usual security detail had not been informed. It was an email which had come only to you, in the exercise, and it asked whether you wanted to do anything about it. If you didn't, there was going to be a big weight of unaccompanied gold sitting on the tarmac at the airport. Probably you should avoid that. The gold wasn't going to be loose and visible -- it would be in 'bags and containers' presumably. But that wasn't the problem.

"Very good," said Gas on the occasion I told her about the in-tray exercise and the talking my way in to the 18th Century. "Why didn't you get the job?"

"Oh, that was the photocopiers," I said.

CHAPTER 5

ĐÀ NẴNG, VIETNAM

Krabi to Đà Nẵng involved a stopover in Bangkok's second airport, Don Mueang DMK, which had once had the IATA code BKK. That honour now went to glossy, posh and polished Suvarnabhumi. The original plan had been to demolish Don Mueang, but it had survived in a niche as a domestic and local hub. It was concrete and brutalist and while less modern than Suvarnabhumi, I liked its austere efficiency and the way it was a reminder of the old Thailand. It had been the only airport on my first trip in 2005. It was a much more apt temporary home for the backpackers on their way in, when they were pale and wondered why everyone was smiling, and on their way out, when they had accumulated enough wisdom for a lifetime, even though they were only 23.

The trip was reasonably uneventful. The business class lounge at DMK offered a free shoulder massage along with the latte, which was so relaxing we almost forgot to go and get on the second plane. This is the only problem with nice lounges. No one ever forgets to leave the busy hell of ordinary incompetent travellers in public zones.

We arrived at Đà Nẵng and found a cab outside the airport. This charged VND 300k for a 12 minute ride downtown. The journey was marked by the driver having an extended video call with his family while on a three-lane highway, not that lanes were of much importance. It was 22C, which I thought was nippy for these parts. But it turned out that Vietnam, unlike Thailand, had climatic variation between North and South and also seasons. It could actually get cold. The streets were full of people standing around coal-burning braziers like they were on strike in the UK in the 70s or 2023.

The cab fare was in line with my heuristic for working out whether I had been ripped off. Or rather my second line heuristic, because the basic principle is that you will always get ripped off. That's just like a cost of doing business if you travel. It still rankles but you have to try to put up with it. But I've always hated asymmetric markets where one guy knows much more than the other guy. Unless I am the guy that knows. The only thing worse than informational asymmetry is forced participation. Which is also why I don't own a car. Or a house. Or anything physical that doesn't fit in a bag I can carry. Physical objects are mostly only useful to the extent that they encode information you can use.

The cab rule is based on the fact that you will pay about a dollar a minute in a cab in London or New York, so if you are paying more than that, you are getting screwed. Nowhere in the world has higher living costs than those two places other than maybe Tokyo. And there, it's a $100 cab ride from the airport but it is an immense distance and the drivers wear white gloves.

The worst place in the world is Cancun, Mexico, where ten minutes costs $50, there is a 20 minute chaotic wait in a maelstrom of confused Americans before anyone turns up, they ask you whether you are the customer or not when they should really know that, which then means you have to fight off a bunch of other people who may also be the customer and then the drivers get out of the cab after the journey to ask for more money.

The cabbies have of course banned the ride sharing apps from the airport so that they can continue to rip people off. Presumably it is so profitable that they can afford to buy everyone in politics or law enforcement who might otherwise intervene. The latest I had read about the situation was that the ban had sort of been relaxed but cab drivers were now beating up the Uber drivers and also anyone who had the temerity to be a customer of Uber. Nice people.

Cancun is basically pointless anyway. Most Americans don't have passports and are not that worried about it. Cancun exists for those who want to pretend to have been abroad, but actually they just stay in all-inclusive resorts owned by large American chains with their own beaches so they may as well be in Florida eating the same massive burgers.

You can go to the ruins at Chichen Itza, which is worth it, because there aren't many sporting arenas you can visit where the prize for winning a game of keepy-uppy is that you are elected to gladly receive the honour of getting your head cut off. But apart from that, it's just slightly spicier than Albuquerque.

When we got to the hotel, I looked at Grab, which was the local version of Uber. The price for the ride from the airport to downtown was VND 47,000. So we had been ripped off by a factor of 6, which was quite a bad result.

After we checked in, we had a drink in the hotel bar, which was very busy as it was also hosting a tech company dinner. We were 15 floors up which gave us a great view of the city, which had some impressive illuminated skyscrapers. One of them had 'I ♡ Da Nang' written up the whole side of the building.

We decided to take a look at the rest of the Liberia file over a couple of local IPAs whose recipe apparently included pizza flour, and were none the worse for that. We used our usual method of assimilating reports, which was that one of us would read it and highlight the key points and also anything bizarre or amusing and the other would ask questions. This was primarily a money doc so I was up for the read through.

The report made no sense. The public timeline started with the Liberian Ministry of Justice saying it was investigating the theft of LRD 16bn which was a vast amount, being equivalent to 5% of GDP for the whole country of Liberia.

"In the US, that would be like stealing a trillion dollars," I pointed out.

"Has anyone ever done that?" asked Gas.

"I don't think so, but presumably it's just a matter of time," I replied. "But also, all statements I make may be are not in fact statements and may be construed only as general observations and further may not be relied upon as financial, regulatory or legal advice," I said, adding a piece of boilerplate for fun.

I read some more. "The son of the former President was a Deputy Governor of the Central Bank," I continued.

"Oh great, nepo baby. Always helpful," said Gas.

"He gets arrested and led out of the bank in cuffs along with four other Central Bank officials. People demonstrate on the streets with signs saying 'Give Us

Back Our Money.' Everyone from the Central Bank gets charged with Money Laundering and -- this is unusual -- 'economic sabotage." '

"If you can get charged with that, then half the politicians in the world should be in jail, " said Gas.

"Half of them should be. But also half of the electorates. And of course there is a charge of conspiracy on top of the others just for fun. Everyone goes on trial. Except the son of the President; he gets dropped off the docket before trial," I continued.

"Amazing," said Gas. "I would never have expected that."

"So then the other four get off on the original charges because there's no evidence any of it went into their pockets," I continued.

"No evidence that that exact money went into their pockets or no evidence that some money went into their pockets?" asked Gas.

"No evidence of anything apparently, apart from unauthorised printing. But apparently that's not a bad thing. There's not a crime of 'unlawful printing' in Liberia."

"That's probably not really a crime anywhere," said Gas.

"The money gets shipped in, received into the Central Bank and then disbursed into the economy. This is all unauthorised but there's also no crime of economic sabotage because the prosecution has to show malign effects. And this cash being splurged around had positive effects because the economy needed some stimulus."

"Doesn't this mean that I can rob a bank and get off because I stimulate the economy when I spend the money?" asked Gas.

"No, because you took the money off someone. Though if you just stole money the bank created, maybe. Even then, it would still be wire fraud in the US like everything else," I said. Everything you did in the US which was illegal was also wire fraud and the DA would usually chuck the charge in with everything else in case it was the only thing which stuck.

"Yeah," said Gas, "it's like crossing state lines. That's an additional violation to be added to whatever you actually did that was bad."

"Right. So the final judgement is that even if this unauthorised printing had been an offence, it wouldn't in the final analysis be one because the government had subsequently ratified it by inserting this cash legitimately into the economy."

"The government laundered it! Did they do that deliberately?"

"It depends what you mean by 'deliberately.' They Central Bank certainly had instructions and intended to insert some cash into the economy. What the exact amount was which they intended to disburse is indeterminate which means you can't show the actual amount was different. But this is all so tenuous that it's a question for Brynjar -- with his philosophy hat on, not his current hat."

"To the extent that his current hat is not a philosophical hat, which is itself a philosophical question," said Gas.

"Good point," I responded. "And in general, good luck convicting anyone when you need to introduce a philosophical account of events before you can decide if a crime has been committed," I said. "Right -- that's it for the public information. No one has done anything and the government prosecutor looks embarrassed."

Gas said "So they get off because the government allegedly authorised their behaviour de facto and post facto even though the government has been trying to lock them up, apart from the son of the former head of the government?"

"That's it, so far. You sound like Brynjar with your 'facto's' there. Next up, a bunch of ex-spooks take a look at what's happened."

"If anything," said Gas. "Who are these spooks?"

"Brynjar isn't going to tell us that. He may not know himself. It's the 'Project Fabre' team." I looked up the name 'Fabre.' Project codenames were often unintentionally more revealing than they were meant to be. This time I drew a blank, because Fabre appeared to be a French entomologist. "We need to keep our eyes open for anything to do with insects," I said, as a result of that piece of information.

"Maybe bugs ate the money," said Gas.

"Actual bugs or code ones are both on the table," I agreed. "The local FIU gets involved; that'll be how Brynjar has an angle." Brynjar had sometimes regaled us with stories of things we potentially couldn't do because we were in his opinion possibly bound by a document determining the 'effective institutional design, mandate and powers' of Financial Intelligence Units like his. But I thought that that was probably not his real opinion as long as we delivered some results that were not obviously associated with a smell more fishy than Tsukiji Market.

Gas had often asked me rhetorically what happened when there was a conflict between 'effective' and 'legitimate.' We basically took the view that how useful you were in any organisation depended on how you answered that question. It was about what you could get away with combined with a cost/benefit analysis of exactly how non-legitimate your procedure was. It might be in a grey area. Most things were.

"Fieldwork takes a year," I said. "They determine that banknotes were printed in Sweden. "There's a bunch of 'physical walkthrough assessments.' That's like 'going somewhere and looking at something' but much more expensive."

"I've done a few physical walkthrough assessments of bars in my time," said Gas.

"They were probably also very expensive for whoever was paying. The actual formal purpose of the investigation is to determine whether an investigation is appropriate," I went on.

"Isn't that question already answered by the constitution of the investigation?" asked Gas.

"It's whether more should be done than has already been done by these Fabre guys. To which the answer appears initially to be yes, since they found 'discrepancies at every stage of the process.' Basically no two numbers are the same. The Central Bank was authorised to print LRD 5bn; they gave a contract to these guys in Sweden to print LRD 15bn; the Swedes actually print and deliver LRD 15.506bn. And then amazingly, documentation exists that purports to show that that amount of bank notes actually arrives at the Central Bank."

"That's good, so far," said Gas.

"Not so fast. Internal Audit Memorandums show LRD 15.506bn arriving but but packing lists for the containers show LRD 17.450bn."

"This is a new way of getting screwed by couriers. When you're just an honest dude trying to steal a few billion, the couriers go and write down what they are delivering. Annoying," said Gas.

"It does also look like the Swedes printed and shipped LRD 17.450bn while being paid to print and ship LRD 15.506bn," I continued.

'Don't tell me the Swedes are going to be bad guys in this," said Gas. "That never happens. They have their headlights on in the daytime."

"That point where the fact that the charge of 'economic sabotage' couldn't be made out, because the government released the banknotes into the economy, looks odd. Because apparently the Central Bank did that without approval from the legislature, which it apparently needed, and because the printing of most of the banknotes was also not approved by the legislature," I said. "We also have a letter from the Acting Executive Governor of the Central Bank to the President -- i.e. he is writing to his mum -- explaining why they need all these banknotes. The reason is all the ones they have in circulation are 'mutilated'."

"How do they get all these new notes out there?" asked Gas.

"This is one of my favourite parts. The Central Bank has 'small teams,' which is described as a risk by the spooks, that basically go out and buy old notes from Bureau de Change and businesses. One of the objectives of this operation is to 'flush out' large holders of legacy banknotes."

"Yeah, I bet those guys don't want to be flushed out," said Gas. At this moment, someone started singing Karaoke, which was unremarkable, except he was clearly using a 10k rig because the venue was several blocks away. "So what's the conclusion?"

"Officially, nothing can be said about whether a container of money went missing. Because every number examined is unreconcilable with all other numbers, and all investigations revealed further problematic discrepancies. No-one went to jail. Nothing further happened. The circus moved on and there was another scandal. The President was replaced with a footballer."

"So this is basically exactly what it would look like if it joined up with our previous $100m from Bangladesh to make up $201m in the tanker?"

"Yes," I confirmed. "Except these notes were in LRD and have to either get changed into USD or someone accepts LRD for oil. Which isn't impossible. It's a valid currency. But there would be a discount of some sort to allow for the fact that you would probably have to drip feed that cash into the Liberian economy. Or otherwise be happy to hold it for a while. Because it turns out that the legacy notes, which were mutilated and were supposed to be bought up and destroyed, were just also released back into the economy."

"One of our legacy hoarders who needs to be flushed out would happily buy a condo and fill it with cash I guess," said Gas.

"He would indeed. And then he could sell the keys to the condo. You could form a consortium of legacy hoarders. Some of those are people and some of them are corporates, and many are both. Brynjar clearly thinks this is the right track to follow so I imagine he wants us to stick with it."

"Copy that," said Gas. "So we need to find the ship incoming here in Đà Nẵng.

We got on to that the next day, after a breakfast of Bánh mì from a stall opposite, together with an egg coffee. This was very sweet and delicious but somehow balanced with a flavour reminiscent of some type of alcohol. After that we headed down to the port.

It had been fairly easy to find online a photo of the ship from the East China Sea rendezvous. The photo was old, but the ship would not have changed much. Or Gas said she knew what you could easily change and what you couldn't and she would be able to tell if it had every been the Shundli, the ship we wanted.

We found all of the berths in the port where you could conceivably dock an oil tanker by looking at satellite photos. There was an apparently full list of arrivals, departures and currently berthed ships shown online. But it didn't have our ship. We decided they must have got it in off the books somehow.

For a couple of days, we wandered around showing a photo of the ship to people in the port and offering small amounts of money if anyone could tell us they had seen it, but we drew a blank and eventually security decided that they weren't happy with us hanging around, so we had to stop. I thought of maybe looking for a local to try again, but if we tried that we would probably have to wait a bit for the dust to settle and also he was going to ask all of the same people we asked.

"Let's try finding something outbound matching on date and quantum instead," I suggested. "The obvious thing to do with a cargo is to use forfaiting. It's a bit like securitisation."

"I'm not sure how much that helps me," she said. We had come across it a few times but she always wanted a cashflow diagram which I wasn't always able to provide. And she sometimes got hung up on the derivative parts. Especially if they were synthetic.

"Does that cash exist or not she would say?"

"Yes," I would answer.

"You can't answer 'yes' to a binary question," she would object, and I would say that this was one of the occasions when you could. In fact, you had to. If you wanted to be strictly accurate, and there was no-one like Gas for strict accuracy.

"Derivatives are easy. The value of one thing depends -- it 'derives from' -- the value of something else. If the derivative is standard, then the something else is an asset in a box and you could take the thing in the box if you needed to. In a synthetic derivative, you have the same exposure to the thing in the box, which might be anything -- the price of oil in three months from now, say -- but you have a claim on someone else for that value."

"So it's important who the someone else is."

"Exactly," I continued, "because now you're taking credit risk that the someone else pays you value of the oil as well as price risk on the changing value of that oil, unless you fixed that at the outset. In which case you get charged for someone else taking that risk. But as long as the someone else has a good credit rating, like they're JP Morgan or someone, you don't normally need to worry about them blowing up."

"How is this like forfaiting?" Gas asked.

"Forfaiting is used by people who ship stuff but want cashflow now. You won't get paid as a shipper until your cargo arrives, and that could be months. You want that cashflow into your hands now so you can buy other cargoes and turn things over. So you sell the right to get paid in the future when the cargo arrives to a forfaiting house. That creates bits of paper which in principle are tradable."

"They probably aren't very liquid, right?"

"They won't be, no, because not many people want to take a package of risks like this which has a lot going on. There's weather risk, for example, which means delay rather than loss probably because the cargo will be insured. So you have insurance counterparty risk. There's some risk that the cargo isn't as specified and is rejected by the recipient. And if you are a new guy, that kind of risk is bigger, " I said. "So you probably won't be a new guy if you are active in size."

"Probably?"

"There's a price for everything. If someone I never met before offers me $100 for $10 and I can see the note, I might think about it."

"You aren't exactly a trusting individual, are you," said Gas.

"I don't get paid for being trusting. Or what's that phrase -- 'trust but verify' -- I could work with that."

"So what am I looking for?" said Gas.

"The forfaiting firms are specialists; they won't do any other form of business. There's going to be a discount because the forfaiter is taking various risks and also fronting cash. So we should see some kind of percentage discount on the $201m number we are currently looking for. The forfaiter will have a guarantee from a bank, because also the exporter doesn't want to deal with who they are and can they be trusted."

"How is the discount calculated?"

"It's basically the time cost of money plus some risk factors. You know that phrase 'a bird in the hand is worth two in the bush?' That's correct and we charge for the bird being in the bush. But in forfaiting you finance the entire amount of the receivables, so our number should still be stated in there someplace," I explained.

"OK," said Gas, "I think that gives me enough to start fishing."

I busied myself with local things to do while Gas was hacking. This involved some great food, including an amazing avocado ice cream down some remote back streets, findable only by a local specialist who put you on the back of a moped. These were the only way anyone got around here. It looked like you had to know what you were doing to move around and the best options were widely separated, because we crossed the river four times in the course of one evening.

The best part about the river crossings was the dragon bridge, which was basically a huge long golden serpentine structure that actually breathed fire and water at specified times. It was erected alongside a much smaller and less aesthetically dramatic bridge which the Americans had installed for supply purposes during the war. That bridge was solid, squat and dependable and did not breathe fire, unless metaphorically and historically.

One evening I needed a change from the local beers. I sat in the hotel bar drinking a double Singleton with no ice. That was a Scotch I didn't know, which was good. An Indian CEO was meeting a local guy whom I took to be in charge of the local branch. The Indian man was giving a lecture on his strategic child-care policies. These involved making your son hate you. No internships. No Lamborghinis. No handholding.

Your daughter got the handholding from your wife but your sons had to grow up strong and this was the only way to do that. It was left unspecified whether the daughters could have Lamborghinis. I thought about Gas in a car like that and decided it would probably work if she felt like making it work. For her.

This all seemed like a good schema for producing a new CEO and someone else who could achieve other objectives. But then I realised it made no sense to determine who did what at birth. What if you had a son that this guy would no doubt have called weak or 'effete' or something and you had a hard-charging daughter like Gas. Then you still get one poet and one CEO. And that's what you need. It doesn't matter who does what. Jamming people in the wrong box which didn't suit them was ultimately bad for everyone but especially the jammee.

I arranged to meet Brynjar's local stringer. He set the meeting in an odd place up in the hills that was something like an old world theme park. You took some cable cars to get there, up in the mountains through the mist. It was incredibly and unexpectedly misty and the coldest I had ever been in South East Asia.

The place was strange in a number of ways. It was crowded and deserted at the same time. The mist meant I couldn't see much. That probably explained the way you would move from packed crowds to desolate empty spaces -- no one could really tell where they were going or what they were supposed to be doing.

Visibility started at zero and then deteriorated further. The environment began to suck photons from my eyes and visual memories of sights I had previously seen were erased. I wonder how far it would penetrate my cortex and what it would delete there and whether that would matter. And then I got hung up on the usual question as to whether anything mattered.

I decided eventually the purpose of the place was for people from India and China to pretend on Instagram that they had been to Europe. A reasonably credible attempt had been made to reconstruct an idea of Europe. It was as if the buildings had been skilfully constructed by experts but using the method of asking me to describe Europe with no internet searches or drawing allowed.

If you had asked me to describe France, I would probably say that a town square had a light stone buildings with things like 'Boulangerie' written on them on a wooden sign. Also churches would have stained glass windows, or as in this case, blue and green cardboard representations of them. Everything was right but also subtly wrong. This visit would not be the best choice for someone from Europe.

The stringer was an Australian called Phil Murphy. He was half an hour late which was unusual for people in this role. He arrived somewhat flushed.

"Why are we here?" I asked.

"It's great for losing tails. Very busy at all times," he replied.

"I see that, but I don't get a lot of tails. It would be very expensive to tail me. You would need a lot of global teams and a lot of switchovers."

"For me, I like to play it safe," said the Australian.

"Fair enough," I said and explained we were looking for a ship. Murphy said he had contacts in local police and a fixer who could get into the docks scene. He would shake the tree and see what fell out. He seemed like a decent enough guy who was slightly paranoid perhaps. His day job was coding for Motion Capture, which was apparently something to do with dancers and penguins. It sounded fun but bizarre.

With that, some trades and some reading, I killed three days. Gas had not emerged from her room as far as I could tell. She was probably deeply submerged in the netherworld of hacking she would go into for extended periods. It wasn't the healthiest existence, but at least room service was offering some options that were local and fresh. I would occasionally see used crockery outside her door so I could tell she was eating. Or at least, I could tell she was ordering food. I knew better than to disturb her or leap to conclusions from cutlery.

I spent much time at the cafe opposite. I looked around a lot but mostly nothing happened. One time a group of light footed white clad ghosts came past my table with that fluttering laugh that is peculiar to Japanese women. They seemed to exist on a different weightless plane to me; it wasn't even orthogonal to mine, laden as mine was with filthy seams of coal, leaden detritus and tangled code and dirty money.

After three days, Gas showed up at breakfast. I poured her some coffee and waited, trying to keep my expectations within limits.

"I got nada," she announced. "I've been over a bunch of systems and many of them are hard to penetrate. It's not top end security; it just seems to be that a lot of it is paper based. You can't hack paper."

"All this will be on the blockchain one day and either the world will run out of electricity or it will all be hackable," I said.

"Or both," said Gas. "In fact, if it's on a blockchain you won't need to hack it because it will be public. I also got nothing from the banks. You can find credentials but you actually need a bank computer with prop software. Those guys aren't allowed any WFH: the laptops don't leave the bank branches. I can't even see the Shundli anywhere on the Đà Nẵng port status list any time in the last 30 days or the next 30 for Expected, Arrivals, Departures or In Port, and those are all of the possible status flags."

"That is a lot of nada," I agreed.

Gas said "I've been embracing the suck, but I need a new angle."

I couldn't think of anything specific. I said "Take it wide. Look for anything." Gas looked thoughtful and wandered off.

Since I again now had nothing particular to do in connection with the investigation, I took a look at the markets. After an hour reading research from Morgan Stanley, I wound up doing a couple of trades which I thought were a naturally hedged pair. I went long Delta Airlines at $37 and Constellation Brands at $225. 'Beer and planes,' I thought. 'What could go wrong?'

I had drawn four quadrants in my head which was as close as I got these days to formal scenario analysis. The four quadrants were defined by whether I would win or lose on both stocks, so the four squares were 'win-win,' 'win-lose,' 'lose-win' and 'lose-lose.' I didn't like the last one much.

I thought I would do fine in most cases. In one square, labelled with the scenario name 'recovery: work hard, play hard,' both stocks win. In another quadrant, 'back to work fellas,' Delta wins. They had first class on every flight. And they had planes. Not everyone did, after the pandemic. In 'I got fired,' beer wins. Only in 'everyone got fired' did both stocks decline.

I was never that pessimistic. The very next piece I read in the FT said that investment bankers had to be optimistic, because cynicism doesn't get deals done. That looked right. In that spirit, I went to Hoi An which had lots of boats, floating lanterns and a four-hundred year old Japanese bridge which featured on one of the banknotes. I tried taking a photo of the bridge both in reality and on the note but couldn't pull the focus correctly.

While I was there, Murphy sent me a message on Signal to say he hadn't got anything. Were we sure this ship had actually showed up, he wanted to know. I explained about the pings and he agreed to look again. Maybe it had docked somewhere esoteric.

When I got back, Gas was in the lobby. "Now I have something. It's a VNX trade confirmation," she said. She handed me a torn off sheet which bore the following hieroglyphics.

HOSEDISC GELIGMBH LOC USD 201,000,000.00 SHUNDLI/RECS ESPO 568ah0000247-re133756 TENOR 540 DAYS 92% ZBITC 119SPV ZURICH GOLD/DELIV IMMEDIATE/NICOS 17:03:45 EOR

"HOSE is the Ho Chi Minh subsid of the Vietnam Stock Exchange. Obviously the first substantive string

GELIGMBH is just corrupt data," said Gas. "After that it mostly makes sense. We've got the type of document, denomination and amount, name of the ship and some other stuff." She finished with "That quadzip in the middle of the code is very odd."

Quadzip meant four zeros in a row, as I had previously learnt. This was one of the more comprehensible pieces of USN slang which permeated her vocabulary. When you had done something or were something you got a specialism classification which was a four-digit code. Before that, you were a completely useless 0000 quadzip. It worked as an insult as well.

"Probably the quadzip is a coincidence," I said. "This is excellent otherwise. You have ESPO, which is a Russian oil benchmark, the duration of the underlying Letter of Credit, the discount and this outfit that did the original forfaiting using a Swiss SPV. There's a different name for Special Purpose Vehicles probably but this document doesn't care. This is indeed a trade confirmation; the instrument becomes a negotiable security: liquid and standardised, in the jargon."

"So what do we now know?" asked Gas.

"What you have here," I said, "is the cargo being swapped for an LoC and then this trade confirm is a record of that LoC being itself traded on. The amazing thing is that it looks like they finally swapped the LoC for actual physical gold in real time. Who is this Nicos guy?"

"I checked the data format by comparing other confirms," said Gas. "That's not a guy, it's a location. But just the first five characters, and you decode it using a World Gold Council query."

"Where?" I asked.

"Nicosia. Capital of Cyprus," said Gas.

"Capital of the Greek part of Cyprus. Alright, let's go."

The journey back to the airport proved somewhat fraught. I ordered a Grab taxi and the quoted price was VND 44,000. I accepted that and the guy showed up. We got in and did around 100m down the street before he started telling us we would have to pay more money. This infuriated me and I refused to pay an extra VND 10,000.

"Stop the car," I demanded. Gas locked quizzical; the extra amount involved was less than half a dollar. But the basic principle of contracts is that the price agreed is what you pay. We got out of the car in the middle of a load of traffic and I called the guy a fucking prick. I don't think he understood the words but the sentiment was clear.

We walked back to the hotel and another Grab car was already waiting. We got in and nothing was said. The guy dropped us at the airport, which took about five minutes. I was just starting to feel vindicated when I got the message from Grab saying that they had charged me VND 55,000. The extra 10,000 was described as a 'toll.'

"I'm going to report these bastards," I said.

"We haven't got time," said Gas. 'Let's get a beer and calm down. And report them to who?"

"I'm reporting them and I'm having a beer. It isn't the quantum of money; I just hate being ripped off. If they had asked me upfront to pay VND 55,000 I would have agreed it. You can't just agree a price and then make up another number you prefer."

"Contract law in the 'Nam, man. Could say anything," was Gas's last remark on the topic.

In the second cab, Murphy texted to say he still couldn't find anything on the ship. I mentioned this to Gas, and added words to the effect that I had thought that the guy was really slightly weird anyway. I was too annoyed to think any more about it. Maybe I could report the cab driver to Brynjar.

CHAPTER 6

NICOSIA, CYPRUS

The flights had been long. We had stopovers in Hà Nội and Dubai and were either on planes or in lounges for 18 hours. We decided to do nothing serious for a while to recover. Gas hadn't been to Cyprus before so we took a look at the general situation.

The island was still divided between the Turkish north and the southern part, which you could say was Greek in that they spoke Greek, but on the other hand they were pretty clear when you talked to them that Greece and Cyprus were different countries.

The historical situation had resulted in a number of jurisdictional oddities. The first one was that RAF Akrotiri was still there and was diplomatically speaking UK sovereign territory. Other large chunks of the island were also still there and still forever England. The Turkish north was not recognised by anyone apart from Turkey which made some aspects of life there interesting, and created opportunities. The two parts were divided by a Green Line, in front on which we were now standing.

"This is amazing," said Gas. We were looking at a scrap of scrubland with a derelict factory in it, adjacent to a car park that was now unoccupied and probably had been for 50 years. The Green Line ran the whole width of the island, roughly West to East. It was sometimes more of a zone and sometimes it shrank to a fence. It basically marked the point where the Turkish soldiers were held by the southern troops after the invasion in 1974. There was a sign on the fence we were looking at from the southern side. It said, in English, Greek and Turkish 'This is the United Nations Buffer Zone. Stop. No access beyond this point.' A Greek friend had told me that the Greek translation ran 'you are in the 'dead zone' of the United Nations' which seemed not inappropriate.

"This is the normal part," I said. "I've seen a house where the Green Line goes right through it. I don't know if those guys don't use that bedroom or whether they illegally enter the Turkish side every time they go to sleep," I said. "Also, phone navigation can get thrown off. It will send you down a street which is the logical route but you haven't been able to walk down that street since 1974 and you just find a bunch of painted oil drums and a soldier with a rifle next to him simultaneously looking bored but alert. There's the old airport in the middle of the Green Line at a wide part. It just has UN choppers now but the duty free is still there. At leats, a derelict store with that written on it is still there. I assume all the gin has gone by now."

"Did the Green Line originate through an agreement?" asked Gas.

"Not exactly. Basically the Turkish Army made rapid advances but then got stopped and this is where that was. The line is still essentially the interface between the two forces. Everyone is still where they were in the conflict."

The city of Nicosia was circular in theory, but all the maps in the south showed only the southern semi-circle and all the maps in the north showed only the northern semi-circle. The rest was blank silence.

There were several ways to cross. We had used one of the recognised crossing-points at Ledra Street. There was a police station there and you weren't supposed to take photos, but in the days of Instagram, everyone photographed their lunch. So I could not be accused of any untoward behaviour if I did the same. I therefore now had a shot through a bottle of olive oil which also showed the crossing point.

We had crossed in the morning and had an excellent Turkish breakfast just over the other side. It was a surprise how everything could change, in some respects dramatically, from the cuisine to the language to the way that you had to get banknotes from an ATM and they were TRL with pictures of Kemal Atatürk on them. That was a noticeable change after the familiar EUR of the south.

"What's going to be interesting for our guys is probably two things. Cyprus is an EU Member State, or the southern part is, but isn't in the Schengen Area, which is an anomaly. And RAF Akrotiri plus the other base at Dhekelia are British so they aren't in the EU now and won't be in the Schengen Area even if the south joins, and if it does, this Green Line will become a Schengen Border as well as an EU border."

"Is the other thing as complicated?" asked Gas.

"That complexity is what creates the opportunity. Potentially, the other thing is as complex," I replied, "but it is at least simple to state. This place is all-over rotting with rotten Russian money." This was obvious in some ways; there were lots of Russian law firms and real estate agents that were doing enough business with local emigrés with their samizdat banknotes and kompromat trades that they didn't need to bother with signage in English. Or Greek. And definitely not Turkish. The Ukraine was meant this cash was being kicked out, but it was taking a while.

Gas changed tack. "How much is $201m in gold? What would that look like?" asked Gas.

"Not that big, surprisingly. It's quite compact and easy to move around, if you get 1kg bars." I looked up the historical gold price, which had been $58,125.33 per kilo on the day in question. "So we are looking at 3,458 bars which would therefore weigh 3,458kg. They could also have got what are known as good delivery bars, which weigh 400 oz or 12.4kg. That would change the number of bars but not the weight."

"What's a good delivery bar?"

"Everything you can trade has a list of good delivery criteria which means if you show up with a product that matches the criteria, the trade is good. So you can't show up with a 12.4kg of gold jewellery and say you have delivered your part of the trade. It's like standardisation. It gets a bit weird when you are dealing with pork bellies, which are huge in the futures markets."

"So $201m in good delivery bars would fit on a ship, no problem," observed Gas.

"Easily. A cubic metre of gold weighs 19,320kg so that's already way more than we are talking about. Even with the spacing, you could fit 3,500 bars into a cubic metre, and you wouldn't really have to, because a standard intermodal TEU container has a 15 square metre footprint. In fact, you could put it on a small lorry. It might be just too heavy for a 2-axle LGV but you could almost get away with it if you had to."

I knew all this because of events that nearly happened with an Italian post office bond issue early in my career. The price of the bonds when they were issued had to printed in some official gazette, according to the local legislation. Once there had been a misprint, and it would have been possible to buy the bonds at half their face value if you could have accessed that price. The misprint was quickly detected and fixed online, but some excitable Italians rushed over from their part of the bond trading floor, and said that the printed number was binding at Italian post offices. Once you had bought them at half price or whatever it was, and it was significant, you could immediately sell them again, at full market price.

This would all have been dismissed as insane had there not been form. In 1992, the Italian post office had issued zero-coupon bonds. They paid no interest -- hence, the 'coupon' was zero, in the jargon -- but gave you back three times your money after 12 years. This worked out at a very healthy 9.6% a year if you could afford to wait. Banks could wait forever or we could sell to someone else, which basically meant paying them to wait. You didn't have to worry too much about the money not being there because the bonds were guaranteed by the Italian government.

And you basically split the profits with the guy you were paying to wait. He didn't mind waiting, because that was all he was doing, and you made your profit immediately and got paid your bonus and were permanently on the beach long before the end of the story and any surprises.

The offer was aimed at individuals, so you had to queue up at a counter, but people from Japanese and Swiss banks in London started flying to Italy, which is always fun, rocking up at the post office with a police escort and banker's drafts for $50m and buying the bonds.

This had been stopped after the post office had sold $3.6bn of bonds in a few days, which had meant loopholes were closed eventually. But people could still believe afterwards that unusual stuff sometimes happened in Italy. The theory now was that you could access this new opportunity but you could only get the 'wrong' price if you showed up with 'cash.' The Italians we had on our floor said that gold counted as cash under the regs and I was roped in to figure out how much gold you could put on a private jet.

The answer turned out to be 'not enough.' Your problem was weight not space. An example of a small private plane was the Learjet 36A, which had an amount of luggage space described in the trade press as 'woeful,' but it was still 27 cubic feet, which came out at 0.76 cubic metres. The maximum useful payload however was more of a constraint at 3212lbs or 1456kg. Not enough. So I looked at the Embraer Legacy 500 in the middle. Loads of space at 155 cubic feet but again not getting there on payload.

So I concluded by lunchtime that we needed an Embraer Lineage 1000 which had a maximum payload of 4,365 kg. They asked me if this was a private jet. I explained it wasn't; it was a regional jet that carried 19 people, if it wasn't full of gold.

I was starting to think about dropping people and going myself in order to fit the gold in. No management, just me and a guy from the Italian bond desk would do it. Why me? Because the guy that does the deal gets the bonus and I was right now writing the specifications for the transaction.

There was about a further hour thinking about who was going to lease us a regional jet right now. There had been some idea initially we were just going to borrow the chairman's plane but I'd now killed that. The question was getting a big Embraer on short-notice and then what it looked like getting fork-lifts and an armoured truck in rural Italy. We gave up, because it probably needed to happen today if it was on. But I still had a rough feel for all the numbers. Regional jet, 4,365 kgs of gold. The gold price was way different now: this cargo was $250m at current value. Comfortably more than $201m. And our guys weren't particularly under time pressure.

But where would they get a regional jet? And how would they load it up and land it when regional jets only used airstrips which would have lots of customs inspections.

I thought about why you might include a precious metal stage. "I think this gold is going to move out of here either by sea again or by sea and road. If you go to the trouble of conversion to a very compact but heavy format like gold, that implies you are not going to use air transport. Planes are terrible for weight. Also the most likely place to convert a bill of lading would be here in Nicosia. That's the financial, political and legal capital. And then there has to be an initial stage by road out of here."

"I guess it's obvious what sort of panel vans they would use," said Gas. "Every parameter will be designed to attract zero attention. They will be new, but not brand new. Not shiny but also not going to break down. They will comply with all legal requirements. They will be white or black. They can take 3,458kg of weight."

On the way back into the Greek zone, a young guy from the Turkish side crossed south with us at the same time. He spoke in English and asked the border guards where there was a phone. He had a mobile but presumably no roaming was allowed from one zone into the other.

There had been a lot of similarly pointless but predictable nonsense about vaccination certificates on the Green Line. 'We will not accept your certificate because it is issued by an illegal entity which we do not recognise' was the line. The Turkish side decided to make their lives simpler by just closing the border altogether for long periods. The contrast between the metaphorical darkness of the paranoia and the bright sunshine impressed itself upon me.

I lent the kid my phone which surprised him. I watched him to see if he would run off with it but that didn't seem to be very likely. People including sometimes myself were often surprised when I lent them my phone or helped them.

On a previous occasion in Limassol I had run into a guy from somewhere Soviet who had arrived apparently with a piece of paper, an address and a phone number. He didn't have a phone so I called the number and explained that Andreas had arrived. The guy on the other end kept texting me because he couldn't believe that I was unconnected with this Andreas guy and the whole arrangement, whatever it was, and had just made the call because I wasn't busy and this guy would otherwise be on the street. You may as well help people if it really imposes zero costs.

"What's the next step?" I asked Gas as we continued walking.

"I'm going to start scraping customs data for trucks leaving from ports and then I'm going to write some Python to filter it,' said Gas.

We arrived at a dead end, blocked off by the wall. There was a threatening soldier on a red sign with various items written on it. The top line was YASAK BÖLGE GİRİLMEZ which presumably meant FORBIDDEN ZONE because that was next on the sign. I was always struck by the way that upper case Turkish I's had a dot on them. The Umlauts did nothing, I had once explained, but someone disagreed with me and said they did the same as they did in German. I had started from the German interpretation and cancelled that out, so we were both right to some extent.

There was an accompanying sign stating that it was not allowed to take a photo or a movie so I took a shot. I wouldn't have thought of doing it if it hadn't been forbidden but the prohibition made me think it must be worth doing.

Since we couldn't walk anymore, we went back to the hotel which was close to the Green Line. I sat outside while Gas went upstairs for her laptop. She came back and sat next to me and then fired up Spyder which was a virtual coding environment and my cue to be elsewhere. Gas had no objection to me being there while she worked but I would probably not add anything and I might cause a distraction.

I wandered around the streets for a while and then found a very good pavement wine bar which was unexpectedly located behind an unprepossessing derelict shopping centre. The pandemic had played havoc with my ability to tell whether something was open or not and that distinction was much more fluid in some places than others. I sat down and read a list in Greek headed with Οίνος λευκός.

I stared at this for a while and decided that the first word might meant 'wine' and the second one looked a lot like the start of the the word 'leukaemia,' which was some kind of problem with white blood cells. So this was probably a list of white wines. I picked the first one, and it turned out indeed to be a local white wine and it was excellent. Hats off to Κολιός, if that's who made it, I thought. The wine was 100% Ιυυιστερι apparently and I was 100% in favour of that after a glass.

Gas wasn't around when I got back so I went to bed. I was just about to sleep when I got a text from Brynjar. It had just one word: 'Vietnam.' Cryptic, I thought. Brynjar must have realised this was multiply ambiguous because he followed it up shortly afterwards with 'new file.' I decided to wait until the next day before I got Gas to download the file.

"Is this another one?" she asked.

"Probably. Our magic number might move up some more. But it looks like they like round numbers. It does keep things simpler."

Gas took a look at the dropbox. "He has a report for you and some code for me," she said.

The report started at the end. There had been an arrest in Sri Lanka. This was unusual. A bunch of MT103s had been sent from Vietnam with accompanying MT203 COVs. The latter were an update to the system which meant that now intermediary banks could see the entire path of a sequence of money transfers.

"The new system is an improvement because it provides more chances to spot something odd," I explained to Gas. "Before it was just like a game of blindfolded pass the parcel where you only know they guy you got it from and the guy you give it to. They could both be fine but you need to see all the way back to the start to be sure that your transaction is good from the outset. And the end. Apparently these guys created MT203 COVs which had good syntax but bad values they made up in the data pattern."

"Who got arrested?" asked Gas, aware that this was an unusual feature.

"So the wires go out to various places including Cambodia, the US and Sri Lanka and some dude shows up and actually withdraws cash. 30m Sri Lankan Rupees LKR which is about 195k USD. Then he shows up again for another 8m two days later and they nick him."

"Amazing," opined Gas. "Something actually happening IRL. These are always the weak points, at the start and at the end. It's like encryption. You can lock it up all you want, but the need of the legitimate user to have access will always screw you up."

Gas went to work. After a couple of hours, I found her in the lobby with her laptop, seated as ever with her back against a wall with no windows or mirrors.

"So, what does your code do?" I asked.

Gas replied "There's a lot happening; I've only gone through some of it. I have something that calls a system routine to find a language identifier for the system locale. It has a check with a list of three system language codes: 0x0419 (Russian), 0x0422 (Ukrainian), and 0x0423 (Belarusian). It quits if it gets a match with one of the last two."

"That's weird. What's the Russian flag doing in there if it doesn't get used?"

"It is odd putting it in there and not checking it. Says false-flag to me. It's impossible to say for sure but the effect of putting it in there in a quit list makes it look like the code has been deliberately written not to attack systems in those three countries, but in fact it only quits in Ukraine and Belarus."

"Which are now opposed," I pointed out.

"Right. But one explanation is that this is someone who wants to make it look like it quits in Russia, thus implicating Russia, but it doesn't do that and it does in fact quit in Ukraine. Anyway, we can't get a lot out of this as far as I can see."

"Could it just be a screwup?"

"Oh definitely. Maybe this is a development version, released by accident, constructed in Russia but not intended for use there. You wouldn't want the test version to quit if you were in Russia and that's where you really are because it will quit before you can test and debug it," replied Gas.

"OK, what else?"

"All the code is in Visual C++ 6.0. That's the same language and version across the Bangladesh, and Vietnam hacks and also originally that time SONY got hacked after they made a movie that was all about jerking around Kim Jong whatever. Or 'taking the piss,' as you would say."

"What does that tell us?" I enquired.

"It doesn't mean for sure that it's the same guy, but it probably is. He's slightly old school. VC6 is a 1998 development environment. That's like prehistory in code. Not as far back as you and FORTRAN, but even so."

"Any fingerprints?"

"Yes. He has some typos," explained Gas looking as excited as she always did by this apparently arcane, esoteric and useless topic. "He's got strings typed in as 'alreay' instead of 'already' and 'FilleOut' with two Ls instead of 'FileOut.' The first one is too weird to be a real error and has to be a genuine typo but the second one he's done twice so he might actually think that's the word."

"Or he doesn't like French girls," I suggested, unhelpfully. "FilleOut Already," I added, pronouncing it 'Fee-Out.'

"Who doesn't like French girls?" rejoined Gas. "But the main action is that I have an idea of your best way to hump gold out of here. You drive it to Beirut."

"Interesting, " I said.

"Think about it. You haven't got that many options from here. You can stick it on a boat but with the migrant crisis, the Med is hot these days. Beaucoup naval action. Lots of checking of small boats. Plus where's your offload location? Has to be on the Med but where they are not likely to take a look at your cargo. Not too many places like that which give you appealing onward options. And the cargo is small but very heavy, so you need some attraction-drawing equipment on a port location you don't choose. You can load a van anywhere. And then if you are on the road, where do you go that's not too uptight?"

"That's a good argument," I said. "Also, Beirut does have a ton of problems which means a lot of options of that sort. And it's not clear where else you can go from here. Certainly not Israel because they look at everything three times." I said.

"No. North to Turkey but then what? Your options are much more constrained when you exist physically in the material world. And you can go south but then you're in the desert. Dudes with AK47s and you've got three tonnes of gold weighing down your technical. Not smart."

"Agreed. What's a technical?"

"A light improvised fighting vehicle. Basically a Toyota with a gun on the back. It could be a Gatling gun, if you're hardcore enough. 6000 rounds a minute. High pucker factor for anyone in the vicinity."

I shivered. "OK, I get the picture. What's your smarter alternative?"

Gas detailed her idea. "So starting from here in Nicosia, you drive north into the Turkish Zone. You can't go through Ledra Street Crossing in a car but you can go through Agios Dometios. After 1h, you've done 73.6 km and you are in the port of Kyrenia. You've now got a sea bus taking 3h 30min but it's only once a day so you have to get your timing right. That takes you to Taşucu on the southern coast of Turkey. Now you're basically just going to drive around the north-east corner of The Med, crossing from Turkey into Syria and then into Lebanon from the north. That's another 685.4 km or 8h 18min."

I objected: "But this means two border crossings with a van full of gold. Plus you'll be going right past the Russian naval base at Latakia. And Syrian border guards … this is all hot and an insane level of risk. Bribing customs officials is one thing; taking contraband past jumpy military guys who are sort of in a war right now is something else."

Gas responded "Special Military Operation, remember. Anyway, you said yourself that it's not a van *full* of gold. And these guys are clearly resourceful and have a healthy risk appetite, to say the least.   But the main point is that I have 'Weikang Xu' on a truck rental agreement and his insurance covers him for Syria and Lebanon."

"Really?" I said, amazed. "Well that changes the whole picture." The presence of the name of the guy who all the way back at the start of this had received the chips in the Philippine casino was indeed a major factor. "You buried the lead!"

"I wanted to get your untainted reaction to the other stuff. But yes, adding that part in does make it much more convincing," said Gas.

"It raises the possibility that if we could actually catch up with him somewhere sensible we could get Brynjar to extradite him somewhere else sensible," I said.

"We never did that before -- we should check with Brynjar before you go All Ahead Bendix on it,' said Gas.

"OK. Let's call him."

As usual, he was right there. He was at home but not asleep, as far as we could tell. He never slept, as far as we could tell. I put the question to him.

He responded with "Extradition looks simple but in practice raises a number of deep philosophical issues." I screwed my eyes up a bit but Gas and I both knew that we should shut up because we were about to learn something.

Brynjar went on. "There's a bunch of implementation stuff but there's also a set of immediate practical issues arising from what's known as the Doctrine of Dual Criminality. This is really straightforward to state. If you want to extradite someone from country A to country B to face charges of X, X has to be a crime in both countries A and B."

"That sounds like no problem at all," I said. "Money laundering is a crime more-or-less everywhere these days."

"It is. But of course you have to show reasonable indications that an offence has been committed. And that gets tricky because there can be a number of ways of cashing that out," said Brynjar. Cashing something out was a bit of a stock phrase with him from philosophy days. It meant something like 'now you have clearly stated the problem, what different ways might the question be read? "The canonical example is if you want to extradite someone from the UK to Switzerland for tax fraud," he continued.

I failed to resist the temptation to interject, saying: "That's got to be easy." Gas rolled her eyes at me. Tax fraud is 100% a crime in both locations."

"Indeed. But showing this is potentially a mess. Let's say the particular offence was lying to the Swiss tax authorities. We have, in a positive scenario, a document which contains a claim which we can also show is false and where we can provide reasonable indications that the author of the claim knew or should have known it was false. But we have to show an act occurred which was also a crime in the UK."

"The same document is good for that, surely," I interrupted again. Gas was also looking quizzical here -- about the same point, I assumed.

"There are a number of possible worlds in which we could exist here." This was another philosophy trope of Brynjar's. A possible world was fairly straightforward at least: it just meant a set of claims which would define the world where all of those claims would be true.

The way the concept did work was that a particular possible world could be the one we were actually in, or close to it, meaning it was easy to get from the actual world to a close possible world. Or it could be remote, meaning a lot of really strange things would have to change for us to get there. Like a world without dogs was definitely possible but quite odd and different to reality. And a world where gravity was negative was a long way off and might not be possible, or it could turn out to be physically possible but nothing like humans could live there. Of course, you never knew which possible world exactly we were in.

"In most possible worlds," continued Brynjar, "we are attempting to show that actions which took place in Switzerland would also be illegal in the UK. But what precisely does that mean? Does it mean that a statement has been made which would have been false had it been made to the UK tax authorities? Or one made to the Swiss tax authorities from the UK? The document in question showing the false claim will include items like Capital Gains, according to the Swiss definition. Do we translate that definition into English law or do we use the pre-existing definition already there? If we do the latter, it is possible that we come up with a different answer." Brynjar paused for some water. We didn't interrupt.

He went on. "And the translation point brings up something even more basic. It is quite likely that the document in question is in German. That would not constitute a valid submission to HMRC in the UK. So it would be disregarded by them. So it could be argued that no offence has been committed according to UK law because you could write any old nonsense to them in German and they would just ignore it."

Gas began to see the point. "And any translation can be questioned."

"Yes. And not not just the language. You will also have been 'translating concepts.' On top of all that, tax evasion in Switzerland attracts administrative penalties rather than criminal proceedings. Which parts of the hypothesis do you bring to the UK and how? So this is the type of point of which you need to be aware of before you ask us to do it. It's like moving from a Swiss possible world to a British one and you don't really know the distance between the two before you specify them both exactly. Though of course in the final analysis we would love to help if you can creep up on this guy."

"We think we might be getting closer," I said.

"The other thing is to choose your jurisdiction. I know you can't really do that, but some places it is just a waste of time even trying," said Brynjar mournfully.

"If they don't have an extradition treaty with our destination jurisdiction?" I suggested.

"That's actually surprisingly unimportant. So the UAE has no treaty with the US, but Dubai wants a clean image these days and so a Nigerian was handed over recently for online scams. He *was* taking the piss though. Private jets on instagram. And it's safe to say all governments are much more keen on extraditing people who don't have their citizenship. It's basically a cost-free way of acquiring useful goodwill. But in this connection, you have to remember that both France and Poland have extradition treaties with the US, and requests have been made to extradite Roman Polanski for decades, and he's still in Europe."

"How does all this look in this region?" put in Gas.

"It looks like a mess. Often corruption means that the local forces we rely on for implementation can just charge $10,000 for the information that a request has been made. And then obviously they are never there when the officers show up. So you could only extradite people with no money, which only sometimes you want to do. The best way is if I know a guy. Then I can get him to do it on a closely held basis. I know a lot of guys. So you can ask me. Where do you think this target is?"

"We think he went to Lebanon," I explained. "I suppose that will not be something that makes you happy."

"Well, there is precedent. A Senegalese/Moroccan dual national guy did some wire transfers he thought were for drug dealers and got extradited from Lebanon to the Eastern District of Pennsylvania. So it's worth a look.

Especially since your guy isn't Lebanese, presumably," said Brynjar with some enthusiasm.

"Who were the wire really transfers for?"

"The Feds," replied Brynjar, grinning. "But it doesn't matter. Who he thought they were for was the crux of the crime."

CHAPTER 7

BEIRUT, LEBANON

Travelling to Beirut was easy if you weren't carrying a tonne of gold, just a 40 minute hop in an A320 from Larnaca, but getting things done once there was much harder than it ought to be. That had always been true of a lot of things in Lebanon, and was now much worse, but I loved the place nevertheless. Somehow they managed to make some of the best wine in the world despite frequent interruptions of war and varied yet unchanging catastrophes. The tragedy was that the locals were all sophisticated and smart but they couldn't live there. My major complaint was the absence of pavements, but there were workarounds for that.

We were staying with friends of mine who lived in an enormous ambassadorial house overlooking Beirut with an extraordinary view down the mountain to the sea. It could easily have been an embassy with a lot of heavy gilt backed furniture and an internal fountain. They had given us wine for breakfast which was potentially a test of our resolve or culture; it certainly turned out to be a challenge for the rest of the day. That was always the problem with day-drinking -- what to do afterwards.

I was explaining through a headache the predicament of the Lebanese financial sector to Gas. "Whatever this is going to be, I don't see how it can officially or publicly involve the banking system. It has completely collapsed and is locked up."

"So how do people live day-to-day?" asked Gas.

"It's tough. For example, right now, people are going into banks with guns to get their own money out. You can't really call it bank robbery because that would be taking money that didn't belong to you. Also they use toy guns so as not to get done for demanding with menaces."

"That's bizarre. How did they get here?"

"They basically ran a nation as a Ponzi scheme for a few decades. That's where you pretend to invest in stuff but actually you use new money to pay old investors, like Madoff."

"That story ended badly."

"It did. The amazing thing there is that apparently the business was non-viable right from the start in like 1967. Often people get into trouble and try to Ponzi their way out of it, but apparently Madoff was no good right from the outset of a 50 year career."

"Impressive."

"It's rarely attempted on a national scale. In Albanian there was a rash of them in 1997. One of them was apparently run by an illiterate shoe factory worker, which might have been a clue. It went to about a third of GDP on its own and basically everyone in Albania went bust. Now they are all going to the UK in dinghy, which is not obviously better if you ask me."

"I saw that. Apparently your politicians asked the Royal Navy to intercept these boats, or maybe they pretended to ask, and the Navy declined the order. That is exceptionally unusual..."

"Is it even possible?"

"You can refuse an illegal order. But you better be damn sure that it is one because you are toast otherwise. You are probably toast anyway. But you can sort of refuse to guard a concentration camp, if you are sure it is one."

"Did you ever refuse an order?"

"Not exactly," said Gas. "But you rarely need to. Going at a normal speed and enhancing all the snafus is usually enough to stop anything ordered by anyone. So what happened to the Lebanese banking system in the end?"

"It's still unclear. Lots of powerful people don't want it investigated, for obvious reasons. It all collapsed, as they all eventually do, because you run out of victims.

The peg between the local Pound and the dollar broke. People had dollar deposits but they were frozen. If you put dollars in, you can get them out again -- they are called 'fresh dollars.' But there's probably no chance of getting old dollars out. The name for them is 'LOLlars,' which is fun and accurate yet distressing," I explained.

"How do people buy food and pay for essentials?"

"They don't, really. They need to have access to fresh dollars from abroad, or they're screwed. The poverty rate went from 40% to 80%. I remember when I was planning to come here last, the cashpoints stopped working jus before I arrived, which I thought was a big deal. My friends said this sort of thing was 'normal for Lebanon,' and maybe it was, but this time it was also the harbinger of the system blowing up. It also doesn't look fixable which is depressing."

I brought up the case of the former Chairman of the Japanese Renault/Nissan joint venture, Carlos Ghosn. "But on the upside, you can smuggle a guy in from Japan in a cello case, so there are clearly some creative people around."

"It wasn't a cello case, although I think that got in the press," said Gas. "I got a report from Brynjar on it at the time because I thought it could be useful for our stuff. The key point is that his tail didn't follow him into hotels, and the extraction team noticed that. Often there wouldn't even be a tail of course, for a non-live package."

Gas went on. "So the team which was mostly former Green Berets went into the hotel one by one. Hotels are obviously great for lots of people entering and exiting without anyone noticing. These Green Beret guys leave a few hours after the package arrives with a bunch of large containers and what is described as an 'audio equipment box.' I think that's one of those heavy-duty black equipment hampers on wheels which road crew use for tours with Motörhead and stadium rock bands and all that."

"I always love how au fait you are with British heavy metal."

"RN liaison times. Those guys got us into it."

So they put the guy in this music case?" I asked.

"Looks like it. The roadie case is too big to be x-rayed so it doesn't get done. They load all this up into a Bombardier Global Express with Turkish plates TC-TSR. They go from Kansai Airport in Osaka to Istanbul Atatürk Airport. They take a very weird extra-long route that looks like it has been chosen to avoid China, which means lots of not avoiding Russia. Then they switch to another jet on the apron to go to Istanbul."

"Weird routes are always to do with extradition; it's a rule like 'weird jurisdictions are always to do with tax'," I said. "Russia doesn't extradite its own citizens. But Russia and China are both high on the list of 'you don't have to worry about being extradited from here' so I don't know why you would make that particular move...unless you maybe have friends in the Kremlin and enemies in Beijing. Of course, the whole reason we spend most of our time in South East Asia is because there's no extradition to the US from Vietnam, Cambodia, and Laos..."

"But there is from Thailand. Which the US did nothing particularly bad to in the war," said Gas. "One part of report on the extraction I thought was interesting was that all the passenger records got faked. There were two planes leased. That actually happened, it looks like. But they were supposedly going from Dubai to Osaka and then Osaka to Istanbul and another one from Istanbul to Beirut. Nothing really came from Dubai. And there were definitely no flights filed or registered from Osaka to Beirut because the Japanese authorities would have known about the package's Lebanese heritage and the number of private jet charters from Osaka to Beirut is going to be zero most normal days. Someone might have looked at that."

"Did his passport get checked?" I asked.

"That's one of the funnest parts," said Gas. "Apparently he has three passports and he had to surrender them all to his own lawyers. So there's an ongoing question there. He may have had some VIP thing in the airport or he may have just not existed as a human on the manifest."

"I knew a Swiss guy worked for the firm. He used to have some crazy status with Swissair before they went bust and were resurrected."

"There's an opportunity for an appropriate use of the 'phoenix' metaphor," interjected Gas.

"Well, apart from the fire and ashes part. So he had some card which was colour that wasn't named. Or maybe you could define it, like it was vanta black or something. That's carbon nanotubes which absorb 98% of perpendicularly incident optical photons. Pretty black."

"So what did that get him?"

"If he had to change planes somewhere, which he did a lot because he basically lived in the air, they would move the planes around so that they were closer together," I said. Gas started to look impressed. "And someone would show up in a limo to move him directly from one jet bridge to another. No tedious messing around in the terminal. Sometimes he didn't need the limo because they would park one plane next to the other one."

"That sounds great! How do I get one of those?"

"It's so expensive its probably not worth it. Unless you are spending someone else's money. And that bank went bust remember."

"So yeah, back on our package, he could have had some status so elevated that someone trained in being nice to

VIPs didn't look at him too closely during the journey." Gas screwed up her eyebrows, as she went on. "He finally entered Lebanon on a French passport. He is entitled to one of those, so it may be genuine, or false. Or a copy. I'd vote for legit copy, allowing him to hand his lawyers another one. There are loads of allowed reasons to get a second passport, though apparently the authorities don't advertise that."

I agreed. I had looked at this a lot. "Yes, you can say that you need to visit Arab countries and also Israel. You might have to prove you already visited or you might need to construct a legitimate purpose, which wouldn't be too hard. Arab countries, including even Lebanon which is not that exercised about Palestine, will have guys detailed to look through the pages to find an Israeli stamp. If they find one, they don't let you in. That may even have been true in his case," I said. "Also apparently Kosovo and Libya stamps count as sufficient to demand a second passport in the UK, where the real reason might be that the bureaucrats there are taking so many weeks for a standard renewal that you can't wait for them."

Gas looked quizzical. "Of course, apart from all that," she said, "there is always a conspiracy angle. I don't usually go for those. But Japanese criminal law has some insane aspects. Like the prosecutors have a better than 99% conviction rate. They have to maintain that. So they usually require a confession which they don't have here."

"There would have been a lot of international attention on this trial," I observed.

"Exactly, and they could well have lost, and done so in a way which showed they basically make up their cases and the courts are biased. For example, there is a judge on record in a case denying defense council the opportunity to charge his laptop. The argument was that it's public electricity and the defense lawyer is there as a private citizen rather than a public official. So the idea of everyone getting a fair shake is deeply suppressed."

I worked out where Gas was going. "So you think that he was told how to get out, or told what day would be a good day to get in a big roadie case?"

"Yeah. It could have been one of those intermediate things. Like supplying arms to Zelensky. You can't get caught giving MiG-29 Fulcrums to Ukraine because international diplomatic incident, semi-performative grief with the Americans etc. But you can bus a bunch of Ukrainian pilots to a Polish airfield and then tell them that there's a bunch of fuelled up jets over there in dispersal, just nicely lined up on runway 030. Plus today is national Polish security staff memorial day and they have a spa trip, and Siły Powietrzne ATC goes along with them for a foot rub and a beer with the game."

"Persuasive," I agreed. "Where is the package now?"

"Looks like he's still here. He's fine. Loads of fresh dollars. The people who helped him got locked up though, in the US and Turkey. He had wired them $862,500 in cash and bitcoin and that was too traceable. Some of Brynjar's people in fact. There was only like about one stage involved: direct from initial payor to final payee. Unbelievable."

I was thinking that there were options here for our guys. "But clearly you can find ways of getting packages in and out of here on jets without too much trouble. No one got locked up here."

"No one gets locked up here, for sure. You might not want to go out through Istanbul anymore though. But of course, maybe you would, because no-one would expect that..." said Gas.

"The other relevant development is that there was an explosion in the port. Seized and badly stored chemicals. Apparently it may have been the largest conventional explosion in history. So it's less likely to be a ship coming in to Beirut," I said.

"You don't want to dock in a semi-exploded port where there are plenty of other non-compliant warehouses, no doubt," said Gas.

"Unless you really want to or really have to," I said.

My friends arrived on the terrace and explained we were going to a clifftop restaurant. We had to drive there. You had to drive everywhere in Beirut because of the strange lack of pavements. Even Gas thought the occasional sidewalk would be nice. Street lighting was sketchy. Some sections of motorway were unlit until you got close to Beirut. People compensated for the relative lack of risk when transiting from the darkness to the light by adding 20% to their speed. In fact, everyone did that. You had to if one guy decided to even out his risk level over the journey.

And rationally, that was correct. You could think about your risk budget in terms of micro-morts, which was a one in a million chance of death. The trick wasn't to minimise your micro-morts but to spend them appropriately. You would get about 10 micro-morts a year in the UK from the chance of being randomly murdered. You couldn't do anything about that if you were there.

But you could try to get paid in some way. Scuba diving was 5 micro-morts per trip, but it was fun. Similarly, 9.7km on a motorbike was fun but one micro-mort. Having a baby was 170 micro-morts so definitely a terrible idea, even before you factor in the massive expense and general pointlessness. Getting COVID at 65 was 14,000 micro-morts. A cigarette was not far short of a micro-mort on its own, so you had better really really be enjoying it.

There was a part of the INTERPOL system to which Brynjar had given us access; we were pretty sure this was illegal, but we weren't complaining. It was a bit like the web pages run by the UK's Foreign, Commonwealth and Development Office that listed the points to be aware of when travelling somewhere. The difference was all the information in it was classified. I checked it if I had time whenever we went anywhere, in case it gave us clues as to what we might be looking for in a particular jurisdiction.

In these parts, the story appeared to be Captagon. Lebanon had historically been part of Syria and it still was for several purposes. This was one of them. The Syrian regime had been ostracised until recently and narco was its only source of currency, hard or soft. Legal exports from Syria were $800m while drug exports delivered $30bn, so there was basically no legitimate economy, to first approximation.

The cost of producing a pill was 3 cents. You could sell them in Syria and Lebanon for $1-2. In Saudi Arabia the price was $25, perhaps because there were fewer other things to do. Pretty decent business. The whole point of Beirut in the old days was to allow rich Gulf Arabs somewhere to let their hair down. The civil war slightly put a dampener on that.

Saudi was the largest Arab drug consumer and the fourth largest in the world. You weren't supposed to say that though. You also weren't supposed to ask whether preventing the meeting of young people of different sexes or the same sex if that's what they were into made them look for other things to do.

The Saudis had got pretty annoyed with Lebanon when 5 million pills had been found in a shipment of pomegranates. They had banned agricultural exports from Lebanon as a result; that had been one among many negative factors hitting the Lebanese economy and precipitating the crisis. Lebanon arrested the Captagon King a number of times, and he was in and out of prison, but continued to run his empire whether he was inside or outside.

There was an organisation within the Syrian security forces called Division 4. It was headed by a brother of the president and it had only one responsibility: security of Captagon production and distribution.

One point that jumped out was that army bases in Aleppo, Homs, Hama, Latakia and Tartus had been converted from chemical weapons production to Captagon production. "That's how we know he knows he's won," I said to Gas as I told her this. "He's able to move from weaponry to economic re-development."

"But sticking to the harsh end of both."

"Sure. But he's back in the Arab League now. He's cool, they think."

"Hezbollah say this is nothing to do with them," said Gas wryly.

"OK. Good to know. Syria produces 80% of the world supply of Captagon; it goes on from here to Italy, Greece and Spain."

"How does it move?" asked Gas.

"Syrian and Lebanese ports. Then straight up the Med. Why doesn't someone interdict it? I mean, I don't see why drugs are illegal anyway, but if they are, you should do it properly. It makes much more sense though to just legalise them and then deal with the negative externalities."

"What are those?" asked Karine, one of my Lebanese friends, who had just brought us coffee.

"We are talking about legalising drugs. We don't stop people killing themselves and we let them drink alcohol, so there's no particular reason to stop them taking drugs.

We know a guy called Brynjar who says there is a thing called Mill's Principle in political philosophy. It says you can only intervene in someone's behaviour to prevent harm to others. So drugs are fine."

"What about everyone going to hospital with overdoses?" asked Karine.

"That's the negative externalities," I said. "The costs you impose on others by your behaviour. So each drug is taxed to exactly offset the costs imposed. Ecstasy would get very cheap, since there's two million pills taken on a weekend in Manchester and 30 death a year. Which is the same as zero or the number of people killed by bathroom equipment or horse riding. Other drugs, like I presume heroin, would get very expensive."

"This is all very clever but I am not sure it would work here."

"I suppose I am proposing it for the west. The current approach doesn't work. Thailand legalised Cannabis and nothing changed."

"Wouldn't you be unemployed?" asked Karine, which caused Gas to look at me for a potential breach of

OpSec. Officially I had done nothing since 2005. I hadn't told Karine much but she had clearly put some pieces together. I wasn't worried though. "Isn't it time to eat...?" I asked.

The clifftop restaurant turned out to have spectacular views and a lot of cats. They wandered about on the top of cliffs with a certain imperial majesty that completely refused to consider the way they were burning micromorts in front of you. The food was all well-cooked and not overdone, which was the way you expected things to be ruined if you were from the UK. I reflected, not for the first time, that being a restaurant cat must be one of the best jobs there is.

The food was also fresh and citric with a good balance between sweetness and acidity. More of the local wine was available in liberal quantities; it was a rare exception to the rule that anything ubiquitous would be low quality. The restaurant was also an exception to a rule which generally held and had been expounded by a guy in the FT I thought was good. He said good restaurants have bad views, because if you have a great view, you don't need to care about the quality of the food. That made sense, but not this time.

There was plenty of eastern Mediterranean stuff like hummus, baba ghanoush, a local soft cheese made from live yogurt called labneh but the items specific to Lebanon were the best. Manakish was a flat-bread which like many things included the local spice zaatar, and there was a super zingy salad called Tabbouleh which Gas actually found a bit too acidic. Not me though.

While we were enjoying a vast array of different perfectly ripe fruit and strong coffee, which were also all delicious, I got a Signal message from Brynjar saying 'Ecuador. Report in folder.' One minor disadvantage of staying with friends as opposed to hotels was the security point, but they didn't particularly know what I was doing on my phone and I mostly maintained the appearance of a sunny and carefree disposition, so I got away with it, I thought.

Brynjar hadn't written 'urgent' in the message or used any caps, so I didn't think there was any problem heading off to the Roman ruins at Baalbek in the afternoon. These turned out to be spectacular, and much better than anything I had seen elsewhere. Huge above ground structures had survived, whereas in England we got excited about a mosaic floor. Here you would have 100m tall columns and very well preserved carvings, which tended to be about Dionysian intoxication or to the glory of the emperor Vespasian.

I had told Gas during the trip about Brynjar's message, and later that evening we sat around her laptop to look at the file, before the evening's libations from Chateau Musar began. This was as good as anything the French could produce and was way cheaper if you got it from the source.

The first thing that was interesting about the report was that it was written by a lawyer at West Point. I didn't know that those existed but Gas said it was completely normal. An immediate further point was that there was more on the Bangladesh heist. Apparently the Central Bank there had used cheap routers and no firewall, which I thought was unusual and Gas thought was unbelievable.

"So this one is smaller; just $12m," I reported. "Instructions are to wire from a commercial bank in Ecuador to another commercial bank in San Francisco. Money goes to Hong Kong."

"So our magic number goes to $213m," said Gas.

"Maybe, but the trail so far is to HK, so it may join our package further downstream. Or conceivably it could be someone else. I haven't got to any fingerprinting yet."

"What's the methodology?"

"Standard credentials hack it looks like. Legitimate login stolen. Apparently one problem is that there is not central way of seeing these trades. The system just sees a ton of transactions and only gets told later that some of them were not kosher and then only in an unknown proportion of cases," I explained.

Gas said "Are the credentials gained through social engineering or network hacking?"

"Unclear. Apparently the first SWIFT knew about it was when Reuters started asking them questions. That's embarrassing."

"It certainly is," said Gas. "Which is why there's not so much public disclosure. Good result for the free press."

"Apart from just the embarrassment," I added, "it's not great for banks if the public finds out that cash in large amounts is going down the leg side and being used for bad stuff. We'd better not tell them. That's probably another reason why we don't exist."

I spent the next day doing nothing while Gas worked hard. The rest of us were drinking wine in the garden when Gas arrived looking concerned. We moved to a separate table and she updated me.

"I have some info on the Ecuador thing. Wells Fargo refunded $958,700 of the $1,486,230 it transferred as a result of getting a SWIFT message from the Ecuadorean bank. That amount went to a guy in LA. Reuters say they can't find him or prove he existed, but that's odd because someone with the same name has a law office in LA. He's an ambassador from Honduras as well or something. Could be a different guy of course. This guy does odd things. I have him submitting a petition for an order which would correct the date of birth stated for someone on a certificate of naturalisation. There's a bunch of procedural stages and then the court agrees that this person was born in 1934. Not at all obvious why you do any of this."

"Maybe something to do with pensions. Crazy stuff happens there," I pointed out. "Someone was getting a Civil War pension up to 2020, apparently."

"How is that possible?" asked Gas. "I can't get any bumps from AFPAK and that was a lot more recent." Veterans always thought they should get paid more if they had spent time on the Afghanistan/Pakistan border because they thought it sucked.

I explained the Civil War pension point. "Lots of older veterans would marry younger women in the 1920's Depression, because their pensions were secure. And then they had kids. And this one individual had some problems and was classified as a 'helpless child' and so she could draw money indefinitely."

Gas looked amused by this, but it was just an overlay on her general emotional state of concern. "Then on the stuff here, I couldn't get anything from the border," she went on. "Probably zero tech and therefore secure against anything apart from people showing up in the room and absconding with pieces of paper."

"Customs reports?" I suggested.

"Same same," said Gas, "paper. Can't touch it. After that I restarted by just scraping basically everything photographic. That's a big bag of data which was mostly useless, but there's a bunch of these webcams around that do stuff like give you a live feed of traffic conditions on I-45, is it foggy up the mountain. Stuff like that. Some people just show you their front lawn."

"They don't store the live feed, surely," I said.

"No. Not all of them even have a live feed. Some of them just take a snapshot every hour and display that. If you tried to store a live feed, you might use 1GB an hour or something. It can be done, by various serious operations on core missions, but these are shoestring operations by individuals for fun, often," explained Gas. "Anyway, I downloaded all of this, ran it through OCR for the plates and expected to find nothing."

"Right -- there's almost no chance we've got the guy on one of these, unless there's hundreds of them, " I said.

"There are ten cameras on the road between the Syrian border and here," said Gas.

I couldn't see how this could work. "Not enough to get him at all."

"That's the opposite of the problem," said Gas. "I've got him on all ten. And in at least two of them, it looks like he's used a flashlight to make it easier to see the plate."

"What? That makes no sense. Is he trying to send us a message?"

"Maybe. If the message is 'fuck you'," said Gas.

"Imagine they knew we would be focussed on car in and plane out for a Lebanon stage," I said. "The port was out because it got literally blown up, the banks were out because they got metaphorically blown up, but private jets had been shown to work for illicit cargo and driving a truck will basically always work, even if you have a lot of friction in the form of bribes."

We decided it was time to report this to Oslo. I texted Brynjar and he agreed to call us in an hour. "Get Susie on as well," was his opening line when he did.

"She's on." The first thing Gas wanted to know was how she got fooled, after Brynjar gave us the devastating news that our last three sectors were fake right upfront.

"So nothing we got from Đà Nẵng onwards was correct?" said Gas, astounded.

"That ship never arrived in Đà Nẵng, correct," said Brynjar. "My guy there, Phil the Australian, is pretty thorough. Also, the gold in Nicosia is not real. The trade confirm is fake data too."

"How could this be?" asked Gas despairingly. I was inclined to give her some slack on this but she wouldn't give it to herself, I also knew.

"Your analytic methodology was sound on the ship," said Brynjar. "It's just that the AIS data were planted. Remember that in Scandinavia we know about shipping, even though I know you do as well, and there was something odd about your story."

I contemplated introducing the term 'shipshape and Bristol fashion' into the conversation but realised that Brynjar would point out that his Scandinavian expertise in shipping derived more from actual experience rather than osmosis from having been born in a port city. And that I was very likely the person on the call with the least amount of actual naval experience. And that this was no time for levity.

Brynjar went on. "So you told me that you were dealing with a transponder, which responds when pinged. But any serious ship nowadays is going to have a transceiver. It doesn't wait to be asked for the information. You might have thought differently because civilians can be slack."

"Right," said Gas, who was now listening with her head in her hands.

"So I thought that was worth further examination. I got our technical department to look at the pings. They said these pings were entirely accurate in terms of what they should look like for a ship doing those voyages, but also that there was no reason why someone with access to the system couldn't just write them in. Generating them would be a technical challenge, for sure...but we know our players like that sort of thing and are resourced for it. And there was an obvious place to plant the data."

"Damn," said Gas. "And I went to that easiest place."

"Exactly," said Brynjar. "That environmental protection agency you don't name in your report in to us is well known, which is why you didn't need to name it. You went to the tree with the lowest hanging fruit. The guys we are chasing know that's the right tree as well as you did." Environmental agencies drew a lot of well-meaning interns with lax password discipline.

"I didn't think they were going to be this sophisticated. How could they be certain I would go there?" asked Gas.

"They didn't know that for sure," replied Brynjar. "But they did know that if you looked anywhere else, you would see nothing, which was no problem for them, and that that was the most likely place for you to look. If it helps, my guys say there was no way from looking at the data that you could distinguish it from genuine data. They got it by seeing that it wasn't in other datasets, which is possible for us and [difficult] for you."

The slight twist Brynjar put on the word 'difficult' here meant that he knew that we could do it and we knew he knew that and that everyone knew that if we did it was illegal and if his guys did it, it was fine. If we did it, it would be one of Brynjar's 'victimless crimes,' that were worth doing, net-net.

"What particularly bends me out of shape about this is that I wrote a technical report on Magruder's Principle when I was at the Naval War College in Rhode Island," observed Gas with noticeable acidity and chagrin.

"Which says what?" I asked.

"The Principle states what you could also state as being the CIA's first law of deception,' explained Gas. "As we know from Sun Tzu, deceiving the enemy as to everything you are doing and all your capacities is half the battle. Magruder's Principle dates from the civil war. It says it is easier to convince the enemy to carry on believing something false he already believes than to give him a new belief."

"Like Norway in the war," added Brynjar. "Hitler thought that Norway was the 'zone of destiny' in the war, because of iron ore, and heavy water, the proximity of the Royal Navy and how there had been landings already in 1940. He also got his only early black eye in Narvik. So the Allies kept making him think that

Normandy would really be here and he kept a crack division there ahead of D-Day."

"I remember this. There was a load of fake radio chatter made up in the UK about tank engine performance in cold weather and obtaining ski bindings for a fictitious British Fourth Army. And like the Germans, we also saw what they wanted us to see, " I added.

"Quite," said Brynjar.

"And this is why I got them ten times on traffic cams," said Gas. "This is all a huge distraction."

Brynjar did his Uff Da thing while exhaling. It would become clear that what this meant was 'it's unfortunate you think that' rather than 'it is indeed a shame that this happened." 'What this means is that they weren't sure how many you would get. They were over-successful or you were in that you got all of them. The point was to lead you to the airport and then make you give up, because there is nothing much to be done there quickly. Or they might have wanted you to find that and go backwards to the maritime data."

"This is a disaster," I said. "All this time and effort wasted."

"Not at all," said Brynjar. "We think you have established a good picture of one of the decoy route sections. This is extremely valuable."

"It doesn't lead to product," I pointed out.

"You are taking a wrong perspective," argued Brynjar. "You have to see these routes as a machine that gets switched on periodically. The decoy sections are there to cut you and the other trackers out of the chain if you are there. Now we know that when we see these sectors active, that some of the real product is moving through other sectors. This is excellent intelligence."

"What exactly is the big picture here?" I asked.

"We don't know. We are waiting to see what you find. It isn't exactly money laundering. It's hard to define what that is, and it wasn't even a crime in the UK until 1990, but this is bigger. It involves laundering, but it looks like the prime objective is just to move large sums of money around to an end location where they are expendable. The laundering is a *method* not an objective."

"Some sectors might be legitimate on their own," I said.

"Indeed, though, I guess it's also relevant that all the money was stolen in the first place," he added, mordantly. "We could call that a predicate offence in terms of money laundering regulations or an original sin if we were being more poetical."

"Alright," I said, "but our position is that we've dropped significant resource on these sections, and we don't currently have a line on product."

"I understand. One of the other teams is in touch with an asset." Brynjar said that people were 'in touch with' an object or some data if they did not possess it, but could obtain it with reasonable certainty and within acceptable cost and time parameters. "I don't know the value or exact nature of the asset."

Clearly he didn't know the exact value and in fact he probably didn't know the approximate value since these pieces of data would be radioactive for him. My concern was with the number of other teams but I knew I wouldn't get anything out of him about that and that the answer was probably indeterminate anyway. None of this was real, officially, and there was a fine line between stringers, freelancers, informants, 'assets' and people who were just 'around.' Gas and I were as formalised as it got with Brynjar and there was nothing linking us on paper and anything not on paper was highly encrypted and would evaporate on observation, like a virtual particle that lived for 10^{-18} s.

"How do we get hold of the asset?" I asked.

"I will arrange for it to be sent to you." he replied. "In the circumstances, I suggest you go to Bangkok to receive the asset. And then you can get back on the trail from there. Maybe take some time off."

Bangkok was indeed a good combination of convenience and enjoyment. You didn't have to persuade me to go there; especially not if there was going to be a payday as well.

"Are these assets legitimate?" I asked.

"Enough," replied Brynjar. I wasn't sure whether he meant the assets were sufficiently legitimate or that was enough questions, but either way, this was probably a good time to stop asking them. Looking briefly at Gas, who indicated with her expression that while she was disappointed at what she saw as having dropped the ball on the pings, she was happy to go along with the proposal.

Gas jumped in. "I have something else." She looked at me. "I haven't told you yet."

"Go ahead," I said.

Gas explained that she had been tracking private jet charters of the type that apparently had been involved in the Ghosn extraction, and she had found two unusual developments. "The first odd thing is that there are lots of these, moving into and out of Beirut. And the second thing is that the rate has a step function in it. I mean that these flights were fairly sporadic for a long time, but then from about five years ago they became very regular. In and out. Like breathing."

Brynjar and I both agreed that this was interesting and should be looked at further. Then we got on to the topic of Weikang Xu. Brynjar explained that he was indeed in Lebanon, apparently in the fertile yet remote Bekaa Valley, but that they weren't going to bother trying to extradite him. "Too much trouble," Brynjar said. "Also, the local guys can just pick him up and see what he knows. They are quite good at that sort of thing. It might not be admissible but we will worry about that later. I will let you know what we get."

"OK. One final question," I said. "These assets in Bangkok are worth our while?"

Brynjar didn't officially have any idea of the valuation, of course, because it would be very unhelpful for him if he did know. "I believe that this will tide you over, and that Bangkok is the right place to be" was what he said. Sometimes Brynjar's English was almost too good. He never made a mistake and also he never deliberately screwed it up, as a native speaker might sometimes, for fun. He seemed to have a flawless lookup table matching colloquial expressions to scenarios. Nevertheless, this whole package was working for me.

"OK," I said, "we're in."

CHAPTER 8

BANGKOK, THAILAND

It was a long pair of flights, 20 hours via Riyadh. We consoled ourselves in the usual way with free business class alcohol, apart from there was none on the stopover or in Saudi airspace. This was not a big problem because we pregamed it. The air hostesses were happy to work with us on that, once the curtains separating business class from economy were drawn. Gas told me off slightly for not using the modern term 'flight attendant,' but she seemed in general to realise my heart was basically in the right place, so there was a limit to the spanking. I decided I could probably update my vocabulary to include 'flight attendant' since it was not dramatically counter-intuitive. And also because 'air host' did not seem to exist while those individuals definitely did.

Something had happened right at the outset with some passengers from economy who decided to use luggage compartments in business because they were all full, I imagined, behind us. People in economy always had much more luggage even though they had to pay for it, which I didn't really understand. Our FA, as I was now calling her, took issue with this. I didn't really care about the objective, but there was a lot of puffing and undirected movement in my vicinity, which I did care about. It ended up with the passengers and their luggage being sent back to the rear of economy, and also the FA said the passenger had a 'stupid face.' I looked to check and it was true.

After that I focussed on the welcome champagne. We never saw those passengers again. They might have been offloaded. Never argue with an FA. Even if you're

231

right, which you won't be, it has no benefits. And if you're nice to them, they often find a way of being nice back.

We made our first destination in Thailand the excellent Novotel which is in fact inside Suvarnabhumi Airport. You could actually push a baggage trolley there direct from the arrivals hall. We did that because it was fun even though we could have waited for a shuttle. This walk took place entirely underground so you didn't deal with the heat blast and the humidity until after you had got rid of your luggage. That was still important even though both of us had dropped back to one duffel bag each to cover basically the entirety of our physical possessions. I thought that Gas owned a cabin somewhere possibly and I had a flying jacket at my brother's house. But that was it.

You could check in at the Novotel at any point and the room was yours for 24 hours from that moment. This took out a lot of difficulties with getting cabs and luggage into the city and out of it again if you had an overnight stopover. We didn't have that this time, but we just wanted to arrive and sleep or if we couldn't, dwell numbly in that netherworld of partially-conscious jet lag without any requirement to do anything immediately.

In some ways, Las Vegas is the ultimate place to fly to from anywhere, because the airplane limbo doesn't end. Hotels are free, which is great, because everyone except me spends a ton of money in the casinos. Everything is in the same building and there are no windows. If you need to go somewhere, you can probably do it without stepping outside and finding out what the temperature is or whether it is night or day.

We waited in the Novotel for a few days, both of us putting in some gym time. We bounced into town a few times using the Airport Rail Link, which was clean, cheap, fast and perfectly located. A courier brought a package to my room on the third day. I looked inside it. It appeared to be an envelope and box with some unimpressive bits of glass in it. The envelope had a Kimberly Certificate, which apparently meant these were diamonds, as well as a short handwritten note.

The note had the words 'Tag RJT, Dieser Typ ist bei uns, Tschuß' written on it, which meant 'this guy is with us.' It was written on a compliments slip from a gem firm, RJT in a place called the Bangkok Gems Tower. The note was was signed 'Angelika.' Informal but effective. Brynjar had described this as a 'letter of introduction,' which I thought was somewhat overplaying the hand. It was like someone writing their phone number on a beermat in a rough pub in Kilburn and later calling it an 'RSVP.' Though using the RJT firm's own compliment slip did add some authenticity.

The Kimberley certificate was from Israel, and although it was notarised and apostilled, it looked fairly fake-able to me. I didn't look too hard in the gift horse's mouth however. The worst that could happen was that I had a bad cert or bad stones. That might fail to add positive value but I didn't see a probable scenario in which it could add significant negative value. I could get arrested for passing counterfeit materials, but Brynjar could get me out of that one.

We decided to base ourselves in town around Silom, one of the lively central districts. Our new hotel was opposite the Skytrain station at Chong Nonsi. This was convenient since the Silom Road was a six lane superhighway that was always packed with the infamous BKK traffic, so you had no survivable chance of crossing it on foot. The metro had been built along the line of the old canal, which was still there, to add a water feature as an extra obstacle to anyone who thought they could cross the road. The metro station was labyrinthine, but you could use its dozens of stairways and escalators to get across the street.

We chose the hotel because it was also close to the Gems Tower. I had had misgivings about this Tower, because it was one of the unexpected stops that Farang tourists were taken to when they were supposed to be going somewhere else. It was standard to get a tuk-tuk to a temple or restaurant or other stated destination and have it 'coincidentally' pass by 'my cousin gold shop' or 'gem store my aunt' and it would take a lot of time and assertiveness to get moving again.

"Do you need me for this or can I get a drink?" asked Gas. The hotel had an infinity pool on the roof, where you had a view of the metro station and a bunch of impressive skyscrapers.

"I think I'm fine on my own. I can catch up with you later," I replied. "Does the name 'Angelika' mean anything to you?"

"Not really," said Gas, "assuming you don't mean my cousin who is a realtor in Columbus."

"Very probably not," I said as I was leaving.   "This Angelika sent us the package."

RJT turned out to be on one of the top floors of the tower, which were mostly for wholesale business. I had requested a meeting by email attaching a shot of the note and I had got an immediate response. My meeting was with Mr RJT, which was a good start.

I walked into an office which was workmanlike and unfussy, except for the desk area which was full of high powered lighting equipment and trays containing arrays of magnifiers, small pen torches, spectacles and tweezers. RJT himself looked small but efficient; his eyesight did not look fantastic but I supposed that was his problem not mine. And he certainly had plenty of equipment to boost it up.

I handed the bag to Mr RJT and explained I wanted a price. The first thing he did was a surprise. He looked at the Kimberley certificate first and for a long time using bright lights and magnifying glasses. Then he established who was the notary that had authenticated the certificate and who was the apostille provider who had made the certificate a recognised internationally acceptable document under the Hague Convention.

At length, Mr RJT appeared satisfied with the certificate and its appurtenances and turned to the other item in the envelope.

"Yes," he said, "So, you are friend of Angelika," he stated.

"I am indeed," I replied, only slightly encumbered by the fact that I had no idea who Angelika was.

"How is she doing?"

"Oh you know Angelika," I said. "She never changes."

This elicited a laugh from Mr RJT, who finally turned to the box. He opened it, looked inside, and looked back at the Kimberley certificate, which mentioned carats, and parcels. He looked inside the box and again appeared satisfied. To no one in particular, he said "Wagner. Central African Republic."

Then he looked again at the diamonds which just looked like bits of glass to me. He checked them in the lights and then said "You have 12 stones for a total of 67 carats of octahedral Commercial Rough. No inclusions external or internal, no cleavage, no macles. Very normal material, good in market."

This sounded positive, and a lot better than 'not much call for these nowadays.' It was almost like we had been given the basic sort of diamonds which meant no questions needing to be asked. Which was good, because I didn't have any answers. I looked up 'macles' on my phone while Mr RJT carried on peering at them and found out that it was twinning of diamonds. It didn't look like it was good news so I decided I ought to be happy I didn't have any.

He looked though a device that folded out into a pair of lenses. "Polariscope shows no problem. This is all in order. I can offer you $301,625."

I though for about four seconds about arguing or negotiating but then realised the massive information asymmetry in this trade. So I just said "Great, when can I get it?" and received the answer that if I waited in the coffee lounge for an hour, a wire transfer could be prepared for me. Thailand was one of those places where you could sometimes get things done very quickly if they involved motivated people who knew each other working together and jumping on moped taxis. If you wanted an official to stamp a piece of paper, you could wait a thousand dynasties.

Not that such a thing existed here, since Thailand was the place in the world most prone to military coups. I had actually been on the spot for two of them myself. They didn't seem to make a lot of difference on the ground, apart from the fact that there were lots of elections and alcohol sales were prohibited on election days.

It actually took 35 minutes to get the wire transfer. I could see this had occurred while I was sitting drinking two double espressos in the lobby because I got a ping from my banking app. There are few things more fun than getting a popup notification saying your account is up by six figures. So I quietly said "That'll do it" to myself and wandered off, giving Mr RJT's assistant a double thumbs up with matching grin as I left.

I walked up the enormous and traffic-strangled Thanon Sathon Tai past one of my favourite hotels. The Banyan Tree had a sky bar that was something like 36 floors up. They had good mojitos and a ridiculous view over the whole city. The bar itself felt like a ship floating on the clouds, partly because each end was a raised platform like a forecastle and poop deck. Maybe that was why Gas liked it; I liked the mojitos.

I was heading towards Patpong night market, where Gas was having a beer in the street downstairs from the girlie bars. So I was able to sit down next to her and say, "We have 300 grand in Yankee dollar, so we are officially tided over and not skint."

This was a slight exaggeration, since we hadn't been up against it before. But it was still good to have extra liquidity, and if you flew everywhere in business class, you could use it up quite quickly. Hotel prices were generally not much above $35 a night for four stars in Thailand, so you couldn't really leak meaningful cash that way. The main variable was the length of time between pay days, which could be anything at all.

"Bueno. I like being not broke. All frosty on the sales process?" Gas asked.

"Yeah, they were completely chilled," I replied. "They didn't even flinch when I handed over a copy of a

Republic of Vanuatu passport.   It was a real copy too, made with a photocopier."

"What was that thing again with you and the photocopiers at the Bank of England?" asked Gas.

"There was another exercise after the in-tray thing. You did it with a bunch of other candidates sat around a big round table. Members of staff did one-to-one marking on each candidate and did a lot of writing."

"So they are all sitting around watching what you do? Weird."

"I didn't mind. There was a big office plan on the table with about eight of us sitting around it. We had been briefed before that we were to imagine that we each worked for a director of the bank; we were all executive assistants or something. And the big shot we worked for wanted one of two new photocopiers sited somewhere near his office. Obviously this was not very realistic because there was no way any of these big shots would actually do their own photocopying. But no-one asked that question. Some people were just a bit scared. I never care what the rules of a game are. I just try to understand them and win."

I was momentarily distracted by an improbably loud buzzing sound, which I couldn't be sure was originated by a machine or an insect. After a few seconds, I could see that it was an enormous bumble bee, which must have been more than 4cm long and was banging its head on a closed window behind us that was right next to an open one.

I wondered briefly whether large bumble bees would sting you more, and how they could be smart enough to survive but not smart enough to handle windows. Then I realised that probably things you can't see but block your path probably didn't exist in the evolutionary environment for bees.

Gas said "Surely though it's easier if the rules of the particular game you are playing make sense, or are well-motivated."

"Maybe. But I understood it was a game and the stated objective was to get a photocopier close to my boss's office. That was good enough."

"So how were you supposed to do that?"

"That was the fun part. They didn't tell us anything else. We just had to negotiate. So I started off by deciding that my guy had gout and couldn't walk very far. Also he had to do much more copying than anyone else because I decided he was director of counterfeiting or something."

"How did that go down?"

"The other candidates weren't too happy -- some of them anyway. They started saying that this wasn't in the notes but I just smiled at them."

"I somehow think there is going to be some kind of problem here," said Gas. "And not just because I know you didn't get the job. So what was the outcome?"

"I was told that my success level had not been matched in the entire history of them running this game. I'd got both of the photocopiers sited actually inside my boss's office. So I was quite pleased about that and surprised me when they canned me."

"Did they tell you why?"

"Yes. They said that while I achieved the objective, I wasn't supposed to make people cry."

"Amazing. They didn't state that as an objective, then," said Gas.

"No. Maybe they thought it was implied."

Gas said "Perhaps they were trying to find out if you would treat subordinates badly."

"They don't find that out with this exercise," I said. "I would never treat subordinates badly because you don't get the best out of them. The same way I am always nice to wait staff, and flight attendants. You have to be super weak if that's who you bully. They should have designed some collaborative exercise. This was competitive. They chucked me in a shark tank and I ate the competition."

"Maybe you're just not a public sector guy."

I supposed not. "I requested written feedback later, and it added that a woman who had interviewed me had complained that I made 'aggressive hand gestures.' I couldn't work out what that was but I thought about it and remembered I had been explaining bid-offer spread changes in option pricing by making sort of scissor opening and closing movements with my fingers. She had started back in her chair at the time and I had thought 'what on earth is your problem?' but not made enough of it. I mean, her reaction would have been excessive if I had said 'this is how I'm going to cut you up;' it would maybe have been about right if I had actually produced a weapon."

"Yep. You belong on the trading floor," said Gas. "No one cares about you doing Edward Scissorhands to illustrate a price. In fact that's probably the recommended method."

"Well, that's what happened. So you must be right," I said.

"I was thinking about next steps," said Gas. "Also I am confused about the vehicle on the cams going to Beirut. That definitely happened because we saw it. Even if there was no gold inside the vehicle, that journey happened."

"Maybe it was just some other contraband, not connected with our guys," I suggested.

"Could be," responded Gas, "but that doesn't explain the wanting to get spotted. In fact, it anti-explains it."

"Nothing explains that," I agreed. "What are the next steps?"

"We have to go back to the last thing we know, which is the oil getting transferred in the East China Sea. I'm going to download some industry specialist trade flow software and get some credentials and see if I can get more data."

"Sounds good. I'll maybe look at money trails," I replied. We went for highly authentic Currywürst mit Pommes at one of the Old German Beerhouse places off Sukhumvit. I enjoyed German food in Bangkok more than I did in Germany because they made it with passion. We got started in the afternoon.

We were now back to exactly $201m as the target amount. I checked disclosed cashflows plus or minus three days around the critical date but found nothing, having looked at 17 international trade databases. Or more accurately, I found 3 transactions that were of that amount among the millions listed, but they did not appear as though they had any possible connection with our $201m. One was a purchase of stock in MRK, a major US Pharma company I had owned slices of myself in the past. It was done by a nominee fund on behalf of an undisclosed client. Standard. One was a Singaporean sovereign fund which was exiting some tech and real estate in Beijing for political reasons. Less standard, but nothing to do with our guys.

The third was some hedge funds combining to bet against a sprawling Indian infrastructure conglomerate where a short seller had alleged one of the main listed entities was audited by an accounting firm with four audit partners. Using tiny audit firms you could capture was one of the major red flags that no-one spotted with Madoff.

I looked at this one slowly for a couple of hours. But I couldn't see how any of this could be linked to the oil, and all the counter-parties were subject to varying degrees of KYC/AML regulation, whereby you can't just do deals for people without knowing something about who they are. Or at least, being able to look to the regulator like you know something, which more-or-less amounted to something similar.

The share price of the various Indian entities had dropped by a combined $100bn in ten days, which was striking not least because the magnitude of the gains made by the short-seller must have been immense. But again, not our guys.

I widened the scope out by 10% either side. This got me a lot more transactions, but again none of them appeared to have oil on the inbound leg. I switched to EUR and got to €187,306,449.36 at the prevailing FX mid market rate. 13 transactions on the day within 10% of that. No oil. £, ₹, ₩ and ¥, same same, nothing doing. I understood ¥ as JPY but apparently the Chinese were also using a Y with two cross-strikes for Yuan Renminbi which struck me as dramatically unhelpful of them.

Then I opened out the window to ± 3 days which gave me a total of 1107 transactions in the six different CCYs on public exchanges. Nothing looked interesting but I saved the file. If the trade had happened in a dark pool, where buyers and sellers meet up in the digital equivalent of a darkened speakeasy and transact bespoke amounts of bespoke asset types with bespoke amounts of disclosure where bespoke now meant zero, I wouldn't get it without a subpoena and probably not with one.

I took a break around 2030. The time difference between New York and BKK was 12 hours, which was actually quite handy, because you could just switch AM to PM and vice versa. This was the only time I would use a 12hr clock.

One thing causing some nerves in the markets was an upcoming CPI print in the US. Inflation had been running hot for a year or more and the Fed had hiked 450 basis points or some massive number. Everyone was freaking out about a hard landing recession but I had never bought it because employment was red hot. How can you have a recession when everyone has three jobs and is spending like a drunk sailor? The data print was 0830 NYC time, as they mostly were. It came out hot which the market initially didn't like at all, but then later on it decided it didn't really care. That was fine by me, even if it didn't make any sense. Most things the market did didn't.

I started thinking about parallel trade arrangements. This happens if you want to do something in a jurisdiction where you aren't allowed to have that exposure.

Imagine you aren't allowed to lend money in Russia, say, but you want to, and you are allowed to sign a contract with me in my London office. I have a branch in Moscow. My branch lends money to your friends in Siberia, you lend me money in London, no problem. Obviously my branch in Moscow will actually have ten cutouts in Cayman etc. between me and it but you don't need to worry about that.

Alternatively you might want to own the Russian stock market. You definitely can't do that out of Washington or London. What you can do though is effectively gain that exposure though by entering into a swap agreement with me, if I am in a jurisdiction where I am allowed to have that exposure and I can contractually agree with you to give you a bunch of $ ± some more $ X where 'some more' is a function of what the asset you aren't allowed to be exposed to does. The fact that X is calculated based on the value of the market in Moscow doesn't concern anyone and this is a private contract that need not be disclosed to anyone. It could be an encrypted smart contract if you want to be super safe, though you will need some people in the tech/legal interface and they are rare. Because lawyers can't do maths.

Or it could be funky. Say your reference asset does x in a year, you might want 'some more' to be 2x or 3x or even x^3 or $16x^4$ if you were some kind of lunatic. This was all also non-disclosable though, and your only potentially declarable risk was to me as a counter-party in your accounts next year.

What all this added up to was that I couldn't see what to do with it next. It was clear there were plenty of invisible things you could do once in the system. It was now way past 2am. I knew Gas would crack on all night if need be but I was done.

As it turned out, I didn't see her for three days. There was a 24hr gym in the hotel; I wandered around town a few times. One day she showed up for breakfast and I waited to see what she would say. This was a practiced routine.

"I started with the two things we knew to a reasonable degree of certainty," she began. "The ship was in a known location in the East China Sea at a fixed time. That was Point Zero. Also we know it was a VLCC."

I refilled my coffee.

"I downloaded a digital map of the world's sea lanes. I looked at what is the top speed for VLCCs because that defines the maximum distance from Point Zero on a particular day. A standard service speed for a VLCC is 15.7 knots, for a typical double-hulled vessel constructed by Hyundai in 1999. You might get 16.4 knots from a 2006 version from Kawasaki and 16.5 knots from IHIMU in 2009. JMU have one doing 16.8 knots that they built in 2018. So you can see they are not getting much faster. All of these are laden or 'with ballast' speeds and they are service numbers that you could reasonably expect to get for extended periods. You aren't going to be doing All Ahead Bendix in these things anyway."

"What was that again?" I asked.

"There's 'normal' top speed on a warship, 'All Ahead Full,' then there's emergency speed for combat, that we call 'Flank,' ' Gas explained with some memories reflected on her face, "and then there's a level beyond Flank which isn't labelled but it's where it used to say 'Bendix Mfg. Co.' who made the gauges. If you say 'Bendix' that basically tells the engine room 'we need more speed and without it we're all dead anyway so it don't matter no more if you fry the engines son.' "

"Clear," I said.

"As of 2020," Gas continued, "the Pierre Guillaumat is believed to be the world's fastest VLCC at 16.7 knots. So I decided to use 17 knots as my baseline top speed. Then I looked at correction factors.   These are displacement, draft, wind vector, current vectors, condition of the hull and the propeller. The last two can only slow you down -- if you have a lot of barnacles on the hull or a u/s prop, neither of which is going to happen to anyone halfway pro. So I ignored them." Gas paused here for a full coffee refill, so I could tell we were still at the beginning.

"Current and wind vectorise down; you basically only care about the component in your direction of travel. Obviously a following current will speed you up as will a following wind, though given these aren't sailing ships, you might want to think of that as an absence of headwind resistance rather than an actual propulsion. Displacement is the weight of the ship and everything on it; draft is the distance between the keel and the waterline or 'load draft.' So then I wrote a Monte Carlo simulation keying off distance and fuel consumption."

"Wow,' I said. I knew what a Monte Carlo was because I had written some of them in my particle physics PhD. It was a way of simulating a range of possible outcomes in scenarios where you didn't know what would happen, but you did know what the key deciding factors were and something about how their probabilities varied. It was called Monte Carlo because random numbers, or rolling dice, was at the heart of how you chose your actual values for various parameters. You basically assessed what might happen by looking at the average of all the things that might happen.

Gas went on. "I started off each run at Point Zero with a randomly chosen heading. I assumed maximum acceleration to maximum speed. Every ten minutes, I assumed a [10%] probability of a course change, where the number of degrees of that course change was between 10 and 90, with the actual number being my first assigned random parameter in that run. I excluded any course changes which would cause you to run aground or undergo an unscheduled landing event. If a new course option became available, such as coming abeam of an available sea channel, I assigned a 50%

chance that the ship would take it. If at any time a ship came within 24 hours sail time of a port that could accept it, I assigned a probability that the ship would cease open sea manoeuvers and would then sail directly for that port and dock at it. That was my second random parameter, where I smeared 50% by a Gaussian."

I was still following this but I had to concentrate. I closed my eyes and my coffee got cold.

"Then I did 100 million runs overnight, looking to see where the ship could be when. This gave me a heat map which expanded out around the world on an hour-by-hour basis."

It was time to make an observation. "Now you need fiducial cuts to account for stuff you wouldn't actually see. Or maybe you already did that by eliminating any possibilities that the ships could go aground," I said.

"Right," said Gas. "I think you mean the next stage, which was I thought about eliminating insane trajectories. But then I thought, 'what's insane?' Heading 90% of the way to a port and then coming all the way back would generally be insane. So would going around in a circle for 98 days of what would otherwise be a 2 day voyage. But stuff like that goes on at sea sometimes, when you have to dock at LA and you can't. Or maybe you are trying to make life difficult for people who are trying to track you. So I left it all in, and decided to check later for the level of insanity and whether that particular flavor of madness could be explained."

I thought this was going to lead to a somewhat unmanageable dataset size but I also thought that Gas could offload all this onto the cloud and use some remote big CPU if need be. The major issue was how she was going to work out which of these millions of trajectories the one ship we wanted had followed.

"Now you're wondering how I tie this back in to real life," she said.

"Yes. It's like a Brynjar thing. You've generated all the possible worlds and now we want to see which of the possible worlds could be identical to the actual world."

"Exactly, " said Gas. "And the key to that is fuel consumption. I know what that is in each sector of the journey; it varies proportionally to the square of the cube root of displacement and the cube of velocity: $F_C \propto D^{2/3} V^3$."

"Amazing. So you really start to burn fuel if you speed up. Double the speed, multiply fuel consumption by 8," I said.

"That's it," she said. "After this I also have to correct for changes in fuel consumption caused by changes in displacement as you consume fuel and get lighter, but that's fine, if a bit meta. Then I have to tie it back into something reported somewhere. And for environmental reasons you mention, fuel consumption has to be reported to the IMO."

"That's a useful cross-check. The IMO is International Maritime Organisation, right?"

"It is. So now the issues are two-fold. One -- not getting screwed up by fake data like last time. Two -- where could the ship be and how much fuel usage would it have to report when it gets there. If it made an accurate report."

"How do we know it would make an accurate report?" I asked.

"We don't know that. But faking this means hacking more databases, which would be interesting, plus as you will see I think I found a check."

"Excellent. So what did you find?" I asked.

"I had to do many more Monte Carlo runs that I thought to get good stats. I needed 100 billion in fact so I outsourced it to the farm. Cost me $10k. But it was worth it. There were about 150m possible arrival port/ time combinations. For each of those I had a fuel consumption number. So I cross referenced the arrival time and consumption report to all the IMO databases of fuel consumption."

"That must have been a massive job."

"It was, but the fuel consumption is reported on quite a granular basis with high precision, so I was able to eliminate basically all of the possibilities except five. Three of them were at the same port, with different arrival times. In each of the three locations, I found the inspector that will sometimes go and make a physical check on consumption."

"How does he do that?'

"Basically, a really big dipstick. It's not rocket science. But even looking at the gauge isn't bad. You can't hack that for someone who is standing in front of it because it's mechanical."

"And what did you do?"

"I basically bribed the three guys to do their job. Not a big deal. Go and drop the dipstick on these ships, tell me if they have made a correct report. Not a breach of duty or confidentiality because this is all public data and I was just, like I said, getting them to do their job. That's worth $1000 to anyone."

This was starting to sound like real information. "So what's the answer?"

"All five of the ships made accurate reports. I then asked the inspectors to give me a basic description of the ships, colour, superstructure, name."

"Yes, why didn't you start with the name?"

"I did. Nothing called the Shundli has ever docked anywhere ever again. They must have resprayed it at sea."

"I suppose you can do anything out there and no-one will ever know."

"Correct. The Shundli became the Evergreen Laurel. Everything else fits and all the other four ships had major unchangeable features different to the Shundli, like extra bilge pipes, number of windows on the bridge or differently configured and numbered VHF antennae, or other stuff that we sailors know about. OK, I guess they could have changed the last thing but I don't think they did because it's a pain in the ass."

"Don't you have to file all sorts of other paperwork, re-registration, name changes and all that?"

"Yes, but there's not really a time limit or an enforcement mechanism. And it depends on the location of your flag. So we would have to chase that up in Togo."

"OK. That's probably not going to be productive in the
short term. In any case, the major question is: where
did it go, Gas?"

"Gibraltar."

CHAPTER 9

GIBRALTAR, UK

Gibraltar was another of the strange interstitial places that fascinated me. It was somewhat like going on holiday to the 1950s. Hotels had a portrait of the Queen and a trouser press in every room. You could get items like condensed milk and strawberry jam at all times. Except Sundays. Nothing was open on a Sunday. Or late. Or early. But during normal hours, you could definitely get those things, and no foreign muck. That included sherry, even though that drink was delicious and manufactured less than 120km away in Jerez.

I had first flown to Gib, as it was known, during the pandemic hangover, which caused the airline no end of confusion. At London check-in, they had had an iPad which told them what the rules were for entry to various destinations. The airlines needed to know all of those conditions because they were on the hook for any violations.

The woman on the check-in desk had dutifully searched for Gibraltar in their system, and drawn a blank. I aimed to explain this: "Technically it's a domestic flight."

"No, it can't be, scheduled flight time is 2 hours 50."

"That's also true," I said, wondering whether I should bring up the Treaty of Utrecht and deciding against it based on a theory of officialdom I had developed. This was an extension of standard policy in a police or regulatory interview. This could be summarised as 'answer any questions in the shortest accurate form possible, say nothing else under any circumstances.'

There was an analogy in coding that Gas mentioned to me once: the MWE or 'Minimal Working Example.' This was usually used, counter-intuitively, to examine problems, so it could have been called 'not-working example.' If you had a bug, you had to strip back the code until it was as small as possible but still exhibited the problem. That way, you had given the bug the smallest possible habitat in which to roam, or be crimped, and then you could see it. Or if you had to get help, the helper didn't have to wade through any irrelevant lines.

This was for me one of many examples of when the clear thinking required to generate clean code carried over to useful habits of logic in real life. But when I told me brother about it, he told me about Mrs Jones's Austin Metro.

He was the service manager in a garage. She brought it in every week with a problem that was somewhere in the transmission or the synchromesh. It was in warranty, so she was within her rights to keep bringing it back until the problem as fixed, so she did.

After a couple of months of 'fixing' the mysterious problem and still having this cursed car return like an avenging Leyland angel, my brother decided he had to fire the big guns.

He explained to me what they did. "We put Mrs Jones's Metro on the left. We put the new Metro on the right. We started the car on the left and looked for the problem to occur. Then we moved a part over to the car on the right and moved the good part from the right hand car to the left hand car."

"How long did this take?" I had asked.

"Forever."

"What was the outcome?"

"In the end, the problem moved to the car on the right but we had no idea why."

"Harsh. What did you do then?"

"We wrote off the car on the right for unspecified reasons and gave Mrs Jones the car on the left. We never saw her again."

"Didn't the insurers or manufacturers want to know why you wrote it off?"

"Yes; we said it was unfixable.   It had had more mechanic hours than construction hours and there was zero new information available about the problem."

So that showed the limitations of the minimal approach, but it was still the right way to go. In practice, this way of interacting could have slightly strange consequences as the interviewers realised that you were not going to respond to anything that would normally be construed as a question but was in fact a statement, like "I see you have several bars of gold in your luggage."

Not a question. If you assume it is, you have to decide which question they have in mind. They may not have one. You may answer one they would not have thought of doing. So don't do that and don't do their job for them.

I had proposed this approach to someone I met at a wedding in Belize who had been the squash world champion. To get to Belize, you had to pass through Miami. And that meant dealing with US Customs and Border Protection, who were surprisingly aggressive.

This in fact was a deliberate policy. The idea was that if you were 90% stressed, because for example you were carrying drugs or wearing a suicide belt, then a bit of extra hostility might push you over the limit and cause you to let the cat/joint out of the bag or explode in the wrong place as the case might be.

I myself had been given a hard time in Miami for 'coming to the US without a pen.' My friend told me later that he had followed my approach and it had worked for him. The border agent had seen his squash racket and asked what it was. My friend had told him, whereupon the agent said, based on nothing, that it was a lacrosse racket.

My friend told me that he had been on the edge of saying "I know what a squash racket looks like because I used to be number one in the world" but chose in fact to say something more anodyne. "No; it's a squash racket." As a result of this forbearance, nothing happened.

So that's why I didn't say anything about the Treaty of Utrecht, or indeed the War of Spanish Succession, and eventually the airline let me board without further checking requirements, because there weren't any. Sometimes these jurisdictions with a strong emotional attachment to a remote location were very useful; it was important to them that travelling from London to Gibraltar meant nothing, the same as travelling from London to Belfast. Same country, nothing to see here.

Check-in for us on this occasion was fortunately much more straightforward. We had the fairly common occurrence of someone from Economy wanting to check-in in the Business Class lane because there was a huge queue at Economy. This of course was the point.

Karen, for it was she, then exhibited the other usual behaviours of not having read any of the regulations and not having any documentation and also entering into extended conversation and complaint. Fortunately this was all concluded relatively quickly once it transpired she had an Economy ticket and they booted her out of our way. I would have started there because it's a reasonable heuristic that if you can afford a Business Class flight, you are organised enough to both have your docs but also business-savvy enough to know what the airline can and cannot do for you.

Gas and I had obviously already checked in online and we had made it through bag drop and security at BKK in 7mins 23sec which was a new PB for us. We had stops in Frankfurt, which I liked and gave me an opportunity for Rinderrouladen, and then in LHR. I wasn't too happy about 'being home,' but it was only for a couple of hours.

Gas had fun with how everyone in the airport had the same accent as me: "So cute!" She was right on the edge of tweaking my cheek but I put on a fierce face and stared her down. She smirked and we argued about beer temperatures instead.

We didn't particularly have much work to do on the first day in Gib, because we had decided it would be a bit obvious to just go straight to the port. So we went up the famous Rock and hung out with monkeys. There was a good view from there of one of the UK's two new monstrous aircraft carriers, which was visiting. While we were looking at it, Gas said "That's actually a fair sized birdfarm for you limeys. On the topic of big items, what does $201m in cash look like?"

"Not huge, actually. You're talking about pallets. Standard pallet footprint in the US is 48 inches x 40 inches. If you stack the pallets as high as they are wide, and use $100 bills, you need just under 12 pallets for $1bn. It's not that big a deal. So you need something like 2.2 pallets. You could get it smaller if you used 1000 Swiss Franc notes, but it's probably not worth the extra effort inbound and outbound."

"The weight though..." wondered Gas.

"Yeah, that's still the problem. For space, even a family car is probably fine of a couple of pallets. But $201m weighs 2010kg. So again you want a light truck because a panel van will be just overweight. But you don't need a full-on artic. If you did have an artic, you could have a full cargo of something else and your two pallets of cash at the back, no problem."

"So if you did this in CHF, how much easier would it get?"

"Well, CHFUSD is not far off parity, so you would be reducing everything by a factor of 10 if you did it that way. So instead of 2.2 pallets, you need 0.22 pallets. The base of the pallet stays at 48 inches x 40 inches but it's only piled 11 inches high. You're almost getting to case territory."

Gas was surprised: "The equivalent of $201m in a briefcase...!"

"Not quite," I said, "but very close. A tabletop...and remember it still weighs 201kg, so you can't carry it. You could push it around though, just about."

"So how do you get packages in here?"

"What we could usefully do is a physical walkthrough assessment of the border," I said. "To see what you can get through."

"Alright. Well let's get some passports and try it. They can only send us back if we have to fill something in."

"There has to be some serious kind of operation here because it used to be a Schengen border." After Brexit, UK passport holders had third country status in the EU. That meant we were allowed 90 days out of every 180 in the EU. This was worse than most people thought, because they imagined it meant you could stay for 90 days, leave for one day and then come back. The reality was that if you used up 90 days, you were then forbidden from returning at all for the next 90 days.

"I'll bring a bag to see what happens to that as well. Let's start by crossing on foot," I said, assuming that this would be more suspicious than otherwise, and we were trying to create suspicion.   We headed down to the crossing point.   "What's kind of insane," I said as we approached it, "is that the UK is not a member of the EU anymore, and Schengen is a free travel zone for EU members, and Gibraltar is part of the UK, but also Gibraltar is in the Schengen Zone."

"That screws up the Venn diagram," said Gas.

"It does," I agreed.   "There's a thing about Spanish police in Gibraltar territory.   It would make things massively more easy, because otherwise Gibraltar police, who are British, have to enforce Schengen rules they know nothing about.   But of course that's too much 'solves the problem' but doesn't fly the flag for the Imperial measures people.   So it isn't happening."

The first unusual observation we made was hard to miss. Crossing the border involved also crossing the runway at the airport and so we now had to wait as a BA A320 landed.   This was as loud and impressive as one might expect.

I remembered a previous similar experience.   "The only thing better than this is Skiathos.   You can stand right behind the runway and planes come over you at about 10m. You don't want to stand exactly behind it though because you will be knocked over by the backdraft. I saw two backpacker girls get rolled over twice there once."

"Isn't civilians walking across airstrips one of the things that's most frowned upon by authorities, in general?" said Gas. "We do shit like that all the time, but that's different."

"Sure, but if you look at the map, the runway cuts right across the peninsula. So they can dislike it but there's no way to avoid it." There were a bunch of vehicles indicating RAF military police and civilian police presence but no actual visible personnel. "There's too much traffic here for the authorities to do anything meaningful, even before when the public sector had any capacity to do anything," I said.

We reached the border crossing in a crowd of mostly Spanish people on foot. The bag got scanned. No one checked our passports. No one knew that one UK and one US citizen had entered the Schengen Zone. "So this is how you beat that 90 day thing, " I said, "but you probably can't get major contraband through this way.

"If you're doing the 90 day thing, you would probably want to go back out this way as well, which would constrain you a bit," said Gas. "Unless maybe Belfast."

We immediately turned back and went back through the border again. No one cared and in fact it did not seem as though there was an easy way for the guards in this direction to know we had done that, because it was a different lane and different guards. This struck me ass not normal practice because in law enforcement, odd behaviour should always go to the top of your agenda.

Brynjar had suggested that Gibraltar might be a hot location so we were vaguely checking to see if we saw the same person twice, and we did the store window thing to check behind us. These were good reflective surfaces that people didn't think it was weird if you stood staring at them for a long time. I always thought it looked suspicious but that was because I hated shopping and would never be looking in a store window under any circumstances other than nefarious ones.

In this mode, Gas asked "Do you remember that kid with the weird t-shirts?"

"No cats, No Nietzsche?"

"Right. What did he look like?" asked Gas.

"No idea. I was reading his t-shirt." Then I realised what she was getting at. "Oh I see. You think that was the idea."

"Could have been. Or maybe he was just a weirdo. But we definitely didn't make him." We had stepped up the paranoia level slightly after telling Brynjar whereupon he said he had 'indicators' that Gibraltar might be a location of interest for our guys. That of course made it all the more imperative that we went there.

I had a friend in town. Jasper Ragg was a psychology professor who played jazz drums in his spare time. He was here for a conference. We had agreed to meet him for drinks, partly to make it look like we were doing standard stuff and not looking at ships in which we had become interested as a result of the outputs of a vast Monte Carlo simulation.

I'd been at school with Jasper in Bristol and Gas had met him a few times. We'd consulted him once or twice on psychological questions. We'd decided he could basically be trusted with much of what we were doing because he clearly had never made any money out of what we told him; he wasn't in the business. And he didn't care that much. If he had wanted money, he would have dressed less like an academic. He didn't actually have the elbow patches on the corduroy jacket, but only because that would have been unnecessarily well turned out. He looked right at home in the 1950s, where we now were.

"How are things in Hull?" I asked. Gas could never believe that there was a town in England which was just one letter away from Hell.

"Freezing," replied Jasper. "But I'm still happy about swapping a two-bed maisonette in Barnet with a tube line in the garden for a four bed detached with a drum room."

We brought Jasper up to speed with an outline of what we had been doing, without giving him anything non-public. He immediately saw lots of psychological points to make.

"The thing with the shipping data was probably what we call Motivated Reasoning. It's related to Confirmation Bias but isn't quite the same. The big meta-review is

Kunda (1990) and she sees it as having three aspects: you have some biases or offsets in three things you do with your beliefs: accessing, constructing or evaluating them. She also says it is more likely to happen if you are under time pressure, and that was true here."

"So what does that mean in practice?" asked Gas.

"I don't think there was a problem with access or construction here," replied Jasper. "But evaluation of the output beliefs may have fallen down. The answer is a more severe critical process, but it sounds like you have already adopted that with your simulation and the real-world check. I'd just in general be more cynical about everything -- though of course, that often makes it hard to believe anything at all and you need to do something."

"We do," I agreed. "But it has to be soundly based. I hate to sit still so much that I prefer to act wrongly, because I usually suspect that by acting I may flush out more data."

"That's a personal choice to do with risk aversion. The other major issue I think you have is what we call Theory of Mind errors. Theory of Mind is the label for how we predict and explain the behaviour of others. You are actually doing a lot of that because you are in fact trying to retrofit beliefs to perpetrators by reverse engineering from their activities -- or what you know of them -- in order that you might be able to predict and interdict future activities. And maybe actually catch them one day."

Gas wanted to know what caused the errors.

"There are two major accounts of how we do this Theory of Mind stuff," explained Jasper. "One of them says we have a theory of other people and the other one says we simulate them. Or a bit of both. If you simulate them, you are going to be implicitly assuming that they are like you. And that is going to give you systematic errors in predicting their behaviour if they aren't like you. And that's the case -- they are very different to you."

"This is interesting," said Gas. "So really I need to try to get into their mindset."

"Ideally, yes. But more realistically, you should try to examine where you are going to be systematically different to your targets. If for example you have a ton of training and experience -- as you do -- then the answer to many questions about what someone else would do is not going to be generated by asking yourself what you would do. That's the hard part. Becoming someone else who is less capable than you in many ways. Actually it's also hard to become someone else when they can do things you can't. But you can aim to operate with more intelligence than they do, and you can aim to consider a wider spread of options including ones you would dismiss."

"I've seen a ton of this in military history. People assuming that the other guy is going to do what they would do, but the other guy might just be a madman..." said Gas.

"That's exactly right. In fact, a friend of mine has written a book showing exactly that," said Jasper.

"I'm confident we are smarter than they are," I said, "but we are operating in heavy fog."

"Everything you know is helpful. You have been improving your picture of the sort of things they do. While there is not really anything like what ordinary people think of as 'personality,' that does help you see how they make decisions differently to you."

279

"How can personality not exist?" asked Gas.   "I know what Burgoyne's personality is like."

"Actually," replied Jasper, "I would say there that what you have done is improved your Theory of Mind in relation to him by observation.   But how different is he to you anyway?"

Both of us looked indignant at this.   Jasper went on: "What matters here is training and experience and both of you may be more like each other in those respects than your targets are and that's what's making it difficult to predict target behaviour."

"Surely there are stable patterns in how people behave?" I asked.

"Yes, but they are more driven by stably intelligent responses to situations.   It's always a good move to pick up a £20 note off the pavement.   Though people never do."

"No?" I asked.

"No. They don't believe it can be real and not have already been picked up by someone else."

"Cynical."

"Right. But even if you find something that is always the right move for everyone, that doesn't mean you have identified that someone has a stable personality feature. What you can observe falls into a categorisation called or defined as OCEAN. There are five parameters on which everyone is located somewhere. Openness, Conscientiousness, Extraversion, Agreeableness and Neuroticism."

"What's Openness?" I asked.

"Something like being interested in new experiences and seeking them. Both of you are probably very high on that parameter which would form evidence for my claim that you are not that dissimilar. Anyway, once you have established where people are on these five parameters, you have explained all the data. You don't need anything else to explain the limited amounts of non-situationally determined behaviour stability we observe. So that's it. Anything else you are calling personality is made-up."

"This doesn't sound too helpful," I said.

"It's not too bad," said Jasper. "For one thing, we don't think these parameters are set in stone and for another, I don't say you couldn't replicate or imagine being somewhere else in the OCEAN parameter space. I suppose the key distinction between you and the targets is that you and your friends in Oslo are presumably somewhere up the top end of Conscientious and your targets are at zero. Actually that's not quite true. They may be very focussed on serving the ends of their organisation."

"I think I can see the sort of problem you mean with this Theory of Mind," I said. "I always think it looks super weird for me to be staring into a shop window because I have no interest in stuff. I mean objects that you could buy. I want to own lots of assets that I can convert into interesting experiences, but I have no interest in things. But people do it all the time so it must be normal."

"That's the right way to think about this," said Jasper. "Try to be less yourself when simulating others."

"Haven't you just said I don't exist?" I objected.

"No, I said you didn't have a fixed personality in the way most people think. You very clearly have different and unusual skills and experiences. Which will throw you off when predicting others."

"OK, got it," I said, but I wasn't completely sure I had.

"But going back to the original problem with the shipping data, maybe you should be aware of Confirmation Bias as well."

"I've heard of this one," said Gas. "It's where you believe things you want to believe..."

"Approximately," said Jasper. "There are various flavours. The two ones I think are probably key here are looking for evidence to support claims you already believe and then not subjecting incoming data to even-handed and rigorous evaluation standards when those data support claims you already believe."

"Aha," said Gas. "That sounds like a statement of Magruder's Principle. So the answer is, don't believe anything unless forced to and don't give information a free pass because it supports a claim you believe."

"That's it," said Jasper. "Also you might misclassify information, or as we would say, code it, as the wrong thing. Or not code it at all."

"OK, we've got our marching orders then," I agreed.

"On a more pressing issue," said Jasper, "how is it possible that there is no sherry here?"

"I can't understand it," I said. "It's inexplicably catastrophic."

Gas wasn't so sure about this. She was more of a Bourbon gal. She thought that sherry smelt rotten. Of course, we knew that and that was what made it good. Though also we had once got into a fight with someone who said 'that smells like it comes from Uncle Pedro's finca' when we knew that it was precisely that roughness we liked.

We walked back to our hotel, dropping Jasper at his which was close to ours but lower quality. His University booked it, which meant it had to be inexpensive. This was somewhat annoying for Jasper since he was effectively being limited in spending his own money: he had won a research grant which included a travel component. He often had end of year issues with a 'use-it-or-lose it' component and I had to find ways of spending a research budget on Krugerrands without that being too obvious. It was harder than in physics where you could just buy a ten grand oscilloscope and then fence it off.

The next day began slightly unusually. Gas was saying something about a cousin of hers with whom she used to play being in a car crash. I wasn't paying that much attention because I had been looking for an opportunity to get exposure to Air Liquide and this looked like it. There was a global shortage of computer chips which didn't appear to be going away. It was too late to play that by buying the chipmakers, but fabs, the huge fabrication plants where chips were made, used a lot of industrial gases to keep their manufacturing clean. And those stocks hadn't moved yet. I was dipping in and out of the Call Options in Frankfurt but eventually just got out of that and went long the stock, because that was more consistent with also drinking coffee. I made $17,000 over breakfast though so that was fine.

I looked up and saw that Gas had gone so I spent the morning on the terrace of the hotel. This had a good view of the harbour, a pool and was a pleasant place to be. I noticed however that very few people used this place for enjoyment. They just took pictures of themselves pretending to enjoy it. They would not actually lie on a sun lounger, but they would do so just until they had the shot. Then they would move to a table and pretend to read a book in the sun.

You could say that strictly speaking, this wasn't fake news for social media. But they were not really conducting the activities in which they purported to be engaged. They were, in fact, in the claimed location. But they were just presenting that image rather than inhabiting it. It was also fairly normal for a small family to spend more than an hour taking these spurious photos, which struck me as an extraordinary use of time. It's a frequently made point that people present their curated lives, but what I observed was not re-presentation, it was completely theatrical.

Gas came back and explained that she was going back to the US for four days. She told me she would buy her tickets out of the operations account. This was fine. Apart from the diamond cash, ops1. acct. had just received one of its periodic infusions of $257,000 resulting from something I had done a while back with a

Long Iron Butterfly Spread in Seoul. Options strategies were incomprehensible unless you looked at the graphs like a physicist and then they were easy. You just needed to read the curves and have some ability to combine them mentally.

This kind of thing was easy for physicists since we spent all our time saying 'what can I do with this cool maths?' That distinguished us from mathematicians who were fascinated by the tools themselves rather than what you could do with them. Presumably that was the reason that financial markets were full of physicists and there were no mathematicians. That and the fact that it was even harder to find a mathematician with a human interface than a physicist.

"I'll see you in four days," I said. "I may still be here or not. I will see if I can think of options for the next sector from here." Gas walked out with her bag, paid her bill at reception and asked them to get her a cab to the airport.

I walked around the town during the day, thinking about what the possibilities might be with a cargo of oil here. They fell into the usual two categories. You could convert this cargo into another one and sail it out, or you could sell the cargo, possibly using letters of credit and the factoring mechanisms and enter the financial system. Gibraltar had a lot of offshore finance, especially insurance, so that might be worth looking at. Just that day, a deal had been announced to run Malaysian life insurance offers out of Gib.

A coffee shop appeared and I stopped for ten minutes. Double espresso. While there, I got a ping from the Ops. Account. Gas's ticket had cost $10,975 which meant she must have gone First Class. 'Fair enough,' I thought. She probably felt like a break after maybe feeling bad about dropping the ball on the shipping data.

I continued on foot. I wasn't walking particularly with any aim in mind. As I rounded one corner, a stunning view of the sea and a rocky headland at an indeterminable distance across impossibly deep blue breakers flecked with clear bright white came into view. This was so dramatic and unexpected that I could not work out what this huge mountain across the water could be. I looked at Apple maps on my phone and zoomed out and was surprised to find that I was looking at Africa. Right there, apparently in touching distance, was Morocco and the Spanish enclave of Ceuta, which was Spain on the African continent and therefore doubly interesting.

I came back to the hotel for dinner. There was a woman playing the grand piano in the hotel bar. I was initially focused on getting a bar stool and obtaining sone of the Laprhroaig which had been matured in sherry casks, which I did, and it was excellent.

Then I swung around on my stool and had a look at the pianist. She was so pretty it was quite hard to look at her. She had loose auburn curls and eyes where it wasn't quite clear if they were light or dark blue. But they were definitely intense.

She was playing something classical with a highly violent level of ferocity and expressions to match. Waves of intensity moved in and out of each other. It sounded almost like there was a carrier signal based on a sine wave which was swapping energy with some internal reference waves in a systematic way. The music was incredibly complex and sounded like what happens after you forget the notes. Or move on to the next level.

There were a few people in the bar but they were mostly doing their own thing or looking at menus. I was the only one transfixed by the performance. I mostly looked at the piano player's hands, which were moving much too fast to follow the individual movements. You could begin to pick out blurred patterns if you looked carefully enough.

She played for about ten minutes then stopped. I wanted to applaud more than I did, but it would have sounded weird among the scattered claps. I turned back around to face the barman and got another whiskey with some peanuts.

"Is that the Laphroaig?" I heard in a central/eastern European accent. I swung back around slowly. The piano player was asking me the question.

"It is. It's great with the hint of sherry from the barrels. Also appropriate for the location. Sort of. Or at least, appropriate for how this location should be."

"Maybe I will try one," she said and took the stool next to me. The barman came over and she pointed to my drink and said "Also for me." When it came, she turned to me and said "Živeli!" which did not appear to need translation since she was also raising her glass and smiling. This was all rather unexpected.

"Cheers! That was a wonderful piece. What was it?"

"Sort of Prokofiev Concerto No. 3, Op. 26, 3rd Movement. Normally played with an orchestra but I didn't have one."

I lacked sufficient musical expertise to talk for long on the topic, and so the conversation came to a natural pause. I found out that her name was Ljubi, which she said meant 'kiss.' That was an arresting claim, though I couldn't tell if it was true because of the slightly impenetrable smile she wore when giving the explanation.

Then she asked me what brought me here. I always had problems with this topic of discussion, and I didn't want to completely make things up, because that was high risk. So I decided on one of the usual cover stories that I was still a physicist. Basically no-one would be able to detect me in this apart from a current practitioner who would be able to see I was extremely rusty.

On hearing this, she said "Marš bre!" and wanted to know more. I gave a brief outline of particle accelerators and what we had been doing in Hamburg.

The brief outline became a fairly long outline, because Ljubi kept looking interested and asking questions. After this had gone on for a while, I asked her if she needed to go and play some more.

"Not really. They aren't really paying me. Do you have a nice view of the harbour in your room and a minibar?"

I had both of these things. She said something like "Hajde," smiling again. We went upstairs. The view of the harbour from the balcony was undeniably impressive. I had gin miniatures so I made a couple of G&Ts. We didn't have ice though and Ljubi said she really needed that, which seemed reasonable. It was a hot evening. So I called down to reception and asked them to send some up.

I almost drank the whole G&T in a single gulp, which looked a little low class, but I was suddenly thirsty. I continued to think about where this evening might be going. Somewhere good, it looked like. What would the next drink be, I wondered. Perhaps I should order a bottle. I asked Ljubi if she liked wine, and she said she did but didn't know that much about it, so we talked about the options.

Ljubi wanted to sit on the balcony, so we started to move together in that direction. It was about then that I simultaneously threw up on my shirt and hit the carpet.

CHAPTER 10

UNKNOWN, UNKNOWN

I woke up with an extraordinary headache and also a lot of neck and back pain. My throat made sense of the French phrase for a hangover which involved something like having a 'wooden gullet.' The back pain was because I had apparently been sleeping on a lot of hardcore, meaning rocks and building debris, rather than old copies of Hustler, which would have been more comfortable.

I took a look at my surroundings. I was in some kind of derelict house, which was low and made of stained concrete. It was warm and the apparent location of the sun suggested midday. I could hear the sea but nothing else, apart from seagulls.

It was no fun at all moving out of the shadows into the bright light. In fact, moving in any fashion was no fun. But I nevertheless managed to stick to the darkness. And now I got another sense switched on which told me that the building stank of piss. 'Nice touch,' I thought. It mixed well with the dry vomit on my shirt front, giving what a wine buff would have called acidic undertones to the earthy core. I wondered how long it would be before any positive elements entered the scenario analysis.

There was a sort of unfinished concrete stairway around the inside of the interior walls. The building looked more like it had not been completed and then become derelict rather than fallen out of use. No-one had ever lived here. The stairway was somewhat dangerous because it had no guard rails and the concrete had perished in parts, leaving holes with stained rebar which you could fall through completely or just break an ankle in if you were luckier.

I went through four complete rotations of the jagged stairwell and emerged on to a flat roof. The rebar here definitely took on thrusting threatening shapes as if the whole arena had been constructed as a trap. And the concrete was stained orange with rust. I squinted into the sky, which was apparently grey and cloudy, but also appeared unbearably bright to me. I could see a marina, but it was much smaller than the ones in Gibraltar. I turned around and I could see the rock. So I hadn't been moved far.

The inside top floor of the building contained the only sign of life. Someone had spray painted 'I am awake in the place where the women die.' I thought about this. Did the writer mean that we were all in the world and that was the place in question but only he, or quite likely she, was alert to that fact? Or did the writer mean that this specific building was that place, and he was there to observe; enjoy; deplore; report? No available interpretation was encouraging.

The first order of business was to find something to drink, ideally a non-diet coke or something else with a lot of sugar. I patted my pockets. No wallet. Nothing at all. I went back down through the building and out into the street which was completely deserted. It quickly became clear from a street sign that I was in La Linea de la Concepcion, the Spanish dormitory town just the other side of the border with Gibraltar. It was unnaturally quiet and very run-down, even when compared with Gibraltar.

No phone, no wallet, no passport. But I was authentically covered in concrete dust and this was a very soft border. I walked south and found the pedestrian crossing point; I was by now extremely thirsty. I knew it would also be a good idea to eat something, but heavy nausea had kicked in.

Once near the customer point, I hung around trying to look inconspicuous. This was hard without any possessions. I did a lot of looking at a fictitious watch and staring up the street. After about twenty minutes, which was about the most I could cope with waiting, I was just about to take the risk anyway when I saw what I wanted arriving.

Three old Spanish construction-type guys in heavy boots and very used overalls were walking towards the border. One of them had paint spatter and the other two had undefined dustiness. They must have not got casual work today or they were hoping for a late shift. I tacked in behind them and we crossed the border together. I nodded as though I was agreeing with something one of the guys I was following said. No questions asked.

I started to feel better and worse at the same time. It was abstractly positive that I was now through the border and coming back to a location where I had a room and I could get help from Jasper. But physically I felt abysmal and it didn't feel like it would improve quickly. Just getting through the day was going to be a challenge. And then there was the damage to the operation to determine and assess.

My first port of call was the bar in the hotel. The same barman was there. He smiled as I walked in but then his expression took on cooler undertones as he realised that something was not right with me. Quite a lot of things in fact.

"Everything alright, sir?" he said, rallying.

"Not really," I replied. I ordered two cokes and downed one immediately. Then I started sipping the other. "That woman who played piano yesterday. Does she work here?"

"No. She came in during the afternoon. I never saw her before."

"How did she get to be playing piano?"
"I love pano. She asked me what sort of music I liked. I said Blue jazz like from 1957 and more modern stuff. She thought for about ten seconds and then went over to the Grand, saying 'This is how Keith Jarrett might improvise Giant Steps." '

I knew he was talking about cool old-school American sax from John Coltrane and then a more modern, open, breathless style. I could just about imagine what that combination might sound like. A lot slower, for a start, than Coltrane's train-like driving original. Putting the two together would require a lot of expertise and specialist expertise at that. Almost zero classical pianists could do that unless they had an extra couple of modules. They could learn it, of course, but those guys were purists who didn't want their music minds polluted, and who worried about the absence of notes in the sheet music.

"And she did that? Jarrett meets Coltrane?" I asked.

"She did," replied the barman. "It was unbelievable. Then she said she was a pro, she was just in town for a funeral and it was bad for her if she didn't get some keyboard time every day. So with that, and..." He tailed off.

"And what?" I said, then worked it out from the barman's expression. "You mean the way she looked meant you would have given her the piano if she'd wanted it?"

"Yes, I would have. But anyway, we just agreed I would give her a bottle of wine if she played for an hour or two in the evening but actually I don't think she collected it, come to think of it. Then you arrived towards the end."

He smiled broadly without quite winking, suggesting he had seen us leave together. "Top effort mate!" I was too tired and despondent to correct him. "Can you put those drinks on my room please?" I said and went to reception, where I got a replacement room key. Once there, I did another inventory. Now I also had no laptop to add to all the other things I didn't have.

I walked to Jasper's hotel, slowly. He wasn't in his room, which was unsurprising since it was the middle of the day. The conference was also being held in the same hotel, which was helpful.

I did the German airport trick. I showed the receptionist my credit card, which still had Dr in front of my name, and explained that it was an emergency and I needed to speak to Dr Ragg. They paged him and he came out of the plenary session he had been in.

"What the fuck happened to you?" were his first words. He looked somewhat amused until the gravity of the situation became clear to him.

"I got Micky Finned by some Serbian femme fatale," I said.

"Wow. Was it worth it?" asked Jasper.

"Definitely not. I need your phone. What's your number?"

"OK,' said Jasper and handed it over. I sent an email to gators-bump-0r@icloud.com which read:

10-21 ABYSSINIA URGENT

followed by Jasper's number. 10-21 was the police 10 code for 'call by telephone; and ABYSSINIA was our code word. URGENT spoke for itself.

Jasper was looking like he was expecting me to give him his phone back but I wasn't going to.

'You can't keep my phone!" he said. "Someone might want to call me."

"Who? The cardigan mending shop saying you can pick up your repair job?" I responded.

"The girls. Something might happen at home."

"If your family calls with an actual emergency to do with cash, or fixable with cash, or legals or docs or insurance or motor vehicle, they are probably better off talking to me," I argued. "If it's something more likely, it can probably wait. I will page you again if it's a big deal but it really isn't going to happen. Go back to your conference and I will carry on throwing up and wanting to die." Jasper reluctantly agreed. I had to promise to switch up to URGENT on contacting him if it was anything to do with the cat, Luna. However, Luna was super cute so I was fine with that. She was also pretty robust so any news to do with her was likely to be that she had killed something, a bird, a postman, a tree.

I knew it was still early in the US. So it wasn't obvious when or if Gas would call, but she had flown First and she was only stateside for four days so she would probably remain basically on European time. In fact, she came back within the hour. I could hear slightly depressing organ music in the background at the start of the call, which was odd, but I didn't have the time to go into it.

"This had better be good, Burgoyne," was her opening.

I explained in the minimum number of words what had happened and that we were now minus one laptop and one phone.

"You did what? I only left you for about ten minutes!" was her initial response. Then she said she would get started on it very quickly once she was done with what she was doing. Someone in the background said "Susan put that phone away this instant!" and the connection dropped.

Probably the initial emergency response was now in place, I thought, so I felt it was acceptable to go back to the hotel and crash. I didn't feel physically as though I had a lot of choice anyway. Once there, I had a couple more cokes and three bars of chocolate and fitfully slept while intermittently listening to Podcasts I had selected to not be too interesting.

Sometime mid-afternoon Gas called again. "Whoever has your devices hasn't switched off location tracking on the laptop but they did on the phone, so I think they probably don't have full access or any access yet to the laptop. Both devices were in Cordoba and the laptop still is. The location is non-stable, so I think they are just driving around so we can't show up at their crib. What was on them, anyway?"

"I don't think there was anything on the phone. You could use it to get in to the cloud stuff maybe. The laptop has some actual files downloaded maybe. I'm not sure."

"The laptop is probably the bigger problem, but on the other hand you have MFA on there, so they may not be able to crack it, assuming you still have your face." explained Gas. "There will be a local image of Brynjar's Dropbox on that. That's probably their target. Their strategy is probably to try to use the phone to get on the laptop so they can get to the Dropbox. That's what I would do. They can get in the phone initially using your comatose face probably, but that might not last them to Cordoba."

"What's the plan?"

"Remote wipe. It's good that we had FileVault switched on. The fact that the disk is encrypted is going to give them a really hard time."

"How long is it going to take?" I asked.

"A day if I also wipe the disk. In theory I don't need to do that because it's encrypted. But I will do it anyway. So I got that started an hour ago. We have to assume that anything you might had on there is compromised. The more interesting questions are who wants to know what we have and why."

"That's right. Presumably the target organisation," I replied. "They want to see how close we are."

"What are we going to tell Brynjar about this?" asked Gas.

"I think probably nothing. I don't think there's any upside for us and there's plenty of downside. So we'll just keep schtumm."

"That sounds right. I still can't quite believe you did this," observed Gas sadly.

"Neither can I. Can I go to sleep now?"

"Yes. This is in hand," said Gas reassuringly.

"Great," I said, and then slept for basically the rest of that day and the next night. I was woken up the next morning by a tap on the door. The concierge was there with one large and one small package with a lot of Apple logos. I signed for that and put them on the bed.

I was feeling simultaneously much better than yesterday but much worse than I could have felt. I looked at Jasper's phone and found an email from Gas where she explained that she had ordered me new kit and said that the wipe had been completed with status zero, which meant no problems.

I replied that I had received the items and saying that I thought I should probably leave.   Gas called immediately.

She started with "I think you should hang around.   I want a good look around that harbor.   Also have you taken a look at the outbound options?"

"I don't need to be here to check outbound.   I've had a look in the usual places for transactions anywhere near $200m and I haven't found any yet.   There seems to be pretty clearly nothing in Gibraltar.   I was going to look more in Spain on the IBEX.   They have a lot of data in Spanish and I need to translate some key terms before I look again.   But the Gibraltar systems are more hooked up with The City in London really."

"I can help with that, " said Gas, "the Spanish thing.   In the meantime, you should do two things today: start cloud recovery/install on your two new devices and go look at the port."

"Alright," I agreed. I decided to start with the phone. It was pretty amazing that with a full cloud backup you could start from zero on a virgin device and after some time hooked up to the internet it would become your old device with all your data except new and shiny. I kicked that off, and walked down to the port.

Security was not amazing; the harbour like the whole island was quite sleepy. It was a peninsula rather than island, but it felt more like an island given the political situation. While getting in to the soft outer core looked quite easy -- I did not actually do it because I was on recon rather than execution -- the central area was fairly convincingly fenced. I could probably get in, but only at night. And then I wouldn't see much.

Nothing much had changed on Gibraltar for three hundred years. You knew this because the Spanish Naval Museum in Madrid had a scale model for the purposes of constructing attack plans. There were some ponds where the airport now was, but nothing much else looked different. There were some taller buildings. The Spanish plan of attack involved climbing up the sheer face of the rock under bombardment. It didn't work.

Looking at the model, you could see there weren't a lot of better options, so it was a smart move on the part of the English to ask for it as the price for backing the King the Spanish wanted. And it was the gateway to the Mediterranean, as U-Boat Captains had been well aware.

I went back to the hotel to find that the phone needed a few boxes ticked. I did that and it was ready. I then started on the laptop which was a very similar process. That was going to need a few more hours so I left it plugged in and started looking for vineyard surveying services on the phone's browser.

There were a few companies offering the service. There were no vineyards in Gibraltar, but there were many just across the border in Spain. The availability of drone technology meant that you could now manage your vineyard at a microclimate level, which meant the climate around a single vine. Then you might have AI enabled farm equipment which would deliver the right amount of water and quantum of missing nutrients on a per-vine basis. This was all worth it if you were making premium wine, which plenty of people were in southern Spain.

I found a company called WineSkyScan which had offices on Queensway Quay Marina. I thought about calling but decided to just go down there, taking some envelopes with me. The quay turned out to be very quiet and mostly residential. The company had it seemed converted one of the residential units to an office, or maybe they just lived there. I pressed the bell for the address and said I was looking for drone services. The guy on the other end said he could come down.

When he did, he turned out to be an English kid who was about 23 called Quentin. He was much more self-assured than he needed to be for that age, I thought, but that was a good sign. He was slushily overweight and ginger, which I thought were not going to be positives in this heat, but wouldn't stop him flying drones.

"We could have gone up to the office," he said, "but it's lunchtime and this place right here is good," gesturing at a Spanish restaurant right on the waterfront. I said "fine" and we sat down. We both ordered some sardines and they turned out to have sherry for €1 which was an amazing price for such a high quality drink. It was ice cold and refreshing and very bitter. I loved it. The kid had some too, which sent him up even further in my estimation.

I made some apparently random small-talk to check him out. He claimed to have an engineering degree from Cambridge, so that was where he had gained an appreciation for sherry. I essayed some non-committal remarks about gowns, the difficulties of finding reasonably priced student accommodation, which I thought they called 'digs' there but we hadn't at Imperial, and asked him about his dissertation. He was on top of all that without making any effort so I gave him a passing grade.

"So, do you have a vineyard?" he asked.

I took a look around. Everyone else was either Spanish or busy talking or both. "No. I want to look at the port."

He looked concerned. "That's highly restricted."

"I mean the commercial port. I don't want to look at the carrier."

"That's good, because they would shoot me down and lock me up. It's still not completely kosher though."

I laid an envelope down on the table.   I said "That's
$5,000. Can you do it?"

He took a quick look inside the envelope to check. He
was good, but still slightly too young to completely hide
how overjoyed he was at seeing the contents were as
described. "I can probably do it," he said, "but normally
I need customer ID..."

He was pushing it a little, but I liked the kid, and I had
four envelopes, so I put another one down. "That's my
ID."

He looked in the second envelope. "I see. Your name is
Benjamin Franklin. Well, Mr Franklin, I think you may
be in luck. I have the equipment and my cousin works
at the docks. I will lend him my pickup and a tarp and
we can launch right out the back of it."

"You'd best switch the plates on the pickup, just to be on
the safe side," I said, standing up and leaving one
envelope on the table.   "You get the second one on
completion. When can you do it?"

"Sunrise is best. We can see, no-one there." He looked
at his phone. "That's 0801."

"Get me as much detail as possible on the whole port area and every ship there."

"No problem. I can even livestream it to you for backup."

"Excellent."

I went back to the hotel, saw that I now had a fully functional laptop and phone so I paired them up to sync automatically and was done. Then I had dinner with Jasper and gave him his phone back. He called home and they told him that Luna had indeed caught a bird in the back garden and they were now trying to kill it with a spade.

"You should put a bell on her," I said.

"We have," he replied, "but she's too good."

I had set my alarm for 0750. I made some coffee and sat on the balcony with the laptop on a table just inside the muslin net curtains. It was hooked up to a non-public webpage that Quentin had emailed me details for via a cutout email address that I generated specifically for the purpose. The screen was currently black with some numbers and details around the bottom in dull yellow that sometimes flashed.

The screen lit up at 0800 just as the sun was rising. 'Good on you, Quentin and his cousin,' I thought. The picture was of the back of a pickup truck and a heavily bearded young guy in the cab. It quickly changed as the drone shot up in the sky. I looked out over the balcony and I could actually see it. It wasn't making enough sound for me to hear but it looked quite big, so it was probably loud if you were at the launch site. I looked to see if there was much traffic, foot or vehicle, around the launch site but there seemed to be nothing. This place really could be quite sleepy.

I watched the screen as the drone looped around the various docks in the port and took a leisurely scan of all the boats there. It wandered around all sides and paid particular attention to the superstructure, any visible antennae and the bridges. I checked again to see if there was anyone around and in particular, whether the screen showed any people looking at the drone, but the entire scene appeared to be deserted. After about 20 minutes, when it became clear that Quentin and his cousin were highly competent, I wandered downstairs and left them to it.

Feeling positive about the day, I spent the morning scouring the trade databases again, still not finding anything. I made some more progress decoding Spanish trading symbols and terms. I was still feeling rough but I could work.

Around lunchtime, Quentin emailed to tell me to go to the restaurant at the marina again. I did that, checking with semi-serious assiduity whether there were any people tailing or watching, but the prospects that Quentin had been caught and that the cops had setup a sting in the time available were very slim. Brynjar could have done it, just, but he would basically have had to turn up on his own. The police simply didn't have much resource sitting around not doing anything ready to be deployed at a moment's notice.

I decided not to hang around, but bought a bottle of sherry from the restaurant. They had all types, so I took a palo cortado. This was known as the PhD of sherries, being dry but also not dry, super complex and manufactured in a mysterious process that owed a lot to accident and luck. Palo Cortado happened when you were trying to make a Fino and failed. I gave Quentin his second envelope and asked him how he would deliver the file.

"It's sizeable. I could just about email it maybe but you probably don't want that. I can put it in a dropbox. Do you handle the IT for your, err..., organisation?"

"I'll have my specialist email you, " I said. Gas would like this guy, I thought. I went back to the hotel and put that connection together securely, and then went back to the trade confirms.

In the evening, Gas sent a Signal text. "Got file. Good work. Yr contact impressive. File is big but can review on plane back. 97 minutes of HD video. You have anything?"

I texted back in the negative and asked whether the devices were still in Cordoba. The response was that the laptop had also now ceased to transmit location data and that Gas thought that they were both in the river now. "Either they gave up or they had gotten everything off there. I can't tell which from here. But I reckon they didn't get much."

We agreed that I could now leave Gibraltar. I decided to go to Cordoba, just in case I ran into the foreign agent who had tricked me. I didn't use her name even to myself because she was now the enemy. I wasn't sure what I would do if I found her, but poison was one option. Gas said she would leave her air tickets unchanged and then follow my route out. You could only fly to six airports from Gibraltar anyway, and they were all in the UK.

The route was once more through the checkpoint into La Linea de la Concepcion and then a train. Why was La Linea called that, I wondered. It sounded political, like the whole town was called 'The Imaginary Line that the English made up to steal our territory.' But it could equally well be something to do with immaculate conceptions. I looked online and the etymology appeared to have both streams of thought involved. Probably about the closest that England came to the Virgin Mary.

The train station on the other side was called San Roque, rather than La Linea, which was slightly confusing. It was also incredibly rural and a fair cab ride from La Linea. The service staff at the cafe there were very friendly but were some of the last people in Spain who spoke zero words of English.

They understood though that a guy showing up at a station was pretty much going to want a bread roll with jamon and queso and a lot of water and they were totally on board with providing that. It looked like everyone else was a school-kid on a trip, which was fine by me and meant I had first class to myself.

I changed trains at Antequera Santa Anna. I realised I hadn't said goodbye to Jasper so I texted him. He was used to this sort of thing. I arrived at dinner time and checked in to a pleasant hotel that had formerly been a ducal palace. It was on the main square which was filled with fountains.

CORDOBA, SPAIN

I spent most of the next day still banging my head on various trade and finance databases. Gas landed without incident and started on the train section of the trip.

She texted to say how much she liked entering the Schengen zone unrecorded. I mentioned how the latest plan was for an electronic system to replace the current method of counting the 90/180 day allowance for non-

EU citizens by looking at a paper document and working it out from entry and exit stamps. This method could only be described as wholly barbaric in the current millennium.

I saw Gas arrive and check-in from the bar. She came over to my table immediately afterwards without going upstairs. She dumped her bag next to me and sat down.

"There's new news," she said. "First, I definitely confirmed that the ship with the repainted name and pending name update in the register which used to be the Shundli is there. It is also completely loaded with oil. This is the seventh time the registration has had its pending update request updated without leaving pending status."

"OK, that's great. So now we just need to work out how the $200m gets out."

"About that. There's another pair of VLCCs in that harbor which are in the same twilight zone of naming registration, have current names painted on the side which don't have any history, and which are fully loaded."

Gas was emphatic: "You can't find the $200m because it's $600m. And that's just the cargo value. Given all this registration stuff going on with the ships, the whole thing may come as a package."

"What's the cost of a VLCC?" I asked.

"Extremely variable, but maybe $100m each for a new build with dual fuel capacity," answered Gas.

The air was starting to get very thin at this sort of quantum. This was territory where some corporates would play, but only the largest multinationals that would be in the DOW or the DAX index of the 30 or so largest listed companies in a jurisdiction. Otherwise it was investment bank territory, and bulge bracket investment banks at that, rather than 'local champion' also-rans. After reflecting on this, we thought it was time to catch up with Brynjar via Zoom.

"Anything up in Cordoba?" was his first question. "I don't think we've seen anything there before much."

Gas looked out of the window, which indicated she was going to let me handle this and wasn't going to risk saying something contradictory.

"No particular reason to be here, but it's convenient and we think there were maybe some indications we got made in Gibraltar," I said.

"Oh really? Anyone we know?" asked Brynjar.

"Nothing concrete," I said. "It's just a precaution really, to be double sure. I thought I saw the same guy twice but really we were done there and it's always a good idea to stay mobile, right."

"Move or die," added Gas in a sphinx-like manner.

"So we think we are potentially around $600m now because we have three VLCCs of crude with unusual credentials," I said. "But we don't have source traces on the other two."

Brynjar looked perturbed. "That could all be SWIFT I suppose. You've seen the Nigeria thing?"

I had noticed a headline that said there was something happening in Nigeria to do with a) an election and b) high denomination Naira banknotes needing to be replaced and c) a cash shortage. I hadn't done anything with the information beyond think 'this is bound to come up' because I had mostly been focusing on vomiting and feeling bad.

"I saw it but we haven't looked at it yet," I said.

Brynjar was still looking perturbed but about something else. "It's bigger in another more complex way as well, we think. The fake thing wasn't fake."

Gas stopped looking out of the window and tried to divine what Brynjar was about to say by staring at the screen. "Was it fake or not?" she asked.

"Yes and no," said Brynjar. "I appreciate that this looks like a binary yes/no answer question but bear with me. Think about a chessboard, but maybe make it 12x12 sides instead of the usual 8x8."

I had no idea where this was going.

"We're not playing chess, just using the board. Maybe with one counter," continued Brynjar.

This was still completely opaque.

"There are a large number of ways for the counter to cross the chessboard. You can start anywhere at the left hand side. Let's assume you can move diagonally up and right, straight right or diagonally down and right. You do one of those moves 12 times and you come to the far right side. You have completed a journey," concluded Brynjar.

I thought this was just setting out how you could do a lot of sectors and you had a wide choice of route options between any two points. That was fine but I couldn't see how that could make something fake and not fake at at the same time.

"Imagine now you have a large number of chess pieces. They all have to go from left to right. Some of them carry hot money or contraband and some of them do not," said Brynjar. "Eventually all of your pieces get across the board and so does all of your product."

"That would be an unbelievable nightmare to track," I said.

"Exactly," said Brynjar. "But not that difficult to setup. Certainly not when you consider the resource levels available to our targets."

Gas said "So what we saw with the guy on camera was an empty sector as it were. He didn't have anything with him that time. But other times he might."

"You're getting it," said Brynjar. "I see it as sort of like that tree that Darwin drew in a notebook. Branches descending off from each other."

I was thinking more in physics terms of binomial branch network but it came to the same thing. The targets had setup an incredible network of options. They could snap fit a sector in essentially with complete freedom and move product or not on an individual exercise of that sector. It would be different every time for every pathway.

"Why did they make it easy to find the webcam sector?" Gas wanted to know.

"What did that make you do?" asked Brynjar.

I answered. "Completely discount that sector as something that could ever be interesting in the future."

"There you go," said Brynjar. "They have now thoroughly protected a sector. They could even switch that one off the chessboard if they felt like it was compromised, but you weren't going to look again at that in all probability. Presumably they are constantly switching options in and out."

"Amazing," I said. "It's basically a trajectory variation machine with constant throughput. How do we know all this?"

"We don't know it. But I have a couple of indicators from other teams and basically it's the only possible explanation of what you observed with the webcams in Lebanon. Anyway, plenty for you to do now. We are going to put in some mechanism where we can see the Lebanese truck sector if it starts up again. Basically, eventually we want to get a picture of the whole board."

This was incredible and disturbing at the same time. The levels of complexity and volume were orders of magnitude above what we had suspected. But it did at least mean we were in an environment with a lot of targets, and it did seem as though there were some consistencies and repetitions to track.

Gas was looking distinctly unhappy after Brynjar disconnected. So I said "Remember we are trying to get paid, not interdict all these flows." She didn't cheer up. Maybe she had eaten something bad.

"Is all this just a job for you, or a game, or what?" she asked.

"I don't think it's a thing at all," I said. "It has some emergent properties, as Brynjar would say. I don't know if those suffice to make it a determinate entity. I just try to make optimal decisions whenever a decision point presents itself and sometimes that gives what we're doing a characteristic. But it's not a job because those involve getting a salary and showing up in an office."

"Sounds like it could be a game," said Gas.

I decided to take the night off. Gas was still disconsolate after a bottle of Marqués de Cáceres Rioja each, so I fired up Netflix to find a movie. There was an extended version of Lawrence of Arabia.

"Have you seen that?" I asked. "It's great. Won lots of Oscars." She agreed to give it a go. "There's been a rumour in my family forever that my uncle was an extra in it. But no-one has ever found him."

We watched in silence for 1hr and 31 minutes and then I jumped up in my seat. "That's him!" I exclaimed. A soldier was presenting arms as Peter O'Toole, playing Lawrence, came through an ornamental doorway, while talking to General Allenby.

We stopped watching the film while I tried to work out where the scene was shot. The scene was the British Officers' Club in Cairo, and the family belief was therefore that my uncle had been in Egypt. However, that did not really work since the last British troops had left Egypt in 1956, just ahead of the Suez crisis, and the film was made in 1962. It won a lot of Oscars in 1963. Moreover, the internet was adamant that there had been no filming in Egypt. The scene in the OC was supposedly filmed in Seville.

I took a screenshot of one of the frames with my uncle. There were some unusual large triangular door lintels in the rear of the shot, which I expanded and enhanced. Gas listlessly but effectively found the lintels. The scene had been shot in the Plaza de España, Seville. Some texts quickly established that this soldier was indeed my uncle and that he had been stationed in Gibraltar. As we knew, that was close.

"How far is Seville from here?" I asked.

"45 minute train ride," said Gas, after looking at an app.

"Well, we don't need to be here. I can look for the $600m or $900m anywhere. Let's bounce in the morning."

"Alright. Goodnight," said Gas. She said it somewhat lightheartedly but I was beginning to be concerned that our ability to be anywhere also meant it didn't matter where we were. She had other concerns, maybe.

CHAPTER 11

SEVILLE, SPAIN

We arrived around lunchtime and checked into a hotel in the pedestrianised historical centre. Or it wasn't exactly pedestrianised. It was narrow and mediaeval so technically it had presumably never been motorised, so then never had to be switched back to pedestrians. The stone was old, tired and beautiful. The effect was enhanced rather than diminished by the torn shabby posters that fluttered in the warm air currents wandering lazily around the streets. The daylight almost appeared pink and slower moving than normal.

Brynjar texted us so we called him. He wanted to tell us what he had from Weikang Xu. "Talked, which is good," he said. "The kid is 23 from Hong Kong, at coding school. The Leb cops leant on him pretty hard. He claims to have been directed remotely, paid in bitcoin from unknown sources. They didn't believe that anyone would go for that, but the kid said you do if they start by giving you a lot of bitcoin and then continue to do so in pre-agreed amounts every time you do something."

"Can we trace the bitcoin?" asked Gas.

"The relevant department is looking at that," replied Brynjar. "But it's been through six mixers so they aren't too optimistic. Also there are a lot of flash loans which really greatly enhances the power of the people doing the transactions."

"I think I know what a flash loan is. What's a mixer?" I asked.

"I can tell you something, but your associate Gas is probably best placed to describe them," replied Brynjar.

"Yeah, they are also known in the game as laundry services or tumblers," began Gas. "The formal name is probably 'anonymiser.' The definition of crypto is that all transactions exist on a blockchain, which is just a file that has copies in multiple places and where a bunch of computers that aren't controlled by an individual all have to agree that a transactions has occurred."

"What if one individual does control all the computers?" I asked.

"That's known as a 51% attack. You basically just need to own the decision-making majority. You can then change the rules of the coin to say interesting stuff like 'person X now owns all the coins.' If your system allows that, it's really badly designed. Some guy managed to do it using a flash loan for $100m for which he needed $1m of actual cash."

Brynjar jumped in. "One of the most intriguing features of the nature of these areas is that it's not even clear that a crime has been committed. It basically means that the rules of the system permitted that to happen at the outset and transactions that were legitimate within the framework took place and that's what happened. You should have been aware of this possibility when you signed up or put your money in."

"How many people who buy a crypto are aware of this risk?" I asked.

"Hard to say," said Brynjar. "But what's very clear is that they don't want our help and we have our hands full already anyway."

"So what does a mixer do?" I said, turning back to Gas.

"It's code. Like everything is. The universe is code. A mixer obscures the sequence of transactions on a blockchain. It bundles up a bunch of transactions from one wallet address and sends them all off together but using a different address. If you do this multiple times, which is easy, it gets very hard to deconvolve the transactions. And the wallets are not necessarily tied to an individual anyway."

"When we have done this in the past," said Brynjar, "we quickly regretted it. Because it was a vast amount of work using very expensive people and the guy we got at the end was a cutout. He didn't know anything, did what he was told, got paid, ran a shrimp shack the rest of the time. It's a nightmare. Though also one time it really was the guy and shrimp shack was a cover. You have to ask them about prawns and listen to their accent."

"The mixers are actually really cool pieces of code," continued Gas. "You need a lot of dummy transactions which are complex and random enough to allow you to generate a large number of hard-to-track transactions but not so random that you don't end up tending in the general direction of the transaction you eventually aim to add up to. You can sort of simulate how you will move there and how quickly before you do it."

"Yes, there's a lot of stuff going on in simulation to do with how random random numbers really are," I said. "Because for example in a Monte Carlo simulation like that code you wrote on the shipping destinations, you need random numbers, but computers can only follow an algorithm. Which doesn't give you a random number. It only gives you a pseudo-random number. The difference is a big deal. You might turn up in the same place every time by accident."

"Right," said Gas. "The key step is that the mixer 'commingles' the key questionable transaction with a large number of other user transactions. Lots of them get reversed back out as part of the general fog they want to create. But the end result is that you cannot tell which is the target transaction being obscured and which wallet paid which wallet and even then, you don't know anything about who owns the wallets. It's so ugly it's beautiful."

"And in case you needed more," intervened Brynjar, "if there is an ID information associated with the blockchain wallets, it will be in multiple jurisdictions and multiple entities within those jurisdictions. They have a variable level of enthusiasm to respond on a timely basis to subpoenas. Though sometimes in the rougher places, you can generate enthusiasm among law enforcement by pointing out that certain bounties might eventually become seizable. Which is sort of the genesis of this whole thing we are in, I guess..."

"OK, so this is all a bit huge. It might be worth looking at later on but it sounds unproductive for now. On the Weikang Xu guy you interrogated. Did you ask him how to spell 'file'?" I said, but Gas jumped in.

"There's no point," she said. "Even if he's that guy, it's just a typo. He wouldn't do it every time." I had to agree. Gas continued "Just get a list from him of languages which he's proficient in and how good and does that list include Visual C++ and is his installation a bit old, 6.0 to be precise. Then at least we know if he is a cutout or not."

"He's basically what we call a 'smart cutout,' said Brynjar. "He's not the guy, but he knows what he is doing as far as it goes. Not like the purported address of a major transaction hub in South East Asia for that German online payments company that was a big fraud. It was the proverbial shrimp shack in that case, which is why we refer to 'smart cutouts' and 'shrimp shacks' to distinguish the two types of player."

"Does anyone ever pretend to be the other type of cutout?" I asked.

"Everything that is possible has occurred, or will do," said Brynjar gnomically. "Anyway, this guy is no shrimp. He told us that he gets his instructions via secure email which is encrypted. Or doubly encrypted -- first the email system itself is encrypted, then the actual text he receives is itself in need of decoding."

"What's the encryption method?" asked Gas.

"The kid is reluctant to give that up. Although he doesn't know who he is working for, he knows they will be unhappy if he does that and they can find him. On the topic of locations, why are you in Seville?"

"Personal reasons," I said. "Nothing major, we can be ready to jump if something comes up."

Gas had something else to report, or she thought this was a good time for a change of topic. "I have been looking at those other two ships with pending re-registrations. I know where they came from. One was from the Jose terminal in Venezuela and the other was out of the Malongo terminal in Angola. Burgoyne is going to try to track the input financial legs and I will keep looking at it."

I agreed I would look, but entered a caveat. "Of course, it will be useful to track the sources, but where it goes to going forward is probably more critical. Also, I can already see that the Venezuela input is sanctioned crude, because the U.S. Department Of The Treasury reported it. But the in/out leg to the Venezuelan state could have been anything. It could have been Cuba supplying doctors. And there won't be much to be done in Angola.

I've got some documentation in Portuguese. It could be large denomination banknote replacement or SWIFT as we've seen before."

Brynjar said "All information is useful," and then continued cryptically that if you were looking for a red herring, finding a black shoe was a minor but positive step, because you had found an object in the world which was not a red herring and therefore were closer to determining the location of the red herring if it existed. I thought that this was inefficient because you would effectively have to look at all the objects in the world to see if they were a red herring or not but Brynjar said "that's what you have to do every time."

Gas looked like she wanted to not think about this because it fell into the large and amorphous category of 'true but not necessarily useful right now.' Then she said "We need someone in Berlin because the ship re-registrations appear to originate there."

I interjected "You have that German woman Angelika, right, Brynjar?"

Brynjar said "Actually she's Serbian, I think. She often goes by the short form, 'Geli.' She adopts a German name when she is there to save time."

I paused but remembered not to react visibly otherwise. This was probably nothing. "What's her real name?"

"I don't remember. But it means something poetic, like 'kiss,' in the local language."

I froze. This time it was hard to cover. Gas was looked perturbed but had the presence of mind to stand up and get out of shot where she started looking through files on her laptop with a focussed manner.

"Why do you want to know?" asked Brynjar.

"I suppose it's just nice to know something about our colleagues or whatever you want to call them, in...whatever this is. The network," I said. "Have you ever wondered if it could be ... compromised ... in any way?"

"Define 'compromised,' ' said Brynjar.

This was a good question. How could something that didn't have a name until I just baptised it 'the network' be compromised?

I tried again. "Do you think everyone is working in the same direction?"

"I won't annoy you by asking you to define 'same,' ' responded Brynjar. "It's correct viewed from an indexical perspective. I ask them to do things and they mostly do. They aren't on my payroll. Officially, nothing exists. I sometimes report that I have received information from informants. They are all motivated by self-interest, as is basically everyone. So if by 'same,' you mean 'they will do what I ask provided they can see it leading to information which is valuable to them, or that I will pay for,' then yes. They are all working in the same direction. And if that is what you mean by 'not compromised,' then I can agree to that also. But this is just how you operate anyway, no?"

I could not dispute this.

"Why do you want to know?"

I decided it was time to sign-off and regroup, so I pretended something else was inbound. Once it was just us in the room, Gas said "This is the same Serbian woman that dumped you over the border from Gibraltar, right?"

"I think it must be," I admitted. "What have you been looking up?"

She responded with another question. "Does 'gmbh' mean anything?"

"Yes," I said, "it's the German for 'Gesellschaft mit beschränkter Haftung,' which means 'Limited Company.' '

"So if your name or pseudonym was 'Angelika' and you setup a shell company in Germany, it might well be called 'Geli gmbh?' '

"Yes. Where is all this going?"

"The corrupt string at the start of the Vietnamese trade confirmation. The one that led us to Cyprus. Ages ago. It wasn't a corrupt string. It was 'GELIGMBH.' Now we know what that means."

341

We sort of knew what it meant. It might not add up to a proof that Brynjar's network was compromised. As he had explained, we didn't even know what the truth conditions were for that claim. But what it meant for sure was that we needed to be a lot more careful.

"She might be competition for us in a couple of ways. Finding out what is happening first and getting information to Brynjar before we do. So we don't get paid," I said. "Or she might actually be a player. Or both. Or she might not know."

"She might be part of the thing we are tracking..." said Gas.

"Yes. Which is not inconsistent with her also working for Brynjar. At least some of the time."

This was bad. I didn't see how we could benefit from filling Brynjar in about what we now thought. It was as likely that he would think we were the compromised elements of the network as anything else. I next started to get paranoid again that we might be being watched.

"We have to behave completely normally," I said. "No unexplained changes."

"Alright. I'm going out for a drink to think about where we are," said Gas.

I couldn't think of what I should do so I reverted to my original plan. This meant I went over to the Plaza de España and found a couple of older American tourists who had seen Lawrence of Arabia. I had to start explaining the story quickly because they thought I was going to trick them or ask for money or something. I showed them the research and told them the story briefly. They looked amazed and excited and were very happy to take a shot on my phone of me standing in the same place as my uncle had stood in 1962.

Having got the shot, I wandered around in the square. It was impressive, but I had become overwhelmed by a deep sense of rootlessness, which was somehow magnified by the ornate columns and the tourists. I was struggling to remember what my motivation was, like a deracinated method actor.

In this crowd, as in most places, I was invisible. I moved through it like a ghost, intangible and insubstantial. It had always been useful in the past, but it wasn't necessarily my choice.

I decided eventually I had to return to real life, so I texted Gas to meet me in a square outside an impressively substantial branch of the Banco de España. The square was ringed by imposing buildings, modern and mediaeval, and you could get an excellent cold glass of rosé in one of many bars with outside space. We also got some tapas, which was primarily octopus and squid. It was all high quality but we weren't really enjoying it.

Gas had clearly entered a similar type of philosophical mode to me as a result of the previous revelations. As we ate, Gas asked me why I thought I was alone. I said "I think it's something to do with local minima in phase space." Gas looked at me with an expression that I could only describe as studied neutrality.

"It's like evolution," I explained. "It's only possible to take steps that are incremental improvements on the prior position. So like a giraffe's neck. It has seven vertebrae, the same as us. It would have been a great design move to add some more in rather than just make them extended and weak. But no-one can make that call. Evolution can't make design choices. It can just brute force try stuff and the bad moves get wiped out."

Gas was still looking at me without comment but clearly thinking about what I was saying. Or possibly something else.

"It's not like I don't like women. It's just that at any given moment I am trying to make an optimal decision based on the current state of knowledge and the options available. And there is no sequence of optimised moves which end up with me and a woman being together."

"I understand what you are saying," said Gas, which I took to mean 'you have adequately described the nature of the problem' but not 'I have full sympathy with your predicament.' She continued, changing tack.

"What are we going to do?"

There was a long silence as we thought about what we thought optimal meant and for whom.

"I guess we just have to keep going," said Gas eventually.

"Right," I said, without much enthusiasm. "There's still a target and a payoff here," I added with slightly more.

"So are we looking for another Letter of Credit here, like the one I found in Saigon?"

"Technically what you found in Saigon was a confirmation of a trade backed by a Letter of Credit. So we haven't actually seen a real LoC so far. But yes," I said, "That could be the next step."

"Let's start by getting fucked up."

"OK," I said.

⎯⎯⎯⎯⎯⎯⎯⎯⎯⎯⎯⎯⎯⎯⎯

Mid-afternoon the next day, we continued. Gas said that she had found overnight that the requesting entity for the ship re-registrations was something called Euhemerises Flug DOO which looked like it was something to do with German air travel and interpretation of mythology.

She had then stuck those into what we called The 'Fork.' It was only metaphorically a fork; for a start it had probably about a million tines. She had coded it based on the sort of search we were often doing.

The start of The Fork was to take the characters you had given it, which would often look like nonsense, and see if if could be made into a word or set of words in any language. It would reorder the text into all possible combinations of fragments with at least two letter words and look for anagrams.

The Fork's second stage would ram the results of that through online databases, or Corporae, of every word in a language. There were 17 of these databases just in English; there were also some more specialist ones like one that had the whole enormous body of EU law, known as the Acquis Communautaire, but then jacked through 231 language pairs. That was hugely valuable, both for the combinations and the legal flavour. After this, The Fork would tell you whether what you had were words in any language. Here it was pretty clear that one word was English and the other was German but often it wasn't.

It was amazing how often people ran out of imagination when making up names for companies. The problem was that you often needed hundreds of them. The gold standard solution would be for all of the company names to be like passwords, being some random combination of alphanumerics like fv65fh-wr&enl-#ow9x7 and also being renamed every ten seconds. However, this was massively impractical. So people would do stuff like use the name of their pet with three numbers after it or the river at the bottom of their garden over and over again; if they were one level more clever they would produce anagrams. The Fork found all this.

What it found here was that 'Euhemerises Flug' could also be 'Usluge Hemisfere' which both had the appealing property of being words in the same language, Croatian. They meant 'Services' and 'Hemisphere' in English Also it turned out that the phrase 'Društvo sa Ograničenom Odgovornošću' was commonly abbreviated DOO and was the Croatian for Limited Liability Company. So we had effectively a quasi-anagram of Hemisphere Services Limited.

Gas had found through company searches that an outfit with that name existed. It had done something in Gibraltar that had resulted in an ultimately nullified lawsuit for fraud in providing anti-fraud databases, ironically. It had once shared a Director, now resigned from both companies, with another shell company registered in the British Virgin Islands. That company owned a detached house in Hampstead, a leafy north London suburb.

A planning application had been submitted in relation to that house for a super basement, which would add a pool and home cinema. Fairly standard. There was an email address listed as secondary on that application, behind the architects who provided the primary address.

The secondary email address featured in something known as the 'Sandcastles' data. This we had not heard of before, but it was a compilation of information provided by UAE-based real estate and property professionals. The dataset also drew associations between prominent Nigerian politicians and 800 units of real estate in Dubai property valued at N164 billion. That was $356m.

A generally attractive feature of real estate in Dubai was what was described as a generalised pattern of omission on behalf of authorities in Dubai and a group known rather vaguely as 'corporate service providers.' There was not a lot of basic due diligence being done on foreign buyers. Even simple internet searches were probably a bit too much work, reportedly.

One name came up: James Iburu who had been Governor of Delta Province in Nigeria. I texted Brynjar to ask if there was anything in the files on him. Gas thought they had a cool naming system for provinces and that also they should check out the Governors of Alpha, Bravo and Charlie Provinces also.

One thing Iburu had done was to crowd-fund a peer-to-peer lender. He appeared to be the beneficial owner of a company setup ostensibly to lend money in Nigeria. The fact that he was the beneficial owner meant that he didn't actually own the company; he merely received the benefits of owning it via a contract. This was much better than owning it because that showed up immediately in reports if anyone was looking. Beneficial ownership detection required extra footwork.

The crowdfunding part involved selling a load of unregistered securities to basically anyone on the internet. There was a bunch of semi-legitimate activity where cash raised from investors was then lent out to textile factories in Delta province. But there was also a bunch of transactions all labeled things like 'White Tower' and 'Black Tower' which were not doing anything obviously sensible or useful.

My phone pinged. I looked at at and said "Brynjar's intern has sent us something called a 'lifestyle audit.'

"That must mean he thinks our expenses are bogus," said Gas. "That's exactly what we need right now.

"Our expense *are* bogus," I said, "but he knows that. Our entire operation is off-balance sheet and so is the rest of his shadow network of mercenary mercenaries, however large that may be."

I got hold of the attachment and forwarded it to Gas. A lifestyle audit seemed to be something like a posh name for taking an interest if gas meter readers who were also criminals were driving Lamborghinis. This was quite an exciting area in the UK after the advent of Unexplained Wealth Orders. These allowed you to take golf courses off people if they couldn't give a reasonable explanation of why they were spending £16m in Harrods when they had no job but their husband used to run the Central Bank in Azerbaijan. This was a lot easier than proving that a bunch of money absconded from the Central Bank because that latter task was impossible.

"How does this work with 'innocent until proven guilty'?" said Gas.

"It doesn't," I replied, "but who cares?"

"Do we not care?"

"I can always come up with an explanation for anything. And neither of us are known to be public servants. And our spending has been outrageous for ages so it would have to go to outrageous+ or something. So no, we don't care."

The lifestyle audit was a response to my request for anything related to James Iburu. They had started looking at him for school fees in the UK. Rather stylishly, among other activities, he operated his own 'boutique foreign exchange bureau.' Nothing like owning the shop if you wanted a load of currency transposed into something else as a favourable rate. Actually, if you owned the shop, a rubbish rate was just as good.

State Governors in Nigeria made 7.8m Naira p.a., which had been around £16k in 2020, in which year the average annual fees for boarding schools in the UK had been around twice that. Amazingly, this guy seemed to have millions of kids who were all boarding and £286k of fees had been seen moving in to the UK educational sector.

In a footnote, the report mentioned that 480,000 Suspicious Activity Reports were submitted to the National Crime Agency in 2018/2019, of which twenty-four were from the educational sector. There was some commentary from bursars to the effect that they knew about teaching kids but not detecting illicit financial flows. "This guy was super unlucky," I commented. "Clearly no one in that sector is awake."

"Also these 24 reports are probably all worth a look, whereas 470,000 of the 480,000 others are from devious fucks like you in investment banks drowning the regulators in paper," said Gas.

"I always assumed that they were papering their offices with them."

The next thing that happened when they looked more at this guy was to do with a bunch of company mergers in Panama. This was all sort of public in that someone had helpfully dumped 11.5 million documents from a now-defunct Panama law firm on the internet and investigative journalists were still combing through it. This was why Brynjar had sent us the document, it appeared, because some of the companies seemed to have owned oil berthed in Gibraltar at some points. Brynjar had drawn a big circle in highlighter around one of these companies with a question mark next to it.

"We need a lot of whiteboards," I said. The only way out of this malaise was to get back to work.

About 48 hours later we had covered two walls of whiteboards with diagrams showing dozens of companies that had merged with each other, bought assets, de-merged, changed shareholders, changed names, changed directors and done hundreds of other things which seemed to have no other function beyond representing activity which could potentially be a distraction from what was actually happening. But we didn't get distracted. Tired, and dispirited, yes, but not distracted.

One thing we did get very distracted by was whitespace. One of the documents had extra space after each sentence, and the amount of whitespaces was variable. A normal document would always have two spaces or one after each sentence. This one had zero or one. This stood out for a couple of reasons. The first was that it was clearly visible because no space was ugly. The second was that zeroes and ones meant binary.

We combined up all the bits into real base-ten numbers using all possible window sizes from four bits to ten bits for each number and then looked at the resulting final numbers. We got a lot of numbers but none of them meant anything or had any kind of detectable pattern so we parked it and went back to looking at what the documents were saying on the surface rather than what they might be saying in their metadata. And then we found a set of transactions that added up to something. It didn't mean anything until you saw the whole picture.

The key transaction amounted to an asset swap. At one point, two chains of companies interacted with one another. Somewhere in the middle, two companies merged. The two companies owned shareholdings in a bunch of Liechtenstein Anstalts, which were notoriously opaque. We could only see these ones at all because of the leaked legal documents. One of the chains owned $600m of oil in Gibraltar at the beginning of the corporate mergers. Another one owned some real estate in Dubai.

One big part of the story was Bearer Share Corporations. Gas had found some in the switches in which we were interested and asked me what they were.

"Well, it's a development from Bearer Bonds. Those used to be a big deal up until the middle of the 20th century. The way a bond works is you buy it at the start, with an amount called the Principal. You get paid interest in the meantime and at the legal maturity, you get the purchase price or the principal back. That's how bonds still work today."

"You mean like the bonds the US government issues? And that there is a periodic fight about in Congress, to do with the debt limit?" asked Gas.

"Yep," I said. "Except nowadays all the bonds are just registered. So you don't have a piece of paper. In the old days, you could just rock up to the bank that was the paying agent and if you had the certificate in your hand, they would pay you the interest you were due. Bond interest is still called the 'coupon' because you would literally have a coupon edge of the bond that would get clipped off when you were paid. And at the end, you would get your principal back."

"So all of this presumably got ruled out when people realised that Bearer Bonds were great for money laundering?"

"Right," I said. "Except you can do the same thing still with Bearer Share Corporations in some jurisdictions, like Panama."

"So the company is owned by whoever has the physical share certificate?"

"Yes. Pieces of paper. It's barbaric. But also extremely un-hackable. We only know because the law firm which set it all up got hacked, but you can't rely on that to generally be the case. And no-one knows anything about who owns those corporations now because we would have to find a piece of paper which could be anywhere."

We then got a break from the mixers that we had been talking about earlier. We couldn't understand anything going on with the mixers, because we would need to do years of work. But we could see that one foreign exchange bureau owned by Iburu had the ability to transact with one of the major mixer providers. That meant we looked more closely at that company. It was helpful that there weren't really any legitimate reasons to deal with mixers.

What we eventually worked out was that after the demergers of Bearer Share Corporations and manifold shareholder reorganisations relating to them, the initial positions had switched. One set of guys in Nigeria started out owning a big residential skyscraper in Dubai and ended up owning a load of oil in Gibraltar. That oil then went into the Nigerian national accounts, where it got mixed up conveniently with the vast proceeds of oil actually drilled in Nigeria. That wasn't our concern. Though it presumably should be someone's.

What we knew now was that whoever had sold the oil in Gibraltar to Iburu and his friends now owned a building in Dubai called the Marina Tower, which Iburu had only owned for a month. That was what all the 'Purple Tower' companies ended up funnelling their cash into. We decided to go and look at the building.

CASH-TRAP

CHAPTER 12

DUBAI, UAE

Gas asked me whether I had been here before on the drive in from the airport. She had passed through what must be one of the world's few underground air force bases, which was beneath the southern desert in Abu Dhabi and full of F16E Desert Falcons, and which did not officially exist. She'd been running tests on UAE-specific Black Shaheen cruise missiles. She'd also had some fun in two-person mini-subs. And she'd tried to get photos of Russian and North Korean satellite feeds in the Space Reconnaissance Centre but they had hustled her through quickly. The UAE was odd in that the several emirates had previously bought kit from both the West and the Warsaw Pact, and that post formation of the UAE, everything got chucked in the pot.

"The desert doesn't sound like the likeliest place to find a Navy gal," I said.

"You might be surprised by what they do here," said Gas. "Dubai services more US Navy ships than anywhere else outside the US. Also you guys, the Brits, have signed a secret defense pact that sees 75,000 UK service personnel show up in case of 'emergency.' Same from the the French...so there could be a lot of surprise all at once for some people, if it kicks off in the neighbourhood again. For us, it was our favorite liberty port because it had booze and nightclubs."

"Always good, and yes," I said in response to her question as to whether I had been around here before. "It was a human trafficking and money thing in '09.

Dubai is the second wealthiest emirate after Abu Dhabi. It has to compete and it does that with the premier Freeport in the region and what people used to call 'soft-touch' regulation before that became an unfashionable slogan to use."

"Is it all oil money?" asked Gas.

"That was the start of it, obviously," I replied, "but post-crisis, most GDP is non-oil. That makes life much more difficult for us: in the old days you could start with the oil and work outwards. Now tonnes of stuff moves in and out of the free zones all the time but you can't see it easily."

The hotel was in the middle of downtown and was on the spectacular side, with an enormous golden bowl of fresh rose petals in the ornate entry hall, designed to be the first thing a visitor would see on arrival. Like most buildings here, it was both immense and impressive.

The rooms were even more striking. We had a pair on the ground floor which overlooked an artificial lake. Tourists glided past slowly on boats as they headed over to the far side, from where you could get a great view of the fountain which shot up what looked like 100m or more into the sky, accompanied by lights and loud music every couple of hours. We ordered Lebanese food from room service which came quickly and was excellent.

I took a look at the INTERPOL briefing pages. In this case, the intel was slightly surprising. It appeared that the UAE and Egypt were fighting a proxy war in the Sudan, but that that entire conflict had dropped off the radar of most of the Western media for what were non-transparently described as 'political reasons' with no further clarification.

This usually meant that the powers that be had decided that drawing attention to the conflict would promote conflict, which might be right but looked odd. It felt a bit like Hitler's motivation in invading the Soviet Union. He wanted to prevent the British achieving their objective of engaging the Soviet Union in the war, and his method of doing this was to engage the Soviet Union in the war.

There were two factions fighting in Sudan, the Sudanese Armed Forces (SAF) and the Rapid Support Forces (RSF). One of these was supposed to be the official army, but that sort of thing didn't matter much. And the rebels had a cooler name. What mattered, as ever, was money. These factions controlled 80% of economic activity in Sudan and the same proportion was outside the control of the 'civilian' 'government.'

Delightfully enough, the Military Industrial Complex of the SAF that did all the commerce was actually called the Military Industrial Complex. No point calling it something confusing and unrelated. That was why President Reagan's spokesman was called Larry Speaks and the Chelsea goalkeeper was called Kepa.

The main local ramifications of this were that a lot of Sudanese gold came through the UAE and then an element of that went to the West. Secondly, it was known that the RSF used Emirati dealers to purchase over 1,000 pick-up trucks. These would be converted to what Gas called 'technicals.' I wondered about the resale value of Toyota pickups which came with a heavy machine gun already mounted. Probably pretty good.

I idly fired up what was probably Gas's finest coding achievement. It was a SWIFT terminal emulator. You couldn't use it to steal money. It was just a messaging system. You would have to commit the additional step of pretending to be someone else, who had money, like the Central Bank of Bangladesh, and move it somewhere you controlled. This was fraught with danger, because a large number of official and unofficial wolves would quickly be looking for you.

You could send a mule to withdraw cash, as in the Sri Lanka case, but the guy could not seriously withdraw $100m dollars in cash and move it surreptitiously. Plus he would get arrested. And you faced the standard problems of trying to motivate and instruct him while never meeting him, and not giving him any opportunities to put his fingers in the cookie jar, as Gas said.

Apart from that, as with all activities conducted by humans on earth, it would also be wire fraud in the US. On a grand scale. And that meant lots of jail time, combined with trying to live the rest of your life spending only roubles and renminbi.

What you could do was read logs. There would be millions of them, so it was not quick. In addition, the emulator was backed by a seven-layer VPN Gas had also coded. A VPN, or Virtual Private Network, routed all your internet traffic through servers in many different locations, such that tracking your activity was basically impossible. This slowed things down a lot as well, but you needed the security. And it was handy when you wanted to watch a Chelsea game that was only being broadcast in the US.

I idly fired up the emulator to see what if anything was going on in terms of transfers in either direction between the UAE and Sudan. This produced results quickly.

"Looks like both the RSF and the SAF get their cars from the same guys," I said.

"Not that surprising," replied Gas. "Opposing forces getting resupply from the same source has quite a few examples. Sweden sold the Nazis a lot of iron ore in WW2, and also shipped ball bearings to the UK. That was very tough though and were military operations in their own right."

"Ball bearings?"

"Those are much more important to a military machine than you think," said Gas. "There was also something in the Azores."

"Right. Portugal was neutral right?"

"In theory, though Portugal and the UK have the longest established unbroken military alliance in existence. Dates from some crazy year like 1386 and the Treaty of Windsor or something."

"What actually happened?"

"The Azores are super important from a naval perspective. They are placed right in the middle of the Atlantic in a big space where you don't have any other resupply options. And in WW2, shipping endurance was much lower than it is now. So the Portuguese kind of had to deal with both sides, because refusing one side would be seen as highly aggressive."

"Tricky."

"Right. So a scenario developed in which the Royal Navy were pointed at one island while the Kriegsmarine got another one. Because it would have been a bad party if those guests had met each other."

"Well, I have that but something more. Not only are the two apparently opposed sides in Sudan buying 1000s of technicals from the same car dealers, but they are doing it at the same time together."

"Maybe they want a bulk discount."

"I am sure they get that, but financially they appear to be the same organisation."

"Isn't this war killing a lot of people?" asked Gas.

"Yes," I said. "But mostly civilians. So this appears to be a pretend conflict ideologically."

"I bet the Egyptians don't know that. Or the UAE sponsors."

"I don't know what it is supposed to be about," I said.

'It will be what it is always about. The opportunity to control state power and use that to loot the local economy," sad Gas. "That's how it can be possible that it can be rational for an organisation to split into two halves and fight 'itself,' especially if that then gets international aid and military support in."

"This of course can explain why some conflicts get much more attention than others. The Russians really do want to kill all the Ukrainians, and they will continue trying to do so at massive cost in blood and treasure."

"That," said Gas, "is a different sort of madness."

While we were looking at all of this, Brynjar dialled us. When he came up on the screen he opened with "We got something else from the Hong Kong kid. It's odd material, but we think it's probably OK, partly because it's so odd."

"What did you give him?" asked Gas.

"It turns out he wanted a British passport. Didn't need much else. He asked for two grand in cash as well."

"Two grand? Bizarre," I said.

"It turns out he wasn't at all worried about making money once in the UK. Which seems fair, given his skillset and the fact he would be clean. Obviously we gave him soft immunity as well."

I said "What's soft about it?"

"We haven't written it down. Because making commitments takes forever, as you know. But we have made him believe what is in fact true, which is that we have no interest in prosecuting him, and we won't if he gives us useful intel."

"OK. How about the passport?"

"That turned out to be hard and easy at the same time. The UK already has a programme of passport issuance to HK citizens who are not relaxed about the new restrictions. He just slid into that. But then the bizarre part was that the Home Secretary had to sign off on the individual file, in case she was able to reduce immigration numbers by one. And she actually read the file but then some of our friends from Special Branch shone a bunch of national security lights in her eyes and that was fine."

"Sounds standard," I said. "So how did it go?"

"The next thing was that we couldn't get the two grand but we could buy him an airfare and he said that was cool. He's got all this bitcoin; we don't want it. He'll go to the UK not exactly under witness protection but he has a new name in a new place so if he's not an idiot, he'll be fine."

"He also has to have no connections he gives a damn about," interjected Gas.

Both Brynjar and I looked confused but then agreed that this must be true.

"He must somewhat care I suppose," responded Brynjar, "because he does have some family. The consortium, or whoever they were that paid him, said if he ever touched anything not his then all his relatives would die. This message came with a photo file listing all their addresses. It seems he hopes that if he steps out but does not take their money, they will leave people alone. I'm not so sure, but it isn't my problem."

After a brief pause, I said "OK, so what's the new intel?"

"This is, as I said, very odd. He says there is going to be a bidding process for interested parties to acquire the total funds collected so far. He knows that because he has been told that the whole system is being reset to zero and he was told to be ready to restart his work. This is all fine but the weird part is how bidders find out about the bidding process. He says there is going to be a global announcement on the BBC."

"How is that possible?" I asked. "Sophie Raworth isn't going to say 'and finally, if you are an international crime syndicate or rogue regime interested in acquiring a large pot of hot cash, call the number on screen now' after she reads the news, is she?"

"No. But the kid is adamant. And he doesn't seem to have a good reason to lie. Unless he just wants to throw us off, but he thinks we can revoke the passport. We could, or rather the British could, but it's a hellish nightmare. It's taken years to do that with a woman in a terrorist camp in Syria," said Brynjar. "So in his mind, if he screws us, awe can screw him back at any point by trashing his credentials. We haven't actually said we would shop him to the consortium, but he must be aware that we could potentially do that."

"That BBC thing...that's a lot of output," said Gas. "We will have beaucoup difficulty finding it, especially since we don't know what we are looking for."

"There are constraints," I said. "It can't be a Burmese-language farmers' bulletin on short wave in Myanmar.

Bidders have to be able to find it. It has to be globally available and in English."

"There's one more thing," said Brynjar. "The announcement is happening tomorrow. So the most important thing about all of this is that it means you've caught up with the process. We are now operating in real time."

This was positive but meant we had to move fast. Brynjar's stringer here was a friendly and effective Dubliner called Greg who was the regional lead for a firm which installed the software that ran ATMs. We had worked with him before many times. I'd checked in with him when we arrived and said that we would be in touch if we wanted anything. I called him again and said we had mission requirements that were urgent and critical.

"We need an office and a lot of big flat screen TVs, plus can you fill it with pizza." I looked at Gas. "We might need some extra compute power..." Gas was shaking her head so she obviously thought she didn't need it on-site and could just outsource anything like that to the grid. "No, scratch the computers. The TVs need to get standard TV."

"As it happens," explained Greg, "one of the requirements for a work visa here is to rent an office from the government. So I have one sitting there that I don't really use because I am mostly on the road. There's a couple of PCs in there already. I can get you flatscreens and there's no problem ordering in food. I can do it for you if you want to stay under the radar. Do you have any resource constraints?"

"Within reason, no." I said.

"I should be able do all this for a few grand tops. Some guys from the showroom to plug it all in and pay for the hardware. When do you want it?"

"We must have it by midnight. Spend more if that's going to be a problem. Oh, and we're going to need a lot of coffee," I said. "The second thing is we need to get into the local land registry, for large commercial real estate transactions."

"I'll have to go make some calls on that; it's not something I've looked at before," said Greg. "I'll get the screen stuff rolling and then come back to you on the second thing."

We were now under some time pressure to go and take a look at the big residential tower which was in principle the reason we were in Dubai, so we decided to head straight over there in an Uber and leave Greg to deal with setting up the office for the TV monitoring.

Gas was hoping we could rely entirely on Greg and not need the locals. "You never know which side they are on. The most annoying episode in my career was when I was just about to hit a hunting camp in Helmand that Osama liked and appeared to be in, when a big C130 transport plane with UAE markings landed. The word was that it would have been too embarrassing to 'compromise a Sheikh.' And Bin Laden was here in 2001 getting his kidneys fixed. I could have fixed them for him."

"It is all a bit messy," I agreed. "One of the first things I did for Brynjar involved going backwards from some regular payments that were going in to Al Qaeda fronts. It turned out that the Qataris were paying Bin Laden to blow stuff up elsewhere. Or rather not blow their stuff up. It was only a few million dollars a year so probably a fair deal."

We got out at the Marina Tower which was as enormous and impressive as every other building here. That was useful because it cast a lot of shade and the heat meant you could not be in the direct sun for more than a few seconds. Even in the shade, you had to move directly from the aircon in the car to the aircon in a building with maximum despatch. The heat also seemed to somehow bleach out the colours so they looked like a 70s travel agency brochure. The breeze didn't help because it just moved heat around.

We had found out beforehand that the Marina Tower had 80 floors and 800 residential and commercial units. Major construction was complete but handover of units was continuing, which gave us an angle. Apartments were going for AED 180,000 a year which was about $50,000. Not bad.

As we were walking around the outside of the building, I got a call from our Irish friend.

"I spoke to a lawyer," Greg said. "He says there is something called the Dubai Land Registry and the claim is that you can register a property there in 15 minutes. In reality it's going to take 3 to 8 months. It's supposed to be migrated to a blockchain. There's also something called Taqyīm that supervises valuations."

"How do you access it?" I asked. "Is it a room full of files or a guy you talk to or what?"

"It's a database. But my lawyer contact says that also authority is distributed among many government departments so any transaction will leave traces in a number of places."

"Can he get into any of these places?" was my question. "We are at a building called Marina Tower and we want to know who owns it, who used to own it, who lent money secured on it, anything at all like that."

"The records are online. Anyone can look at them."

I explained this to Gas. She thought what I thought, which was if it was public, it couldn't be helpful. We went into the foyer of the building and sat in a quiet corner. She fired up her Soviet laptop and started looking. After a while she reported who owned the building. "Yes, it's the same situation as we found in Seville. It's now owned by MT Nominee (656) LLC which bought it from MT Nominee (655) LLC. Both in the Caymans. Not tremendously helpful."

Greg was still on the line. I told him what we had found. He said "Apparently when you make a real estate transaction, the buyer and the seller have to show up at the same time. So you could take a look at who is going into the building together. But you would have to stake it out for a long time and we can't go back and do that for previous transactions. And they could do it in a lawyer's office, though apparently it is usual to do it in the actual building being sold. I'd say you have to go to the Caymans shareholder registry."

This looked right and so we parked it for the time being. Given that our guys seemed to be in the business of operating repeated section in a chain, it might be worth doing the stakeout operation in the future. But on the other hand, it might just lead to finding some guys whose day job was running a burger joint or welding who sometimes got paid to walk into the land registry with some documentation they didn't understand and some lawyers who paid them and told them not to worry. The welders might be controlling shareholders and directors of Cayman SPVs for about ten minutes before the meeting and ten minutes afterwards and then get paid in cash in the traditional brown envelope and that was it. We weren't resourced for this in any case so it was probably a dead end.

We walked up to one of the concierges and said we wanted to buy a unit. This was a plausible thing for us to be doing and the guy readily gave us a flyer which had a bunch of appealing facts about the building including pictures of three infinity pools hanging above the desert and also contact details for three estate agents.

Gas said: "I don't know who these realtors are, but that last one CDRE Smythson is a major commercial outfit, isn't it?"

"It is," I replied, "and that may mean that they handle transfers of ownership interests in the freehold of the entire building as well as having some of the units to move also."

The contact name on the flyer at CDRE was Lucy Bond. The picture showed her to be an attractive blonde just about into early middle age. I called the number but it turned out she was in Beirut for a marketing trip all week and we couldn't meet her. They offered us her junior but I pretended that we had had a personal recommendation and only she would do. That was about all we could do on that angle for the time being so we headed back to the hotel.

We got some rest and headed over to the office late evening. The method for doing this turned out to be the metro system, which was incredibly clean, fast and spacious. We looked out the window at what seemed to be kilometre on kilometre of immense new skyscrapers which were visually almost all unusual and exciting. The surrounding desert was on the featureless side, so it was as though the buildings were a reaction to that.

When we found the office, Greg was waiting for us. He was a good looking guy middle-aged guy who had long hair, but his looks meant he could carry it off. He said "I wanted to be sure you had everything you needed and fix any snagging. The store guys just left." He gestured at six large flatscreen TVs which were conveniently mounted on some large brackets like on a trading floor. This was great because you could see all of them at the same time from a couple of expensive-looking and comfortable executive chairs. "I had them hook it up to a global satellite box. Are you really seriously into the footie or something? I don't know anything about that devil's game."

"We need all the BBC channels that are globally available," I said.

"No problem," said Greg. "If you can get them here, you can get them anywhere. And the other way around; if you can get it anywhere, you can get it here."

Greg got a ping on his phone and left, saying he'd be right back.

Gas said "Actually maybe it is good we have the extra computers because we can hook them up to radio channels."

After about ten minutes, we had the screens showing us various 24hr BBC channels, including World News, Parliament and foreign-focused new channels that were in English like BBC America. We decided to ignore channels showing nature programmes and crime documentaries because they were much less likely to have any live material. While we were doing this, Greg came back with large bottles of coke and six immense pizzas. We chose diavola and margarita and he took the others back for his wife and kids.

I switched the sound off on the TVs and hooked up one of the desktop computers to BBC World Service. There were other stations I wanted to listen to, but I couldn't practically listen to more than one and that seemed like the best option.

We then settled in for a difficult period. We sank back into the chairs. The pizza was excellent. The BBC was leading with the Presidential election in Nigeria, which reminded me I needed to look into the Naira angle, President Zelensky saying he was in trouble in Bakhmut and something odd to do with the Governor of Florida taking away Disney's immunity from planning permission requirements because of a disagreement about gay people. Why didn't Disney need planning permission? What was the problem with people being gay? These were deep and unrelated mysteries.

These leads did not change between 0000 and 0400 and then there started to be something about the Japanese antitrust authority looking at bid-rigging for ads around the Olympics. I started to get interested in that because it was new and had some reference to bidding, but there was otherwise nothing to grab on to. The radio mostly covered the same stories with some adjustment due to the fact that they didn't need pictures to cover a story.

At one point, Gas asked me how it could be that someone had corrupted the BBC. I had to admit, I did not have an answer to that that was more sophisticated than 'cash.'

After around 0500, Gas told me I was on my own because she said she wanted to look at the BBC's web-pages. She started working on some code that would download everything posted to any of BBC internet output posted during the 24 hrs from midnight. This turned out to be a large amount of material, but was not unmanageable.

I said "We are going to have a problem if they are using steganography. It could be any picture." This was a method of encrypting data within a photo. The colour of a pixel is set by three bytes each of eight bits of data. If a pixel was completely red, it would be coded with 11111111 of red and all zeroes for green and blue. If you were doing Least Significant Bit steganography, you could change one of the last two bits. That would change the redness from 255/255 to 253/255 which basically meant changing it from 'completely red' to 'only some kind of freak can distinguish this from completely red.' So the image would look the same but you could put hidden data in the last two bits.

"Yeah, that would be hard," said Gas, "but we can use some heavy duty CPU on it because we're not under critical time pressure. I mean, obviously we want to know what's going on, but we don't need to complete our analysis in the 24 hr window. I am setting up to download every picture on every website with a timestamp in the window."

"How will you find the right one?"

"There's no guaranty, but I can compare the amount of white noise randomness in the standard images with the pseudo-randomness in the encrypted payload. Also the picture itself might have a clue. Like maybe it's a picture associated with that Japanese bidding story."

We stayed awake until about 0900. Gas had finished setting up her code and it was running and downloading new photos as the BBC uploaded them. I fell asleep periodically. I would check what was going on with the BBC's output every time I woke up. Various things happened during the day, including the Chinese pretending to be unhappy about the US banning Tik-Tok from Federal devices. Maybe they really were unhappy, but they couldn't actually be surprised.

It turned out there was a branch of Tim Hortons in the building, which was great because it meant more coffee and doughnuts with plenty of sugar. You couldn't watch your calories on a stakeout. We spent the rest of the day and evening watching the screens, napping fitfully in the chairs. Gas wrote her code in Python.

Just after midnight, we had seen nothing unusual on the TVs so we switched them off. We had also heard nothing on the radio, so we killed that too. Gas ran some code to ensure that she had all the photos from the window and that checked out OK. She set off her laptop to begin systematically looking through all the photos for levels of randomness and said "We may as well leave it there. Let's go back to the hotel and sleep and see what we have in the morning. If anything shows up, we can look at it, otherwise we are going to have to physically examine all the photos."

"Can you print them all off?" I said.

She queued them up that but it was a several hour print job so we left.

When we went back in the morning, the printing was done and so was the steganography check. The latter had produced nothing at all apart from what Gas decided quickly was a false positive on a photo illustrating a story about an Indian temple replacing elephants with robots. Then we looked through all the hardcopy photos. It took hours; we found nothing.

We started listening to BBC music channels from the day before if they had live DJs. We found nothing. I started thinking about hidden messages in the initial letters of stories on the webpages. Gas quickly wrote some code to find every nth letter of every story and write them out and then check them against a dictionary. She also added and subtracted all numbers between 1 and 26 to these strings and again looked for words. She checked for the adjusted prevalence of E's, because that is the most common letter in English. We found nothing.

While we were listening to the radio, I said "There's also podcasts. We should listen to those."

"Maybe we are thinking about this wrongly. It can't be this hard to find," said Gas. I thought that she might have a point here but something grabbed my attention. There was a Podcast I often listened to called World Business Report. It was about half an hour long. Yesterday's episode was listed as 1hr 29m.

"This is odd," I said. "World Business Report is too long. Unless they have an extended edition because of some business news that's a big deal -- but then if it was that big a deal, it would probably have made the main output we were watching all day."

We played the Podcast. It was completely normal. The programme ran for a very standard period of 28 minutes and a few seconds. Then it was silence. We listened to this silence with the volume right up for a few minutes but nothing happened. Gas downloaded the file and dropped it into some code that showed us the sound file visually. Exactly an hour in, there was something.

Gas jumped to that section and played it. It was about 1.5s of static. She played it again to make sure it wasn't coming from somewhere else in our setup. "That's interesting," she said. "You can't get static unless you have an analogue system, and this isn't one of those."

We zeroed in on the waveforms and they started to look slightly odd to me. Or strangely familiar.

"It looks like a somewhat modified burst of white noise. Run that through a Fourier transform," I said. Gas squinted, looked at the screen, looked at me, and then looked at the screen again with a shrug. The she loaded up a module to do the transform, which decomposed the signal into its frequency components. When she did this, we got something close to a flat line, because white noise is the same intensity at all frequencies. Something that was close to white noise. But not quite. Every now and then the frequency line had notches in it. They had a periodic distance between them.

"I could convert the distances between those notches to binary," said Gas. "It might be something." She did that and then looked at it. "That's a QR code," she said. She reformatted it into a picture so she could read the QR code by scanning it with her phone. "It's a valid web address. Deep web. Not a burner though. Or it is a burner link, but it's not a one-time one."

We paused to consider the next step. We now at least had an explanation as to how the BBC had been involved. "This could just be dropped in to the standard podcast by someone who is a 23-year old sound engineer. You only need him."

"Right," said Gas, "and no one is going to listen to an hour of silence and find a burst of static and complain about it. And even the guy's boss is at most going to say 'is the right programme there and can people listen to it?' To which the answers are yes and yes."

"That's right. You just need to pay this one guy to do something he knows doesn't matter to him."

"I guess I have to hit the link," Gas said.

"I guess you do," I agreed.

She opened up an instantiation of the Tor browser and typed in the link. A screen came up which said 'name.'

We paused again.

"If this is the bid process, we could screw this up here," said Gas.

"We could," I agreed, "but on the other hand it's a semi open bid process. If you've got this far, your bid was invited. If this is it, of course. It might be anything. Some kind of GCHQ recruitment ad."

"What shall we put? 'Fuck you' .'Division 4?' 'Captagon Heroes?'"

"We could do that," I replied, "but there's a bit too much 'look at me' to all those. Division 4 is maybe discrete enough but might be too frightening even for our guys."

We considered various further options. 'Bureau 121' for the North Korean army outfit of more than 1000 hackers. We decided against that because they could be the sellers and we would be blown. 'Mossad' avoided that problem but was just too bare-faced. Plus we were in the UAE.

In the end, we went for 'alfalasi.' This was a guy who had been busted locally for moving in £100m via money mules. We were relying on the idea that his organisation might still be in play. If anyone managed to check our IP address or timestamp or had any other clever means of determining our location we were in fact in the right place.

Gas dropped the capital letter in Alfalasi, made the colour off-grey rather than black and took the font down to 9pts, because Jasper had once told us that a small font, dull colour and lower case says 'I am not important, go on to the next thing.' The strength of these psychological factors was amazing.

Another box came up. 'Current value of product is $2.213bn. Enter bid.'

"Fuck," we both said at the same time. This was where the iteration of this set of moves across the chessboard had culminated. Presumably they game would be run again with different route variations, different input sources. And it had been run an unknown number of times before. But this was where it stopped this time for a reset.

"What they want is completely clean cash. This is still slightly dirty and still theoretically traceable," I said.

"Well right," said Gas, "after all, we have done part of it. And Brynjar has more pieces of the picture."

"So we have to make an aggressive bid I guess," I said. I mean it doesn't really matter because we haven't got $100m so if we are actually required to stump it up we'd have a problem. Brynjar might be able to get the US to force a Caymans bank to lie to account holders about their balance if we could show a RICO element, maybe." The Racketeer Influenced and Corrupt Organizations Act was an old 1970 law but it provided quite a lot of useful abilities.

Gas said "So what's our number?"

"I think we should go for $1920m. That's a fair haircut and serious. It's a long way north of the usual discount for money laundering but still gives us a profit that makes it worth doing," I said. "Especially if we pay with bent cash."

She typed it in. A new box came up. It said 'You have qualified for product inspection phase. Press enter.'

"This is always the tricky part," I said. "They want to remain anonymous and they want to keep hold of the product but on the other hand, they know that no one is going to wire a billion dollars to someone they never met who hasn't proven they have the product."

Gas hit the enter box with her cursor.

The screen changed to:

```
Key:
XXX.XXXXXX, XXX.XXXXXX
XXX.XXXXXX, XXX.XXXXXX
32.537262, -117.043488
XXX.XXXXXX, XXX.XXXXXX
XXX.XXXXXX, XXX.XXXXXX
XXX.XXXXXX, XXX.XXXXXX
XXX.XXXXXX, XXX.XXXXXX
XXX.XXXXXX, XXX.XXXXXX
XXX.XXXXXX, XXX.XXXXXX
XXX.XXXXXX, XXX.XXXXXX
```

I looked at this blankly for a second. "There must be ten keys, and we have been given one of them."

"It's possible that that's lat and long," said Gas. "Probable. Let's see if it's anywhere viable. Looks roughly like southern California." It took her ten seconds to look it up. "Close. It's actually just south over the border. There must be a key there."

When we pressed enter on the key window, it signed off with the enigmatic legend 43d9 27 Mar FT 13a followed by a larger than normal whitespace and the text C10H8. We told Greg we were done and he could close this down and then we got moving.

CHAPTER 13

TIJUANA, MEXICO

On the plane, I had discussed the mysterious closing sign-off text. Gas had run it through The Fork during a stopover in Charles de Gaulle but to no avail.

"It's got too many numbers to do anything with, really," she said. "27 Mar, that's obviously a date."

"The 43d9 is not part of the date I suppose. It could be another date. 09 December 1943. What happened then?"

"Nothing," said Gas, after checking. "It's a week after an accidental release of Mustard gas in Italy and a couple of weeks before the sinking of the Scharnhorst. So it's in between two famous dates in naval history, but I don't think it's a coded message for me. 43d9 is hex for 17369."

"If that's UK notation, it's another date. 17 March 1969."

"On that day, Golda Meir became the fourth and only female Prime Minister of Israel."

"Possibly interesting. Is 17369 prime? Or special?" I asked.

"Not prime," she replied after typing for a second. "It's 11 x 1579."

This was a dead end. We continued staring at the text on the plane.

I got it on the second stopover in Mexico City. "It could be a crossword clue...in the FT. If you use the other elements we have."

I opened the Financial Times app. Crossword number 17369 was dated 27 March. "Yep, that's it. 13a means we want the answer to 13 across. I'll probably have to do the whole thing." The critical clue was 'Accommodation Tom uses as bordello.'

It took me an hour to do the whole crossword, including a couple I had to semi-guess. But my guesses were a long way away from the critical clue so I assumed it was fine. We drank some really strong gin and tonics and at one point it was looking like I wasn't going to get it finished as a result of the consequent haze. I had a lot of trouble with 'Building from which yours truly might emerge' [C_W_H_D] until I noticed that the name of the setter was MOO.

Eventually I finished, and felt somewhat triumphant. The answer to 13 across was CATHOUSE. "How the hell do you get to that? Tom who?" asked Gas. Then she saw it. "OK, that's actually quite straightforward when you look at it carefully."

"Yes, it's just two definitions of the same word. Some familiarity with Western culture -- Tom and Jerry -- or just that male cats are called Toms, is helpful. I've no idea what we do with it though. Perhaps we have to find a brothel in Tijuana."

"That will be fun," said Gas. She looked like she meant it. "What about the other part? $C_{10}H_8$. It's bad if you don't use all the pieces."

"I have no idea what that is," I said. "But we have the clue solved at least."

We were staying in a hotel in downtown; we got there and slept. There was something going on with the humidity but I wasn't sure what it was. The light was also unique and made me think we were in a different type of desert to the one we had just left. It felt less like one in which a falcon would be at home, and more like a good place for vultures. It was somehow a messier less precise desert than the sculpted artistic dunes of the gulf.

There was something very odd about the other guests in the Tijuana hotel, which was one of the major US chains and perfectly comfortable. Everyone in it seemed to be a very slow-moving, very quiet middle-aged American on the large side. They were all drinking what looked like protein shakes. There was a large gym and a pool. No-one else was ever in either location. No one was in the bar. It was like being ephemerally surrounded by reduced speed phantoms.

The first order of business was to find the precise location of the key. We showered and headed straight out. The hotel was on Boulevard Agua Caliente which sounded a lot better in Spanish than what would appear to be in English 'Hot Water Street.' We had a long walk down what threatened to turn into a motorway several times but never quite did.

We came to a touristy area which felt safer than the motorway. It was odd to see a pedestrian route to the USA signposted, but that was how it worked here. We were very close to the border. At the airport, you could choose different exits and one of them took you to a metro link to San Diego.

Gas was navigating and I was keeping my eyes open. As we got closer to the coordinates, things were definitely becoming more sketchy. The population of generally large Americans thinned out and everyone had a more lean and dangerous look. As we got on to the street itself, the only people around were guys lounging in doorways and kids with scooters and mobile phones. All of them were taking a close interest in us, so I decided to abort before we got made.

"Gas, we need to bail out of this. It's too hot. Stop walking. Do some standard tourist stuff. Look at your phone like the map has screwed you up," I said. She did this.

"OK now make some gesticulations like you are arguing with me, you will never trust my directions again, you don't know why you married me etc."

"I don't know what that last gesture looks like," said Gas, while making suitably annoyed faces. We turned around and walked back out.

"Neither do I. I assume it's general annoyance."

"Can I slap you?" she asked but I didn't think we needed to go quite that far merely for histrionic value.

"This has to go to Brynjar, " I said. "We need either a lot of backup or a lot of stealth." I texted him the coordinates and said it was a location we were interested in. He said he would contact INTERPOL's National Central Bureau (NCB) in Mexico City and come back to us.

That took him a day. That evening we looked into the local wine scene. It turned out to be very good, since the famed wine growing regions of California extended south into Baja California in Mexico. I had told people about this before but they hadn't believed me. They said things like 'Mexican wine sounds as good as an English taco.' Which was sort of fair enough but also wrong.

When he called us, the situation was complicated. "OK, so we have people there but they are mostly in the airport in Mexico City and looking at immigration for international crime syndicate purposes. That's good and bad. Because it turns out that your location is a warehouse building square in the middle of cartel land."

"Yes, it looked pretty spicy on recon," said Gas.

"So it's good in that that our guys are linked into the cartel situation, but they now need to do local liaison to get some Federales cover on the spot. I was expecting some drug links after you were in La Linea," said Brynjar.

"What do you mean?" I said. "That was the deadest zone in the world. It's just for people who work in Gibraltar to sleep."

"It may look quiet, but it's actually one of the hottest zones in the world for drug trafficking. There are 30 active gangs and 3,000 of the population of 64,000 are involved. Every night there are speedboat races between people bringing in gear from Morocco and the local narco cops. The criminals have better boats and they send dozens across at a time so you can't catch them all. And also there's a pipeline for Islamist extremists going into Spain."

"Unbelievable. In that case," I said, "we might find some relevant info on that once we are in there. Or maybe some sectors of what we are looking at involve drugs. I don't know what $600m of coke looks like."

"I thought you used to work on a trading floor?" interjected Gas cynically.

"We can work that out," continued Brynjar. He looked at a document on his desk. "We just got some standard Europol reporting in from customs at Antwerp. Last fiscal year they seized 110 tonnes of coke. It comes in at a purity of 80% and then gets cut down to 60% purity by adding lidocaine and baking powder. So that gets you to, what..."

"The mass increase factor is 0.8 / 0.6 which is four thirds," I said. "Let's say the 110 tonnes is really 120 tonnes because then a third is 40 tonnes and the total is 160 tonnes."

"OK," said Brynjar, "160 tonnes; street price is $50 per gramme, which is $50,000 per kilogram, which is $50m per tonne so that's about half a billion x 16 ... $8bn seized."

"So $600m in coke is of order 10 tonnes or something. Highly doable."

"In an afternoon," said Gas.

"Right," agreed Brynjar, probably with me rather than Gas. "On the financial side though, the trade is easily in your ballpark. The assumption made by both us and the traffickers is that the seizure rate is 10% to 15%. So the cash value moving through just one port is $80bn."

"That's enormous," said Gas.

"Antwerp is big though," responded Brynjar. "It takes about 40 minutes to drive past all the containers. Which I've done a couple of times. It's not widely known but there are police from everywhere in ports, like you can find Antwerp Politie cars in the docks in Tenerife. It gets crazy if they try to arrest someone though."

"That's what international police cooperation looks like," I said.

Brynjar objected: "How would you know? You're from the sovereign UK."

I chose to ignore this. "OK, so where are we on the situation here?" I asked.

"You're going to have to give me a few days to set something up in Tijuana with your location of interest," concluded Brynjar. "It's pretty hot. The Federal government sent the army in a while back and the mayor came back and asked for more assets. Too hot."

Three days later, Brynjar came back and said he couldn't get us in. The whole area was cartel territory and local law enforcement and NCB were not interested in an operation to put two civilians into a building with no likely positive outcomes for them and the most vague of specifications from INTERPOL as to what might be in there.

"The only thing I can do is get you an opportunity to stake it out. You might be able to figure out a way to get inside. I've offered the locals a marker they can call in with me and they have two things to offer us. One is an specially equipped unmarked nondescript van registered in the area. You can park it outside and look out from the rear. The second thing is that they periodically raid these guys. They are prepared to run one of those ops somewhere else and that should distract the cartel."

Since that was all that was on offer, we decided to take it. The van was delivered the next day. It looked suitably shabby. We were told by the guy who brought it to us, who did not give his name or organisation, that we would not be told the location of the raid at any point and we would get the time only when it was about to happen.

We spent some time hanging round in the van watching the building, and saw nothing. We ate badly and slept badly. I could see how Brynjar had got slightly soft. You just couldn't exercise or eat well if this was your job. Plus stress makes people eat junk.

After thirty-six hours of this, at dusk, we were told that it was happening in an hour. We got in the van and Gas drove it slowly and inconspicuously through heavy traffic on Avenida Revolución, which was busy with tourists eating street food and drinking. We got to the location and parked. The kids with scooters were still around but they were much less interested now we were just a local vehicle not a pair of lost gringos.

We observed the building for a while. Nothing happened. No one came in or went out. It looked like a derelict warehouse. After another 30 minutes, the kid on the scooter got a phone call, looked alarmed and sped off.

It was close to dark now and there was no-one around. This was the moment. We walked over to the building and found a window. Gas forced it with a crowbar which meant we smashed the window. That made a lot of noise, it seemed to us, so we waited for a minute or two to see if anyone came to investigate. That didn't happen; judging from the number of broken windows around it was not exactly an unusual occurrence for one to be broken.

We hadn't been able to see through the window because it had had cardboard packaging taped to it with duct tape. That survived the smashing of the glass. We removed it gingerly to avoid getting cut and leaving blood behind. Once inside, we could see that the building looked like a derelict warehouse because that's what it was, with a large open plan ground level. You could certainly store things here, but it did not appear that anything had been for some time.

Gas moved around with her phone and walked around, narrowing down the precise distance between where she was and the exact latitude and longitude we had found in Dubai. Quickly she stopped moving.

"This is it." There was nothing there; in fact the whole floor seemed featureless.

Clearly there was nothing where she was or around her. She stamped on the floor a couple of times. It sounded completely solid. She looked upwards. "We need to go upstairs," she said. "Or maybe down."

There was a metal staircase at one edge and we went up it. There wasn't a way down. Finding the spot was harder this time because the upper floor was not open plan. The location was inside a locked office, but the door was so flimsy we didn't have any trouble forcing it open with some pieces of packing case that were lying around. We could have gone back for the crowbar but we didn't need to.

That turned out not to be the door. Behind the flimsy plywood cover was a solid metal door that looked like it had come off a warship. Thick plates with impressive riveting. It had a typewriter keypad at eye level with just the letters and an enter key.

I typed in CATHOUSE and pressed enter. There was a click. I pushed the door but it was too heavy. When both of us lent our full body weight on it, it slowly swung open.

"Nice with the bordello thing," said Gas. "These bidders better have some semi-literary Brits as well as just like guns and thugs."

"They will probably be well-resourced in all departments," I replied.

I was expecting to see something difficult, like a filing cabinet with 100 drawers where we didn't know which one we wanted and we didn't have the key to get to the key. Failing that, I thought we might find a key sitting on a table. And failing that, maybe the key was hanging on a rusty nail hammered into the wall. But the room was empty apart from some trash and a couple of very old dusty boxes in the corner. So we looked in there.

The first thing we saw was an ancient bill of lading from with DIGITAL EQUIPMENT CORPORATION written on it. "That's amazing," I said. "I used to work for them. A hundred years ago."

Gas said "I have heard of them. I think you can still sometimes find their stuff in banks or running nuclear reactors etc. Places where you dare not change anything."

"That's right," I said. "They were nothing if not reliable."

We removed the contents of the boxes. There was a very old school and very non-flat monitor screen and a box which I recognised as the processor housing, which turned out to be a VAXStation 3100. There was also some cabling and a keyboard, all in the trademark beige.

"So what are we going to do with this?" asked Gas.

"Nothing here. Let's get out and go back to the hotel," I replied. We checked around the room carefully to see if we had missing anything, but there was nothing else unless there was some text written in radioactive colourless paint on the walls. We humped the gear down to the street, which was easy enough because everything was compact except the monitor and got back in the van.

I thought about security. "Actually I don't want to do this here. Let's go somewhere else in a number of separate vehicles." We checked out and ordered ten

Ubers. Each of them took either one of us or an item of luggage or a part of the newly acquired antique computer. Each went initially to a random location chosen to be about 5km away in an approximately equal spread around the compass, and then we added final stops for all of them that converged on a new hotel on the beach.

We thus wound up along Avenida Kukulkan, which ran along a sandbar in the impossibly blue ocean. It was absolutely full of very large, high end hotels patronised by Americans who thought they should get a passport in order to look sophisticated but did not actually want to go to the trouble of going somewhere that did not do a very good simulacrum of Miami. However, this was perfect for our purposes, being anonymous and offering excellent Mojitos and tacos.

"Are you sure you should be drinking before we sort this out?" asked Gas.

"I don't think we are under time pressure and we may need some creativity," I said and she joined in.

Once in the new room, we plugged everything in and nothing happened. They keyboard, while dusty, had seen almost no use. They would normally get worn keys and dirt especially on highly used keys. There were function keys at the top of the VT-220 keyboard which no-one ever used. In this case, the rest of the keys were as virginal as the function keys.

"I think a museum would love to have this. It's pristine. It looks like it's been taken out one time and then put back. The only way you know it's been opened is because they have just stuck it back in the polystyrene guards but without the plastic covers," I said.

"This is super-weird," said Gas. "Why are they doing this?"

"It's the same thing as usual. They have to make this somewhat accessible to qualified bidders but highly inaccessible to anyone who happens to wander in to the process or who is actively trying to hack the process like we are," I said.

"Is that what we are trying to do?" asked Gas. "Or are we trying to apprehend the perpetrators?"

"Both look the same right now. Anyway, the bidders are clearly highly sophisticated organisations so they can probably work out what to do with a **VAX**."

I plugged in the kit and toggled the power switches. After about a minute, three right arrows appeared on the screen. "Console prompt," I said. "That's a phrase I haven't used for 30 years. I typed 'b.' Nothing happened.

"That's not good. It should boot from there." I typed in a question mark and got a list of commands that were available. The list was not long, because computers that haven't been booted yet are not very capable. They are like Hal in 2001 after all his memory has been removed. Except not even that good. No nursery rhymes available.

There was a fair bit of heat coming off the equipment. This was perturbing Gas. "Why is it running hot when we aren't doing anything yet?" she wanted to know.

"That's just how it was. Get used to the old days," I said. Dust burnt up and you could actually see thermal currents moving lazily upwards in the air. "We used to have a joke about George Bush, the first one. 'Read my lips, no new VAXES.' That seems quite apt now."

One of the available commands allowed me to interrogate the status of the VAX/VMS Operating System License. It had expired 20 years ago.

"That's actually not that surprising," I said.

"What are we going to do about that? No-one sells these nowadays I guess," said Gas. "We won't be able to boot it up without an operating system license."

"HP bought DEC so it might still be possible to buy one. And there are these nuclear subs and banks still running it, like you say, so they must have legal installations. But I don't know how we do it, what it costs or how long it takes. However...I have an idea."

I initiated conversational boot mode and got the following.

VAX/VMS Version 4.4 16-APR-1986 22:29
XXXXXXXXXX OPCOM <DD-MMM-YYYY HH:MM:SS.S> XXXXXXXXXX Logfile has been

initialized by operator _FIELD.OPAO: Logfile is
SYS.SYSROOT:[SYSMGR]OPERATOR.LOG;1
Please enter the date and time (DD-MMM-YYYY
HH:MM):

I typed in 16-APR-1992 04:16.

Gas was stunned. "Are you pretending it's 1992?" she
said.

"Yeah. How will it know? It has been sitting in a box
powered down the whole time."

The boot proceeded as normal though with the verbose
switch on, a vast amount of reporting was generated.
After about ten minutes, we ended up with what
appeared to be a pristine installation that would do
whatever you told it to do, but it had limited capacities
since it was not connected to the outside world in any
way. If I did connect it, it would probably freak out
about what the internet had done since 1992.

Now we needed to login. I typed in FIELD as the
username and explained that not only was this a good
username, but it had SYSTEM privileges. I translated
that to root for Gas's benefit.

"It's for field maintenance staff." I explained. This meant she was even more aghast when I typed in FIELD as the password. "It's the old days, Gas. We weren't that paranoid and no-one could boot one of these things. Only experts used computers."

"OK, great," said Gas. "I'll try to remain calm. So now I guess we're looking for anything at all that's non-standard."

"Exactly right," I said. "Bear in mind that we have just booted it rather than re-installed the operating system. So we just need to find a file that's not part of the OS. Something that's been added."

"How many people could do this?" wondered Gas.

"Anyone from Tech Support at DEC. Any of the engineers from back then. Anyone who could be bothered to read the manual. Probably not that many of us left now, but it's not that hard for someone with a comp background," I said. "Apart from the thing with FIELD. You probably have to have been there for that. So I guess we know bidders can find people."

I thought about texting Brynjar to look for anything unusual being generated around recruitment of VAX/ VMS specialists in strange places with great compensation, but decided I could get to that later. Also, why shouldn't old dogs like VAX guys get some unexpected time in the sun?

I set up a bunch of batch jobs to basically tell me the dates and times of creation of every file on the system. The disk span up audibly and generated some vibration. The heat was continuing.

Gas said "I've never seen, or felt, or smelt anything like it. It's more like an engine than a computer. And not a clean engine either. Like a dirty steam powered punk thing."

"Also you could club someone over the head with the processor box if you wanted to. Try doing that with a MacBook Air."

It quickly became apparent that there were a lot of files that had been created at the last installation of the operating system in 1989 and there was one file buried deep in the system that was dated well over three decades later. It was called key.dat.

I fired up the file editor, which was called EVE. The file contained the text below and nothing else, complete with weird pagination.

```
C o l d                                    w a l l e t :
3230363237353634363736353734363536343 26
53635373836333735373336393665363732653 7
3336653631363336623733
```

This was nothing if not opaque. We both stared at it for a while. Gas ran it through The Fork and also a bunch of decipher programs.

"Why are there so many threes in it?" I wondered.

We appeared to be at a halt without some clue as to what to do with these numbers. They didn't look like anything at all.

"What was the part we didn't use?" said Gas. "If you are making something from Ikea and you have a part left over, you did something wrong."

"It was some extra bit of code," I said, and pulled up the photo I took of the screen. "C10H8," I said when I had it. This didn't do anything much run through various conversions. And it wasn't really long enough to do a lot with.

"I'm not very good at chemistry, but I suppose it could be some sort of molecule. Alcohol is C and H and some Oxygen so this could be something organic," I said.

"Are you thinking about alcohol because of the Mojitos?"

"Maybe...but we need something off the edge here, clearly."

"If it is a molecule, what is it?"

I looked it up. "Naphthalene, or coal tar. White crystalline solid."

"What is it used for?"

I looked that up. "Industrial production of phthalic anhydride. I have no idea what that is, or how to say it."

"This isn't the right track," said Gas. We drank Mojitos.

"You can make mothballs from it," I said eventually. "And it's bad if you eat them. You get something called hemolytic anemia."

"Who eats mothballs?"

"People with pico. No, pica. Desire to eat non-food items. Jasper told me about it once. It's a symptom of a lot of DSM-5 items."

"DSM-5?"

"Diagnostic and Statistical Manual of the American Psychiatric Association. Version 5. It's how to diagnose people with stuff, like psychopathy, or narcissistic personality disorder."

"It's good you're this weird," said Gas. "Someone has to do it."

We drank some more.

"The molar mass is 128.17 g/mol," I said. "Can you do anything with that number?"

"Pension legislation in Wisconsin," said Gas after checking. "This is really not going anywhere."

"What's the chemical symbol?" asked Gas.

"A pair of benzene rings.   Two hexagons linked together."

We thought about that and stared at the number some more.

"Double hex," she said and so did I; we both got it at the same time.   Hexadecimal notation ran from 0 to 9 and then continued from with 10 to 16 replaced by A to F. This meant you could represent the value of four bits in one character, which was useful since that meant you could then write a normal text letter, providing you had some way of representing letters as numbers.

Such a standard way existed: ASCII, or the American Standard Code for Information Interchange. Simple but very useful because everyone knew it and everyone knew everyone knew it. Gas put the set of numbers with all the threes through a HEX to text converter and got the following:

20627564676574656642e65786375736966e672e7
36e61636b73

Still not apparently meaningful but at least there were
not so many threes. Since the missing part had been a
representation of 'double hex,' we knew we either had
to double it and do the conversion or vice versa or we
had to do the conversion twice. Gas did the doubling
thing and got garbage but when she did the conversion
from HEX to text again she got:

budgeted.excusing.snacks

This was both very good and very bad. It was very good
in that it was clearly actual plaintext rather than
gibberish, which told us that our process so far had been
good. You couldn't wind up with real words from a
double hex conversion randomly.

The bad part was that it didn't tell us what to do next. If
we had missed a step in the 'bidders instructions' that we
were apparently hacking, then maybe we were supposed
have a copy of 'War and Peace' and find the page
numbers with those words on it or something completely
unguessable if you weren't told.

"I don't like that," I said. "It doesn't make any sense. Maybe we are supposed to convert it into numbers or something. Or it's a password for a cold wallet or another system." I knew what cold wallets were. You could store crypto on them. They were called cold as opposed to hot if they were implemented in hardware rather than software. It was just a drive in someones pocket. Since the original text before the numbers stated 'cold wallet,' we assumed that the numbers were going to tell us where the wallet was, somehow.

Gas looked like she knew what the words meant. She said "It's a place, I think. There is an outfit called what3words who did something supercool. They divided the entire surface of the world into 3m by 3m squares and gave each square a name. It's by far the easiest way to specify a precise location and remember it. This might be one of those codes."

She opened up a website and typed in the three words and her screen went blue. I thought initially she had crashed; I remembered the legendary haiku:

Windows NT crashed
I am the blue screen of death
No one hears your screams.

I thought something like 'kids today, never heard of Windows NT, probably don't even know that WNT follows on from VMS by one letter each...in the same way that HAL is one letter before IBM...' then caught myself doing it and stopped.

"That's odd. It's the sea," she said. She zoomed out and a sandbar of some sort became visible. A road called the A379 ran down the sandbar. "OK, there's some form of civilisation here."

Some more zooming out and she found something called an "Exercise Tiger Memorial" very close to our square. Some kind of Big Game park was her idea. After she went wide enough to see the coastline, we both recognised it.

"Looks like you're going home, Burgoyne," she said. We were looking at the Devon coast. "Not too far from Plymouth. I came through there on flag-flying exercises a couple of times."

Just before we left, Gas sorted out the nature and strangeness of the other hotel guests, by dint of talking to one of them. Apparently it made a lot of economic sense for Americans who wanted gastric band surgery to come to Mexico to do it, and Tijuana, being a border town, was the easiest way to go to Mexico.

This hotel had the concession on some kind of package deal with the local clinic: you could buy the accommodation with the surgery. They weren't eating because they couldn't. They were supposed to take light exercise but going hard in the gym would rip their stitches open. This also explained why room service were very slow. I imagined that when we ordered tacos, we were the first people to do that for ten years and someone had to be brought out of retirement.

The last thing we discussed before leaving Mexico was whether we would have company. What we didn't know was how quickly other bidders would decode the message and where the other keys were. They could and probably would be widely dispersed across the globe, even though they all pointed to one location, presumably.

We had taken a long time to find and understand the announcement and decode our key but we didn't have any instructions. That was positive in a way because it meant all parties would expect only invited persons to be there.

EPILOGUE

KINGSBRIDGE, UK

The 'Exercise Tiger Memorial' turned out to be a Sherman tank on the waterfront. We walked past it and read the sign as we headed to near our target location.

The tank it turned out was one of the 'swimming' variants known as 'funnies.' D-Day rehearsals had taken place in 1944 in the area because the marine and shore features resembled Normandy. This particular tank had sunk during exercises and after a long time underwater, had been raised and placed just off the beach as a memorial.

"It's not that far out to sea," said Gas. "We should be able to see it easily. It might be underwater or floating. We probably don't even need a swimming tank."

We got to a point where we were alongside the specified location. We were at a pub so we had a couple of pints and thought about our next move. There were a lot of tourists on the beach who were excited because there were some seals coming up in the surf.

Gas looked at her phone. "I think it's that boat. It's not actually in the square but it is tied up in such a way that it would be under some current conditions. And there's nothing else. Unless it's a package floating under the water."

"That does happen. The Australians picked up a bunch of product just sitting in the sea at a particular GPS location, waiting for someone to come and load it up."

I wondered how we were going to get out there. It was swimmable, easily, but the water would not be warm and we would be highly conspicuous. As I thought about it, something made my hair stand on end. I didn't know why, but I shivered and looked around. I half thought I had seen some auburn hair disappearing into the crowds alone the shore. I told Gas to keep her eyes open for other bidders.

About 200m away down the beach were some kids with big paddle boards. We finished our pints and went to talk to them. Two of them were happy to take us out to the small boat. Twenty quid now, wait 20 minutes, twenty quid more to bring us back. The boat was so small it didn't look like it would need a long time to search. We got on the boards, which was much harder than it looked, and the sun set as the kids paddled us out. We climbed over the side of the boat. The kids said they would come back for us and drifted slightly away, discussing how they could buy weed with the cash.

The boat was clean and empty. I wasn't sure whether there would be extra levels of protection at this point or whether there was no need or it would be undiplomatic, given only qualified bidders could be here.

There was a small metal box next to what I would call the steering wheel but for which Gas doubtless had some nautical term. The box had a label taped to it with the legend 0x0419, which was the code for Russian language. I didn't know why that was there. We debated opening the box for a minute. It could be trapped. We decided to open it anyway because why would the vendors blow up their bidders?

Inside there was a small USB drive. I took it out, and was confident that I was now holding more than $2bn in my hands. I hadn't ever really done that before.

"All we need now is a 24-word seed phrase," I said.

"How are you going to get that?"

I didn't have an answer to that.

"You aren't going to negotiate with the seller. You haven't got the money. You don't know who they are. You can however be confident that they will do bad things with the clean money they want to get."

"We could give it to Brynjar."

"What will he do with it?"

"I don't know."

"Do you trust him?"

"I suppose so," I said, absently.   I was thinking more about how I could get hold of the money or some money or some money to get this money. So many things were great ideas but you couldn't get them started.   Brynjar looked like the best option, even if I wasn't sure about what would happen.

Gas was thinking about the other players.   "They are all much better armed than we are, and more numerous, and highly motivated.   Just having this thing on us makes us a target.   How do we know that some of these tourists aren't bidders?   If they get it, what do you think will happen next?   And how much enthusiasm do they have for our presence?"

I wasn't thinking about that.   I was thinking that it was worth taking some risk for $1.2bn.   Quite a lot in fact. That was when Gas took the drive out of my hand and threw it into the sea some distance further out.   I watched it as it fell and I watched the part of the sea where it sank.

I didn't say anything. I couldn't particularly think of anything to say. I couldn't drag the sea for the drive, which would be destroyed, and if I did, I still didn't have the code to unlock it. I had played all the cards I had to the best of my ability and there were no more cards. No point being annoyed.

Gas waved to the paddle board kids and they took us back to the shore in anticipatory silence. I handed them their other banknote. They were delighted.

"Have you ever had fish and chips before?" I asked Gas. "It's well worth a try." We sat down at the pub again and drank more beer while we waited. Everyone around us was doing the same thing. More or less.

Made in the USA
Middletown, DE
08 October 2023

40444809R00241